™

SONIC
THE HEDGEHOG

SONIC & TAILS: BEST BUDS FOREVER

SEGA®

IDW

ISBN: 978-1-68405-894-5
25 24 23 22   5 6 7 8

Originally published as SONIC THE HEDGEHOG issues #1, 13, 34 and 35.

Nachie Marsham, Publisher
Blake Kobashigawa, SVP Sales, Marketing & Strategy
Mark Doyle, VP Editorial & Creative Strategy
Tara McCrillis, VP Publishing Operations
Anna Morrow, VP Marketing & Publicity
Alex Hargett, VP Sales
Jamie S. Rich, Executive Editorial Director
Scott Dunbier, Director, Special Projects
Greg Gustin, Sr. Director, Content Strategy
Kevin Schwoer, Sr. Director of Talent Relations
Lauren LePera, Sr. Managing Editor
Keith Davidsen, Director, Marketing & PR
Topher Alford, Sr. Digital Marketing Manager
Patrick O'Connell, Sr. Manager, Direct Market Sales
Shauna Monteforte, Sr. Director of Manufacturing Operations
Greg Foreman, Director DTC Sales & Operations
Nathan Widick, Director of Design
Neil Uyetake, Sr. Art Director, Design & Production
Shawn Lee, Art Director, Design & Production
Jack Rivera, Art Director, Marketing

Ted Adams and Robbie Robbins, IDW Founders

Special thanks to Mai Kiyotaki, Michael Cisneros, Sandra Jo, Sonic Team, and everyone at Sega for their invaluable assistance.

FALLOUT

WRITTEN BY **IAN FLYNN**
PENCILS BY **TRACY YARDLEY**
INKS BY **JIM AMASH** & **BOB SMITH**
COLORS BY **MATT HERMS**
LETTERS BY **COREY BREEN**

CALLING CARD

WRITTEN BY **IAN FLYNN**
ART BY **ADAM BRYCE THOMAS**
COLORS BY **MATT HERMS**
LETTERS BY **SHAWN LEE**

CHAO RACES AND BADNIK BASES

WRITTEN BY **EVAN STANLEY**
ART BY **EVAN STANLEY**
& **ADAM BRYCE THOMAS**
COLORS BY **REGGIE GRAHAM**
LETTERS BY **SHAWN LEE**

COVER ARTIST: **EVAN STANLEY**
SERIES EDITORS: **DAVID MARIOTTE**
& **JOE HUGHES**
SERIES ASSISTANT EDITORS: **MEGAN BROWN**
& **RILEY FARMER**
COLLECTION EDITORS: **ALONZO SIMON**
& **ZAC BOONE**
COLLECTION DESIGNER: **SHAWN LEE**

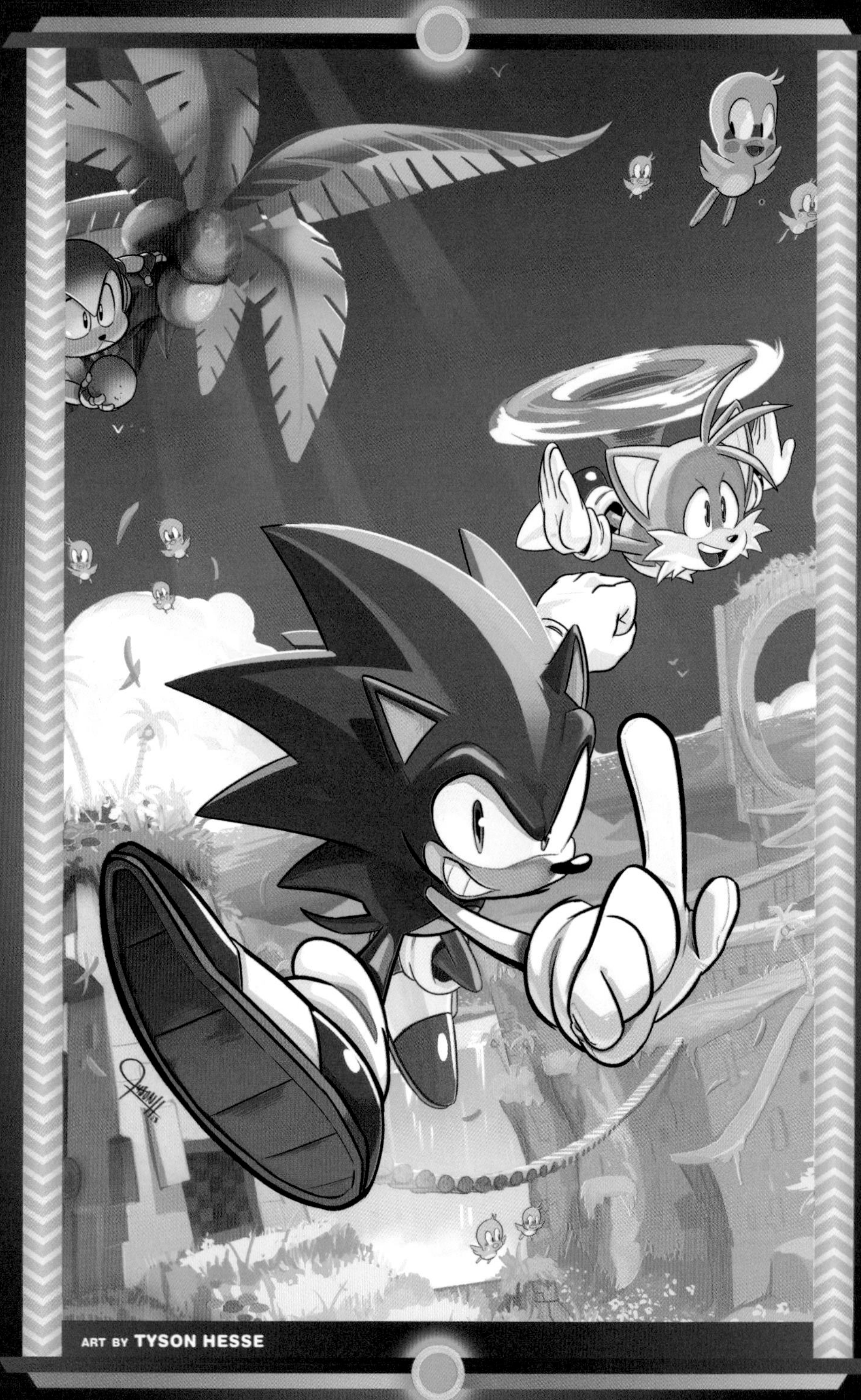

ART BY **TYSON HESSE**

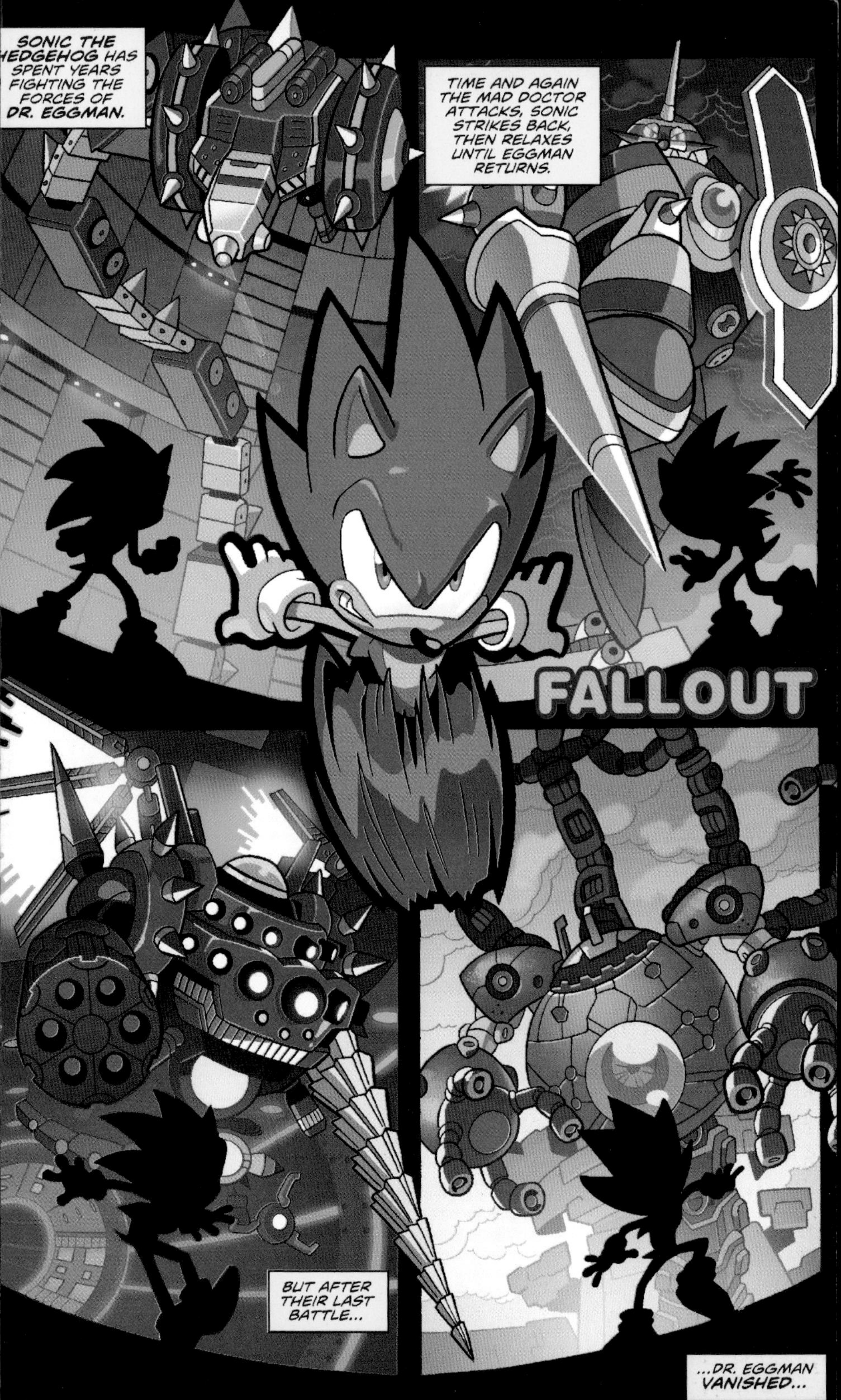
SONIC THE HEDGEHOG HAS SPENT YEARS FIGHTING THE FORCES OF DR. EGGMAN.
TIME AND AGAIN THE MAD DOCTOR ATTACKS, SONIC STRIKES BACK, THEN RELAXES UNTIL EGGMAN RETURNS.
FALLOUT
BUT AFTER THEIR LAST BATTLE...
...DR. EGGMAN VANISHED...

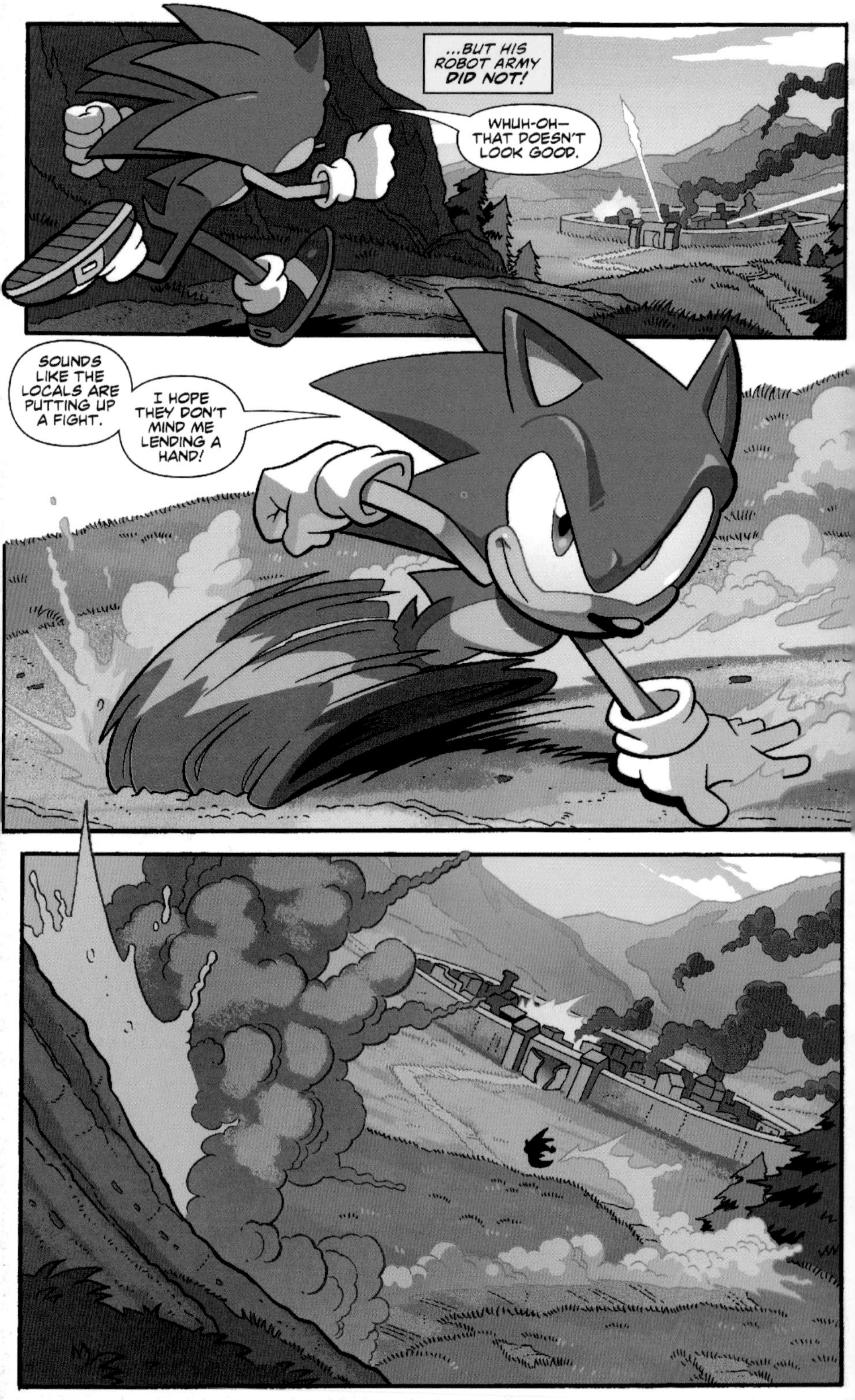
...BUT HIS ROBOT ARMY DID NOT!
WHUH-OH— THAT DOESN'T LOOK GOOD.
SOUNDS LIKE THE LOCALS ARE PUTTING UP A FIGHT.
I HOPE THEY DON'T MIND ME LENDING A HAND!

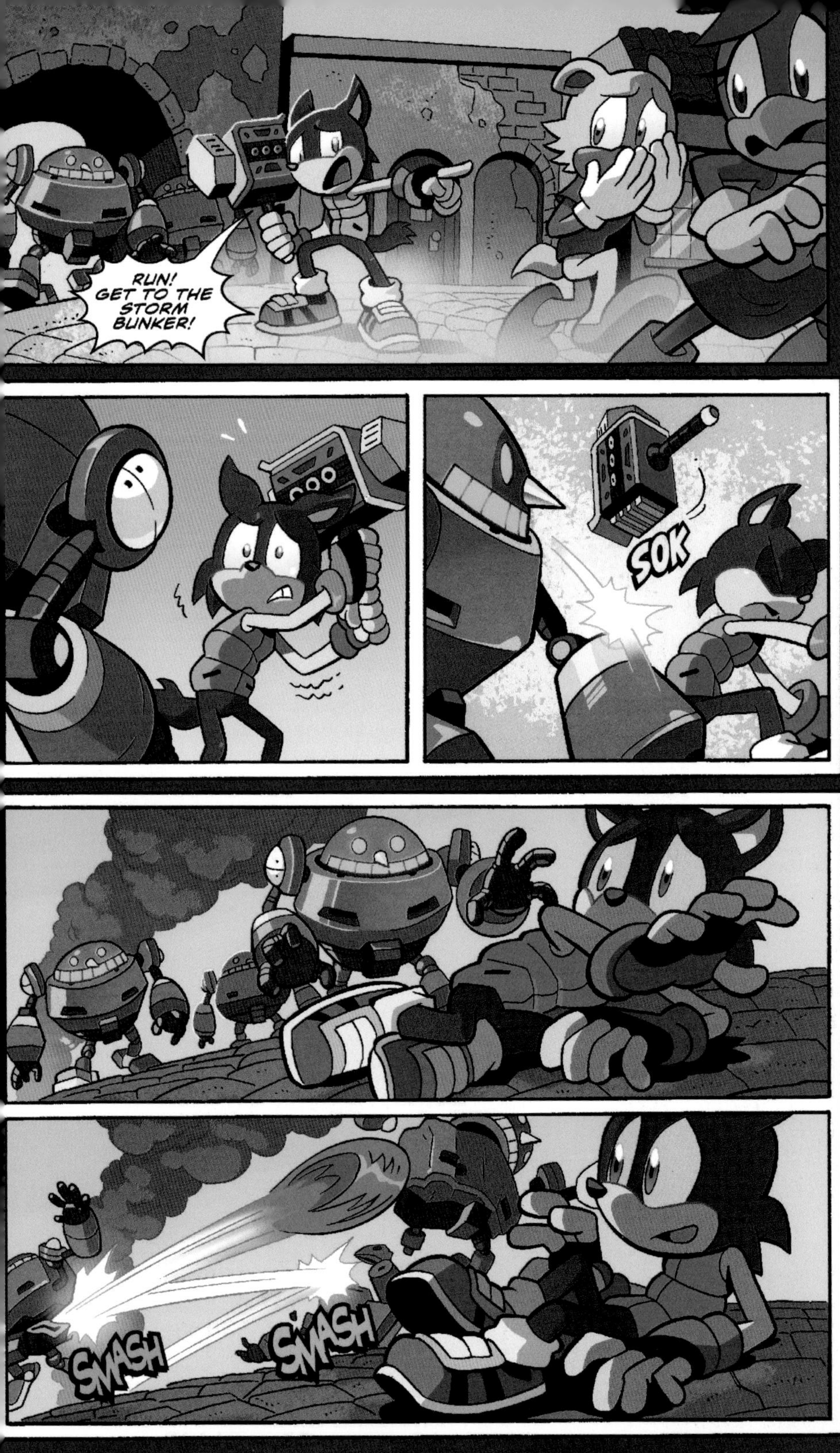
RUN! GET TO THE STORM BUNKER!
SOK
SMASH
SMASH

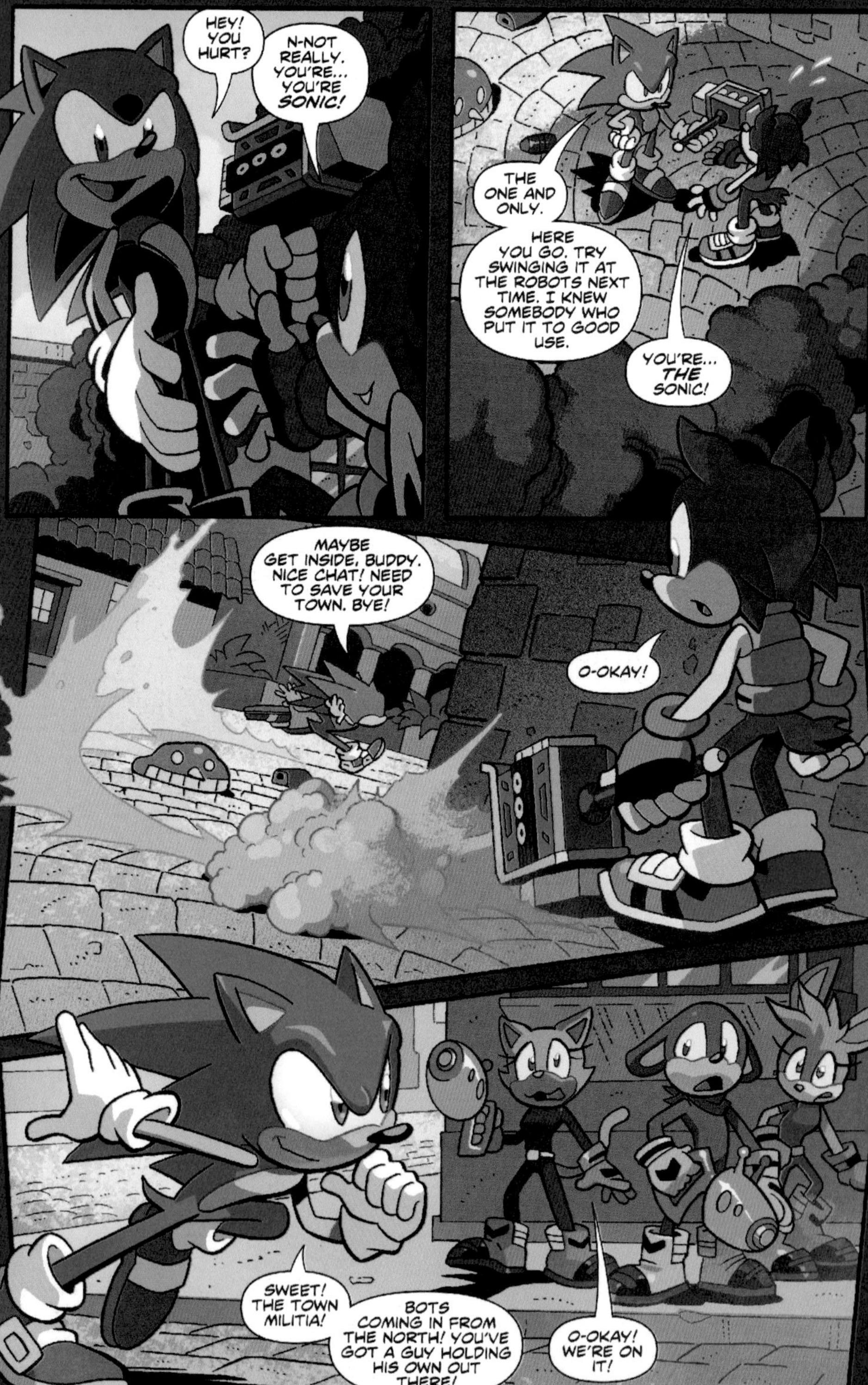
HEY! YOU HURT?
N-NOT REALLY. YOU'RE... YOU'RE *SONIC!*
THE ONE AND ONLY.
HERE YOU GO. TRY SWINGING IT AT THE ROBOTS NEXT TIME. I KNEW SOMEBODY WHO PUT IT TO GOOD USE.
YOU'RE... *THE* SONIC!
MAYBE GET INSIDE, BUDDY. NICE CHAT! NEED TO SAVE YOUR TOWN. BYE!
O-OKAY!
SWEET! THE TOWN MILITIA!
BOTS COMING IN FROM THE NORTH! YOU'VE GOT A GUY HOLDING HIS OWN OUT THERE!
O-OKAY! WE'RE ON IT!

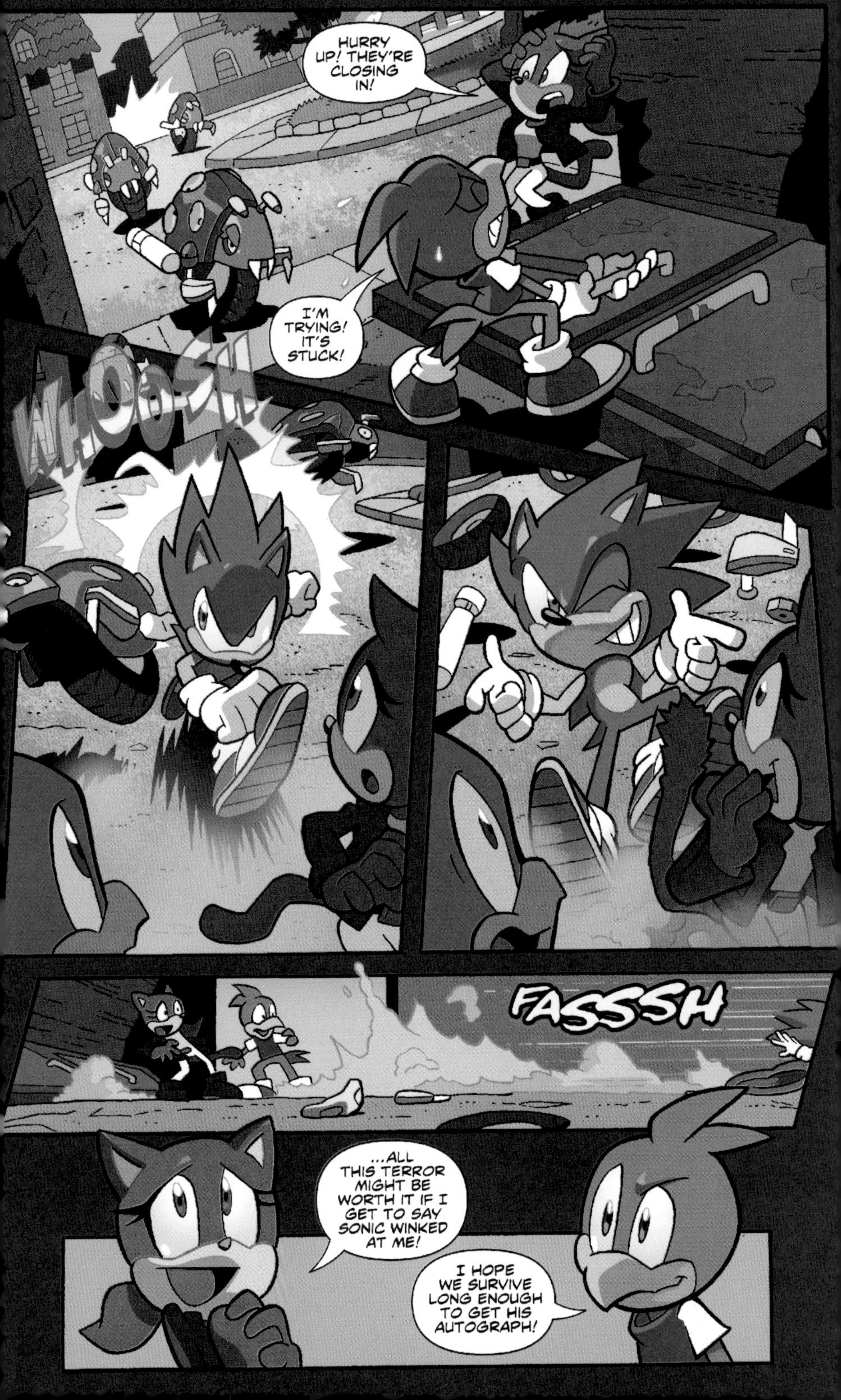
HURRY UP! THEY'RE CLOSING IN!
I'M TRYING! IT'S STUCK!
WHOOSH
FASSSH
...ALL THIS TERROR MIGHT BE WORTH IT IF I GET TO SAY SONIC WINKED AT ME!
I HOPE WE SURVIVE LONG ENOUGH TO GET HIS AUTOGRAPH!

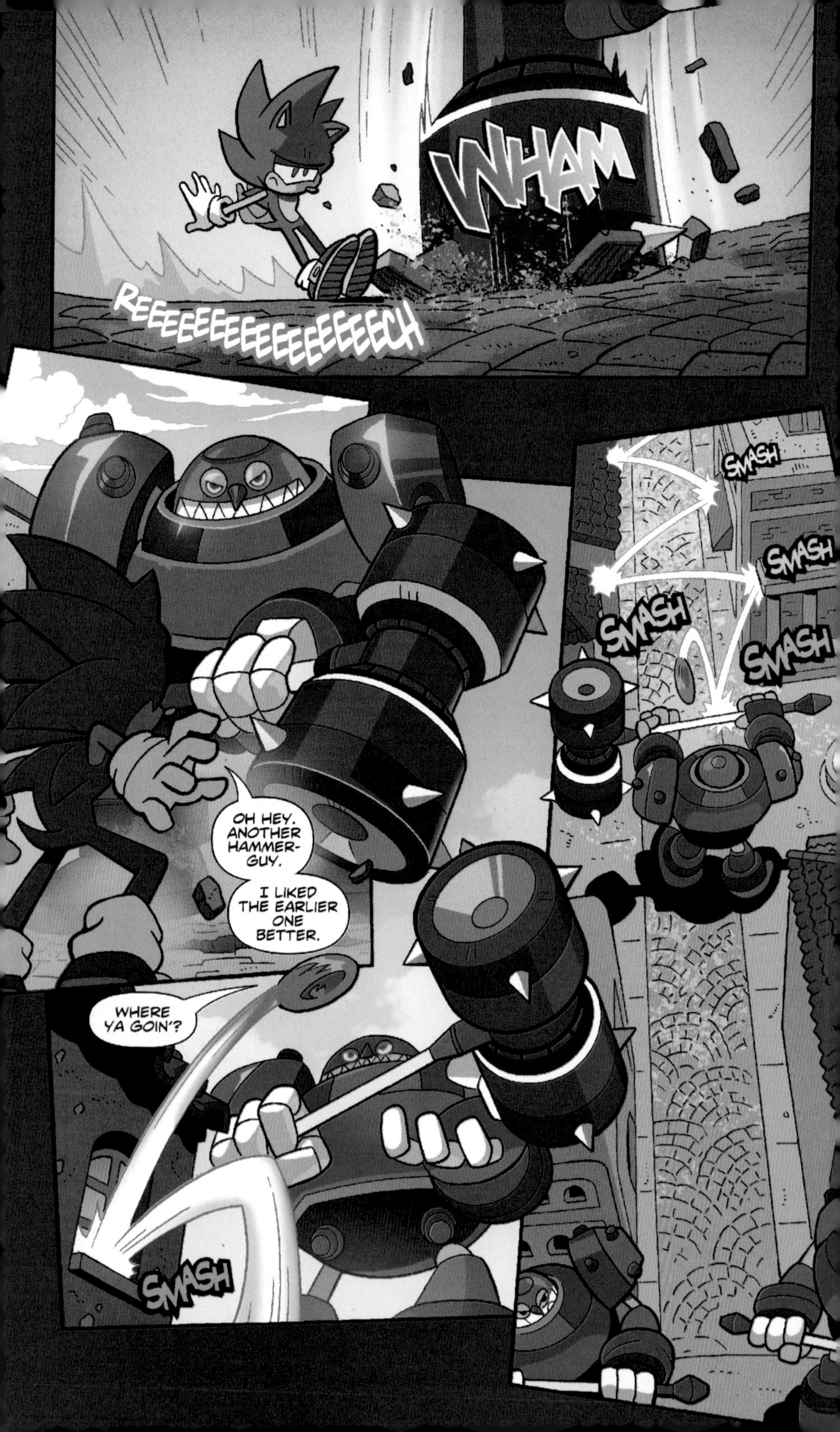
WHAM
REEEEEEEEEEEEEEEEEEECH
SMASH
SMASH
SMASH
SMASH
OH HEY. ANOTHER HAMMER-GUY.
I LIKED THE EARLIER ONE BETTER.
WHERE YA GOIN'?
SMASH

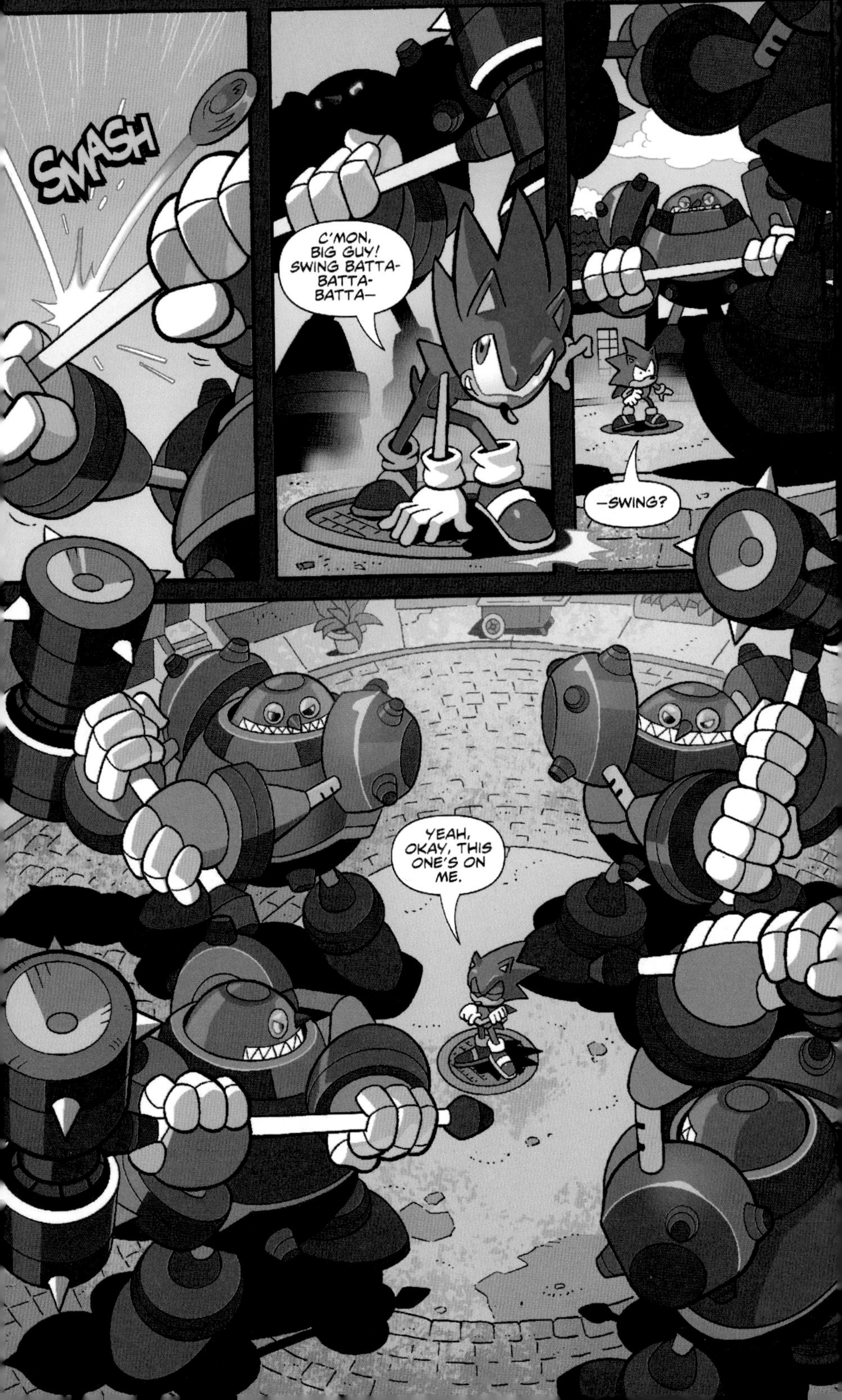
SMASH
C'MON, BIG GUY! SWING BATTA-BATTA-BATTA—
—SWING?
YEAH, OKAY, THIS ONE'S ON ME.

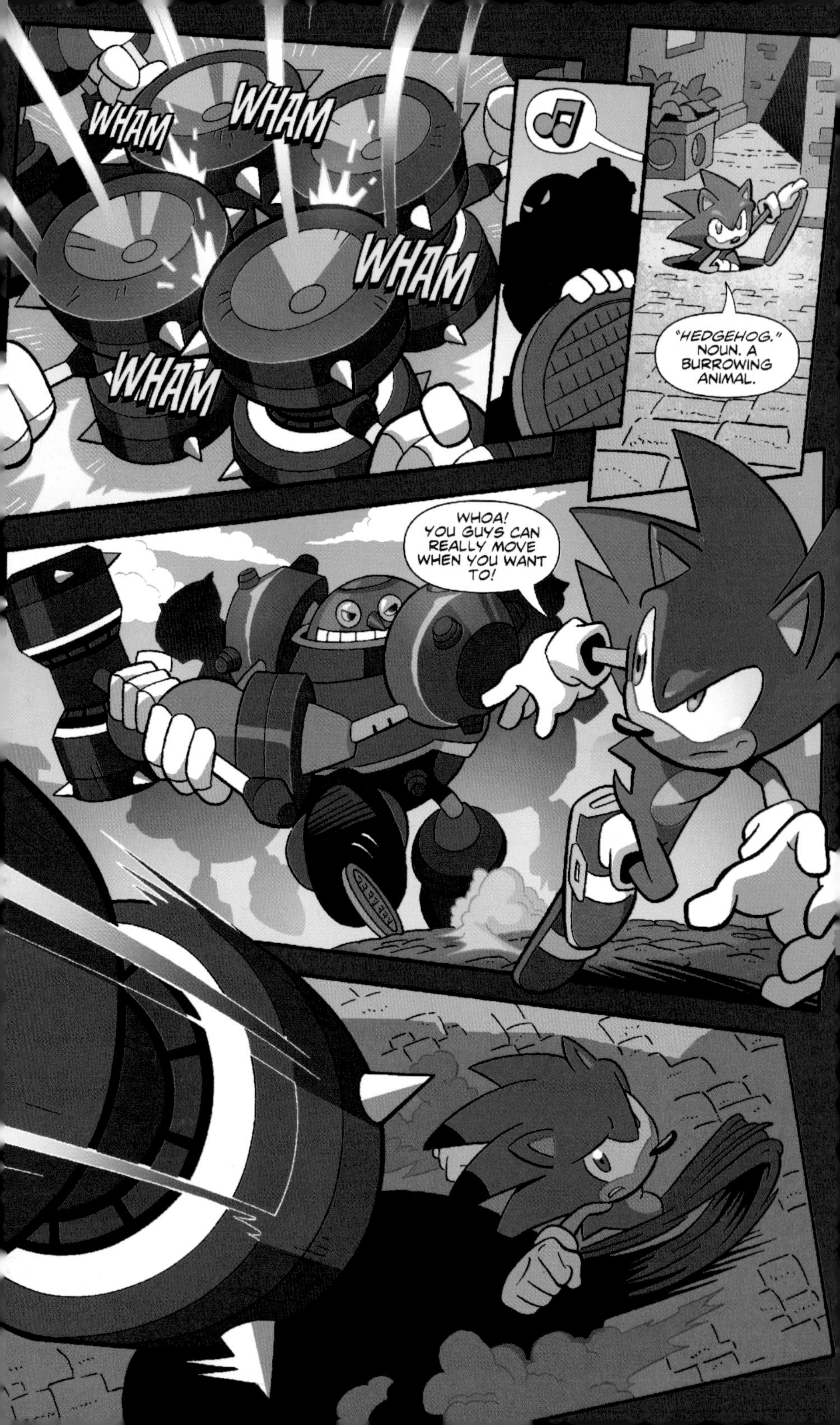
WHAM
WHAM
WHAM
WHAM
"HEDGEHOG." NOUN. A BURROWING ANIMAL.
WHOA! YOU GUYS CAN REALLY MOVE WHEN YOU WANT TO!

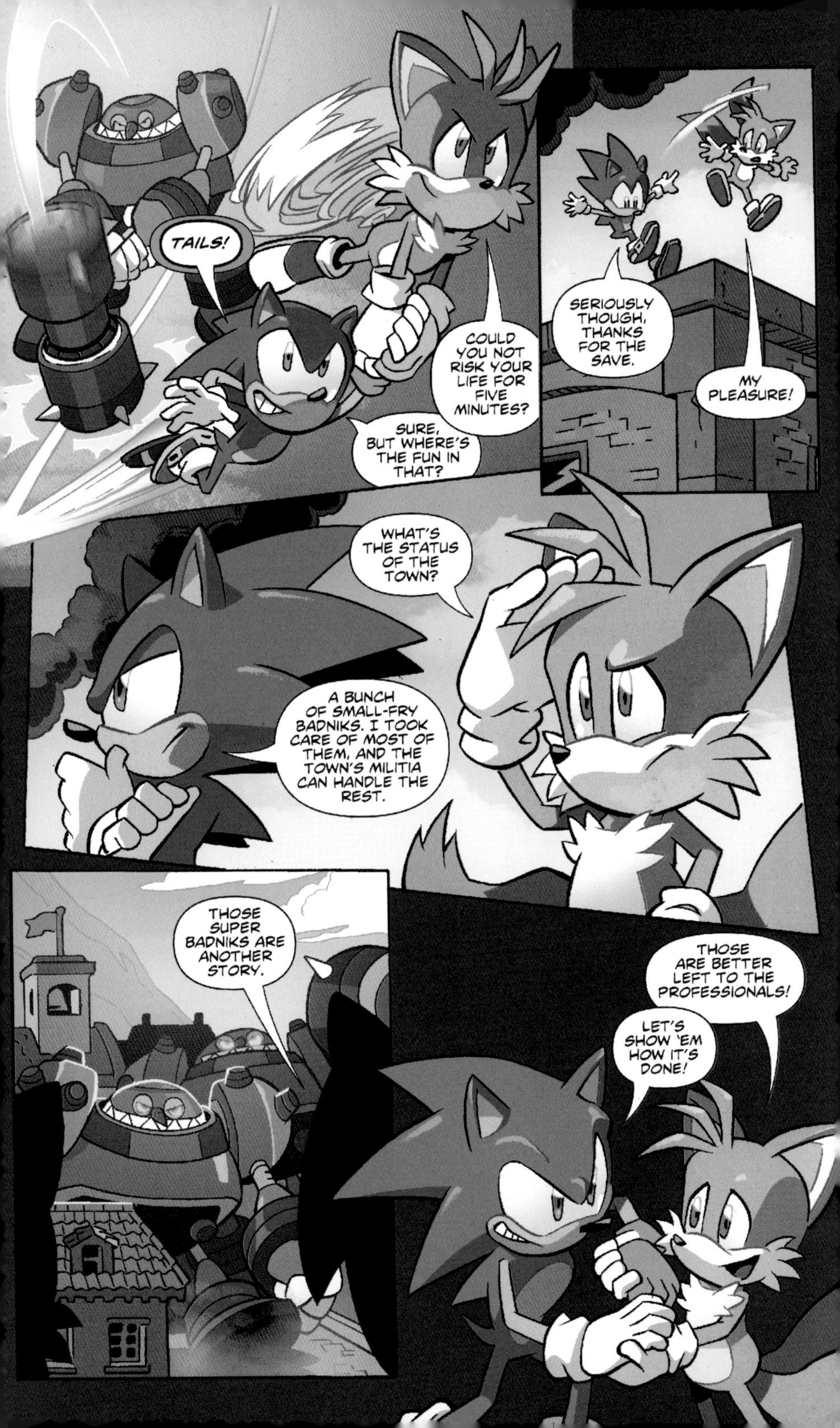
TAILS!
COULD YOU NOT RISK YOUR LIFE FOR FIVE MINUTES?
SURE, BUT WHERE'S THE FUN IN THAT?
SERIOUSLY THOUGH, THANKS FOR THE SAVE.
MY PLEASURE!
WHAT'S THE STATUS OF THE TOWN?
A BUNCH OF SMALL-FRY BADNIKS. I TOOK CARE OF MOST OF THEM, AND THE TOWN'S MILITIA CAN HANDLE THE REST.
THOSE SUPER BADNIKS ARE ANOTHER STORY.
THOSE ARE BETTER LEFT TO THE PROFESSIONALS!
LET'S SHOW 'EM HOW IT'S DONE!

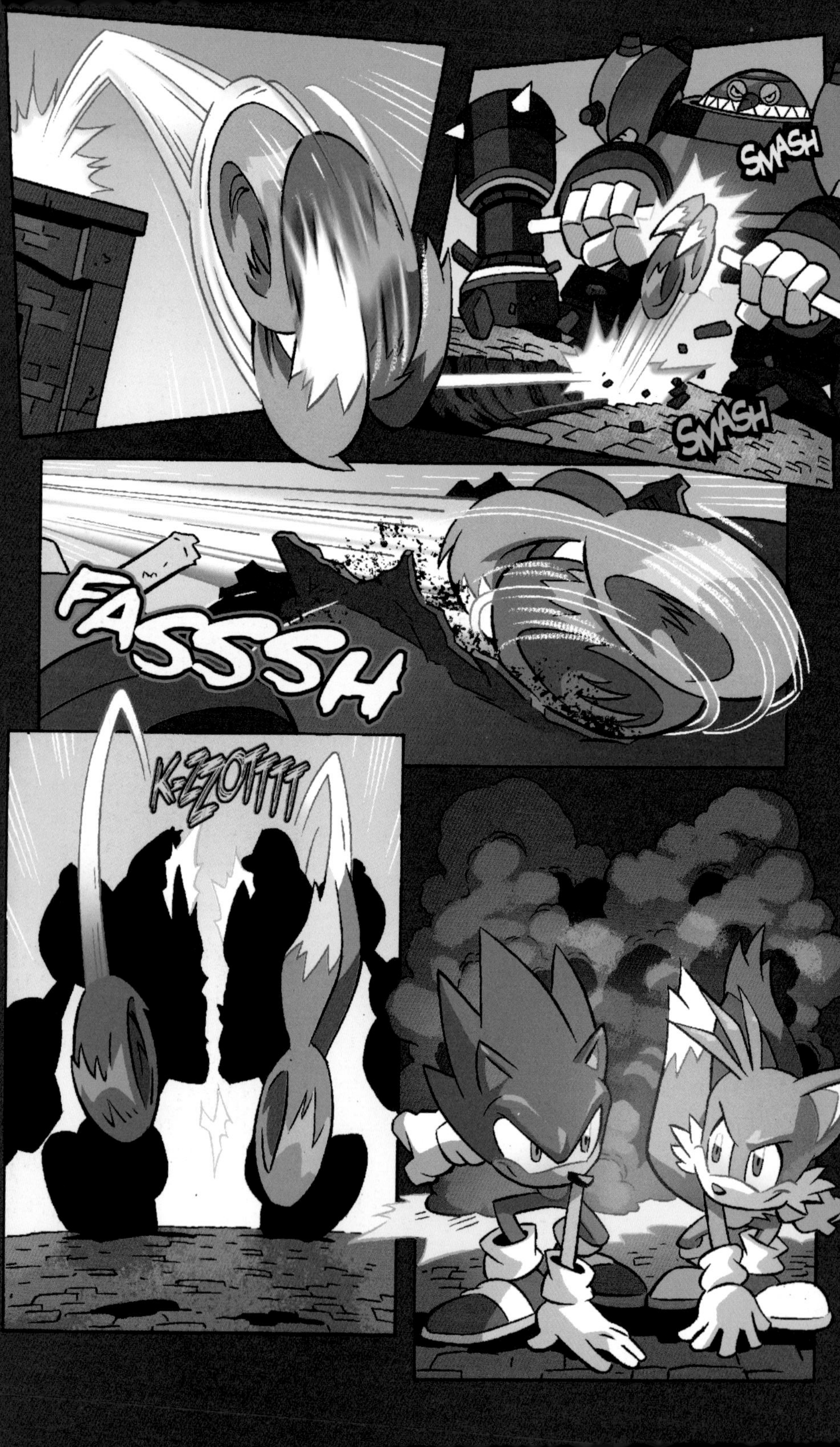
SMASH
SMASH
FASSSH
K-ZZOTTTT

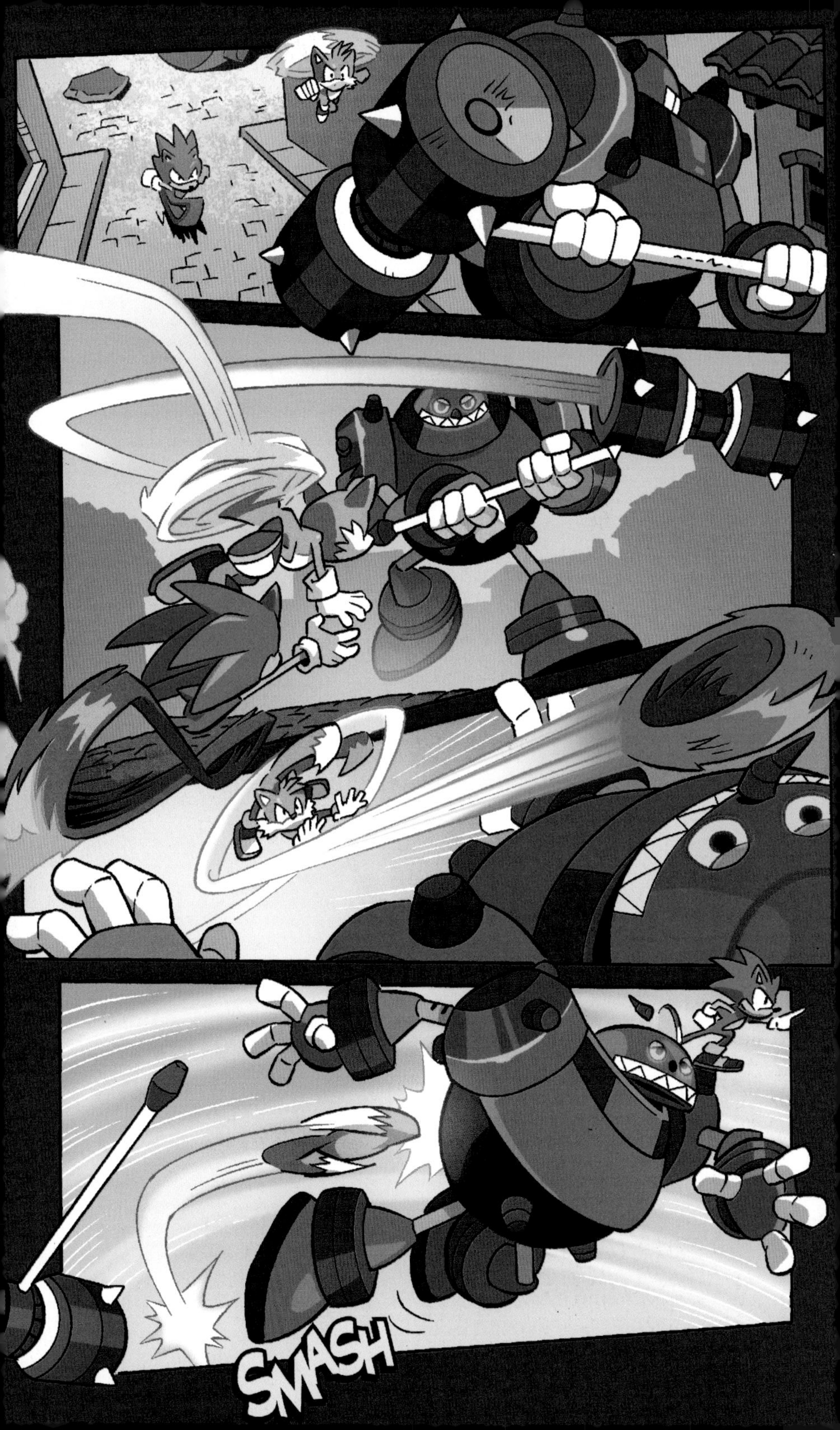
SMASH

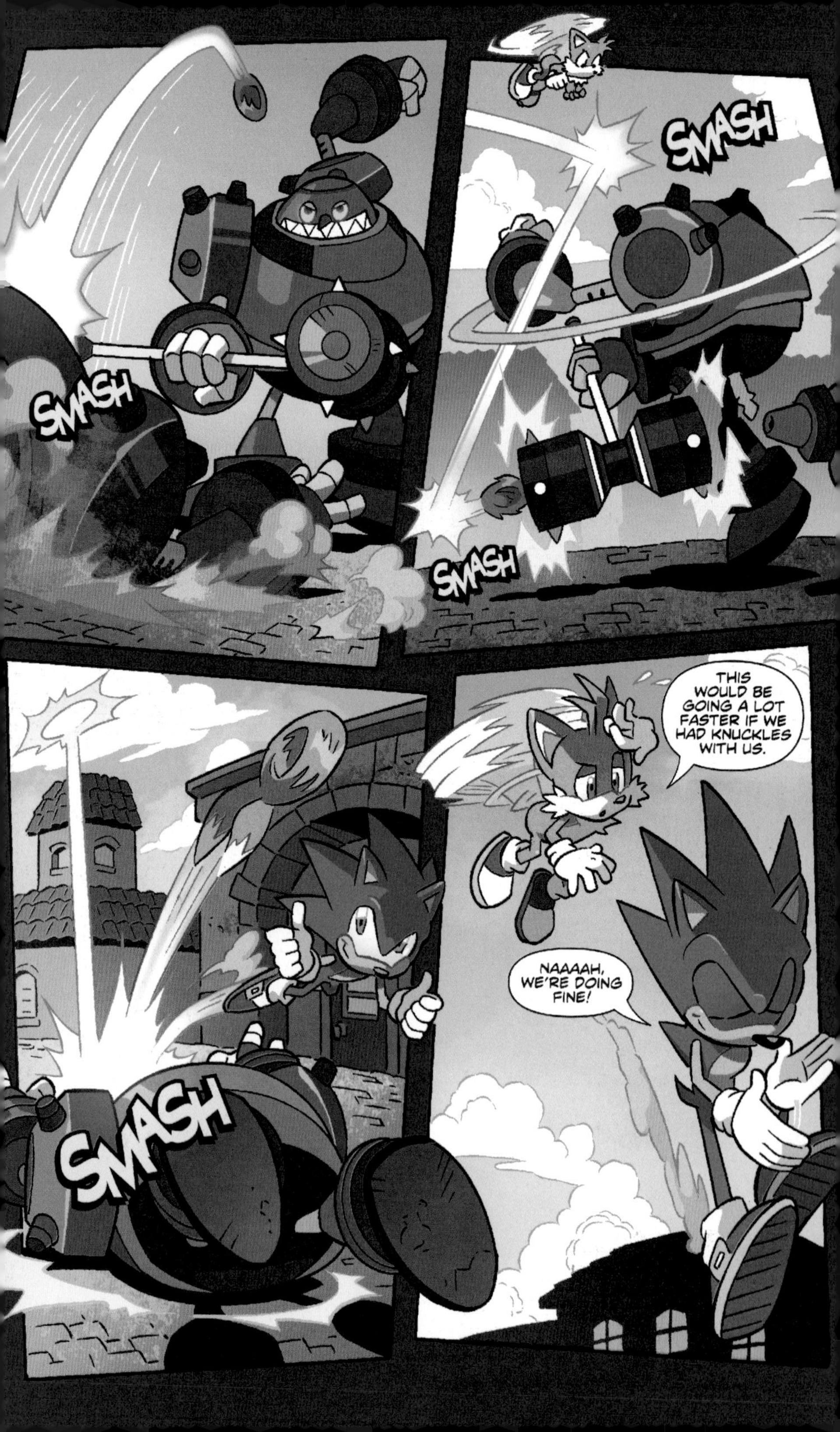
SMASH
SMASH
SMASH
SMASH
THIS WOULD BE GOING A LOT FASTER IF WE HAD KNUCKLES WITH US.
NAAAAH, WE'RE DOING FINE!

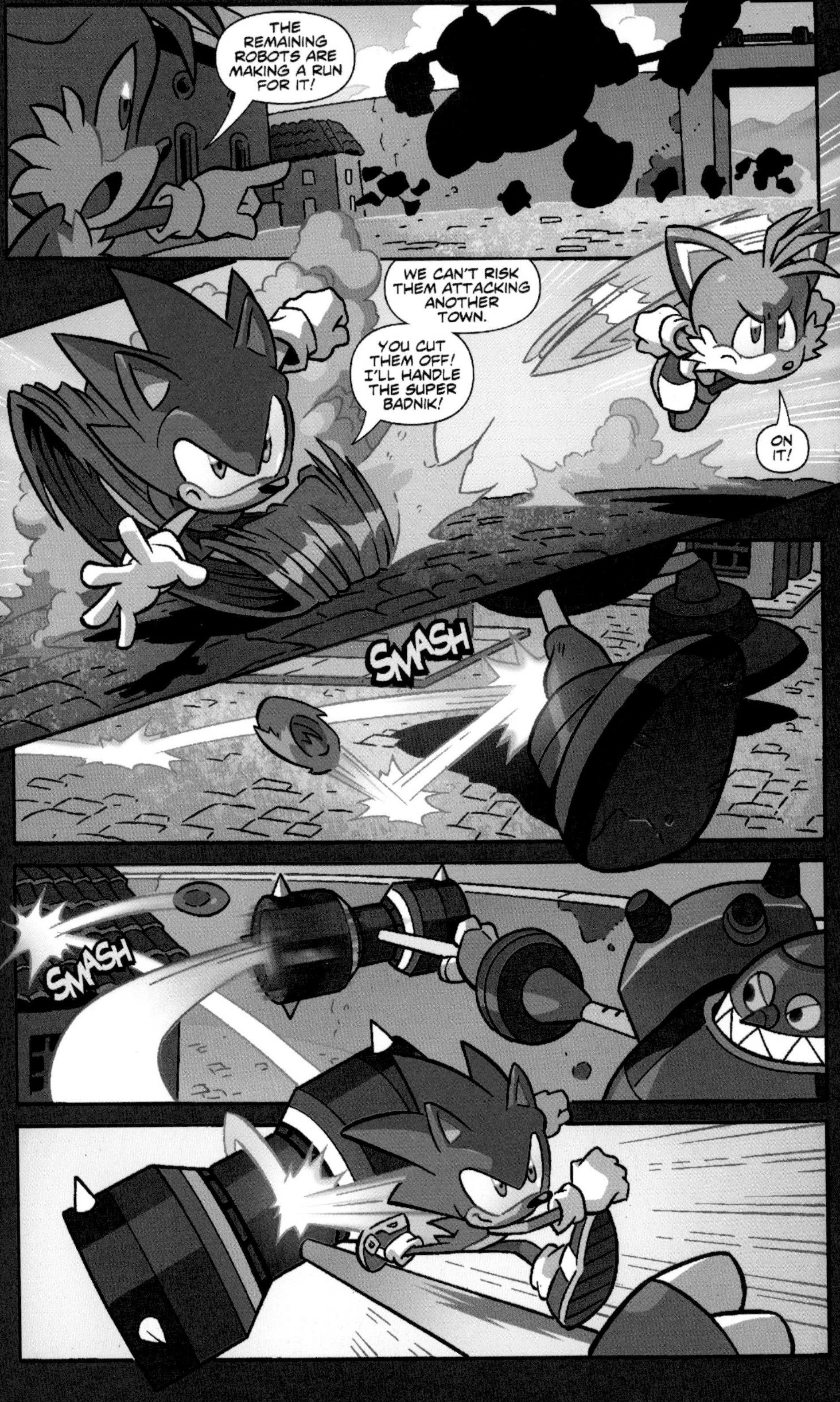

THE REMAINING ROBOTS ARE MAKING A RUN FOR IT!
WE CAN'T RISK THEM ATTACKING ANOTHER TOWN.
YOU CUT THEM OFF! I'LL HANDLE THE SUPER BADNIK!
ON IT!
SMASH
SMASH

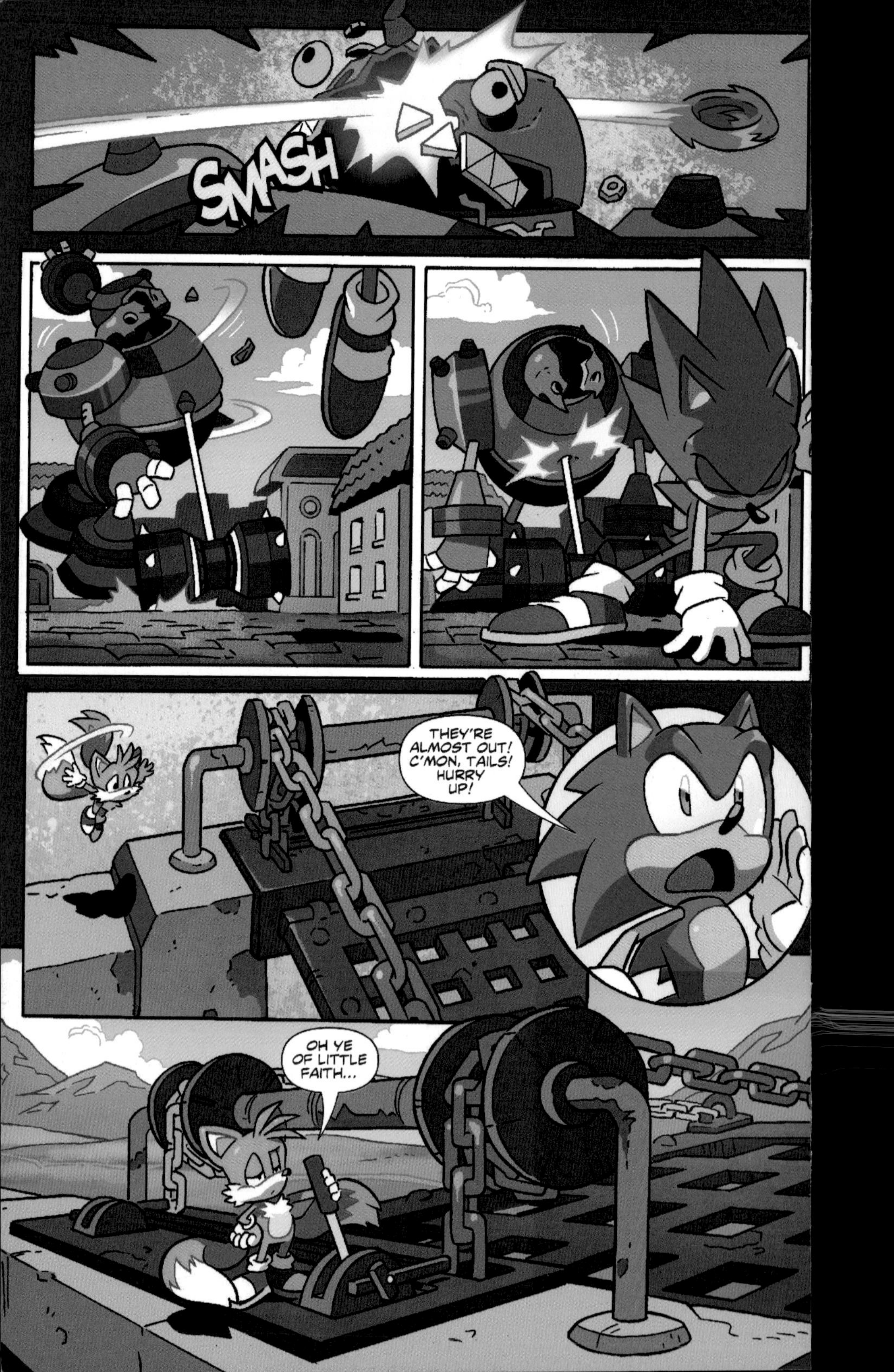
SMASH
THEY'RE ALMOST OUT! C'MON, TAILS! HURRY UP!
OH YE OF LITTLE FAITH...

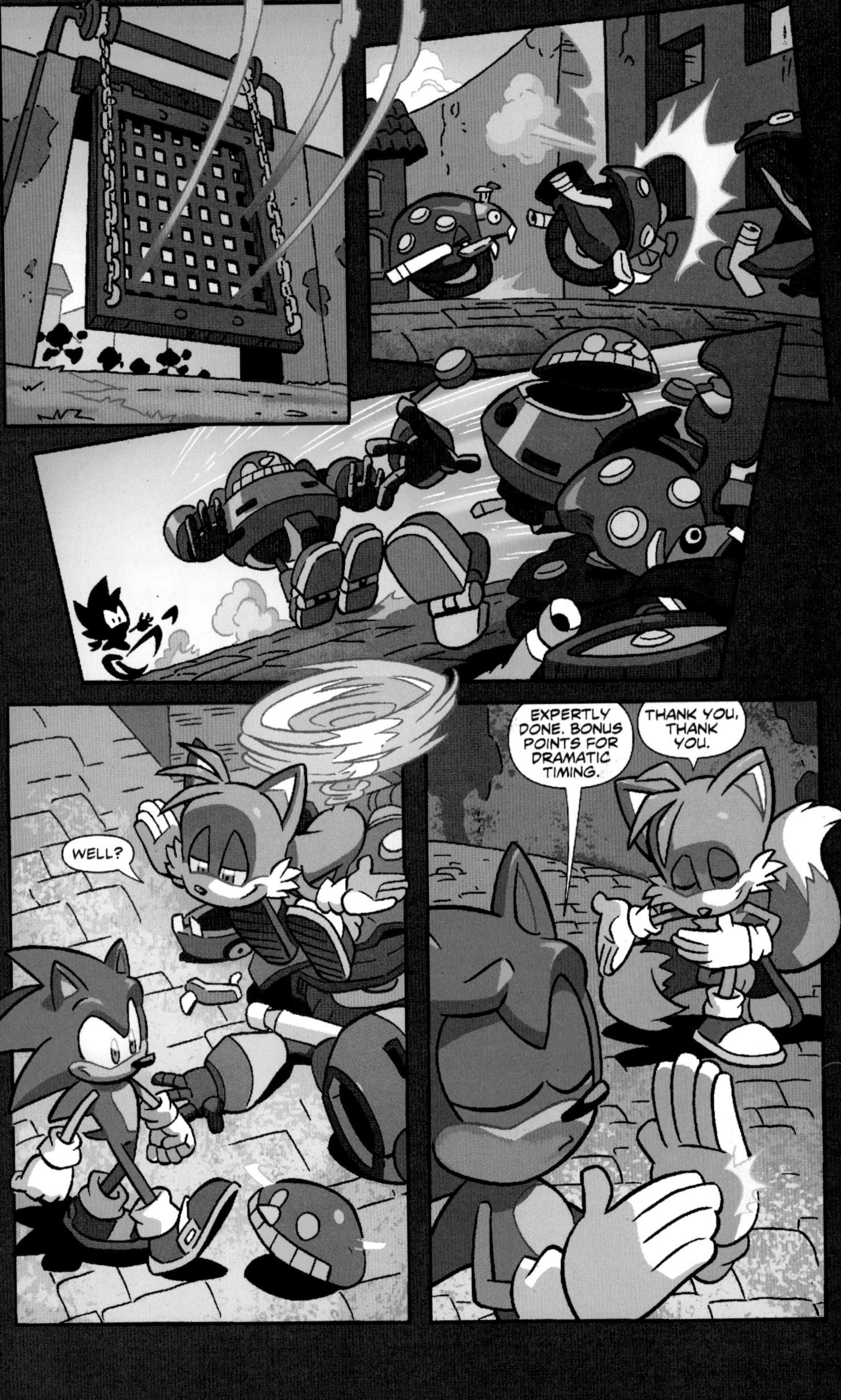
WELL?
EXPERTLY DONE. BONUS POINTS FOR DRAMATIC TIMING.
THANK YOU, THANK YOU.

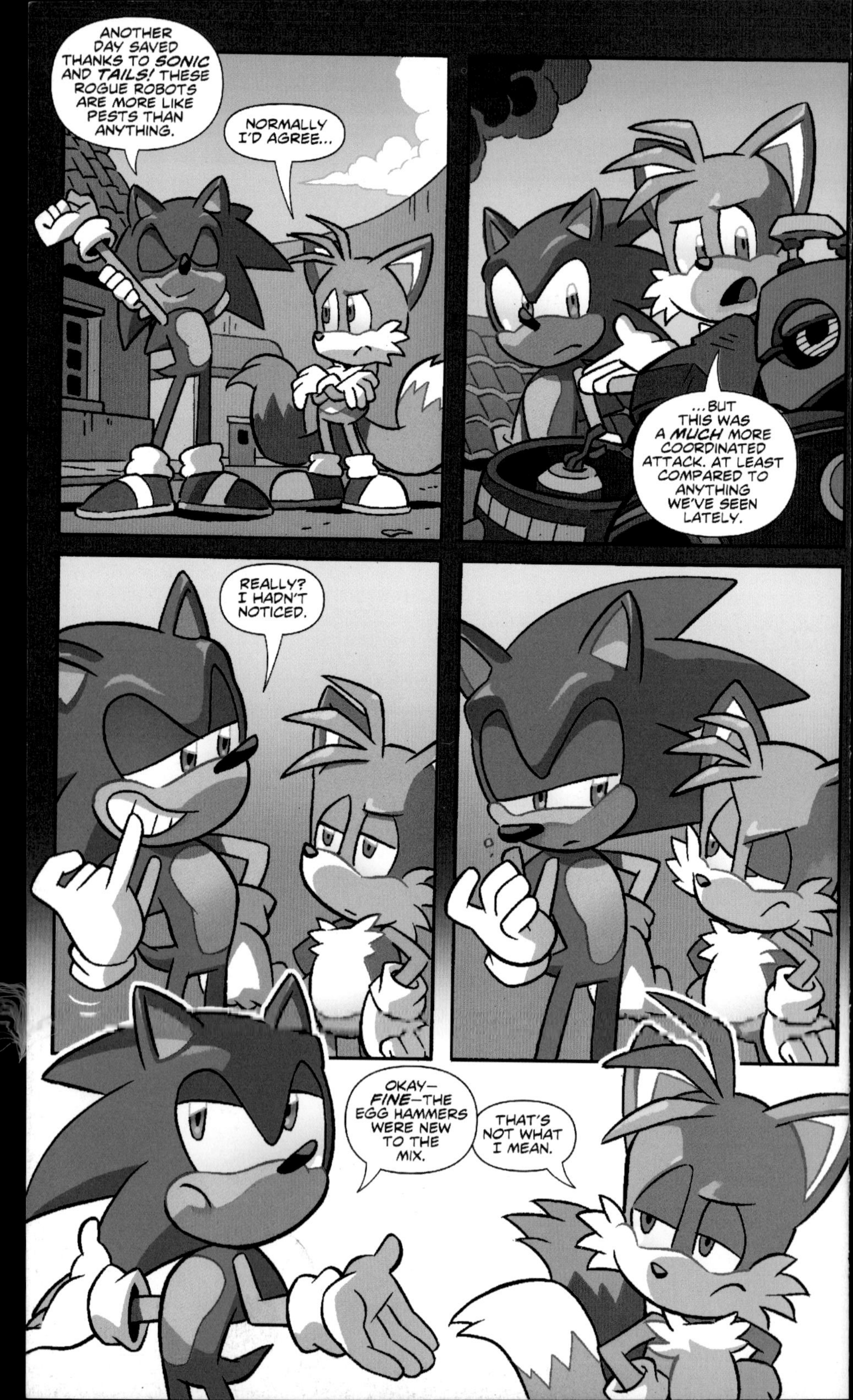
ANOTHER DAY SAVED THANKS TO SONIC AND TAILS! THESE ROGUE ROBOTS ARE MORE LIKE PESTS THAN ANYTHING.
NORMALLY I'D AGREE...
...BUT THIS WAS A MUCH MORE COORDINATED ATTACK. AT LEAST COMPARED TO ANYTHING WE'VE SEEN LATELY.
REALLY? I HADN'T NOTICED.
OKAY—FINE—THE EGG HAMMERS WERE NEW TO THE MIX.
THAT'S NOT WHAT I MEAN.

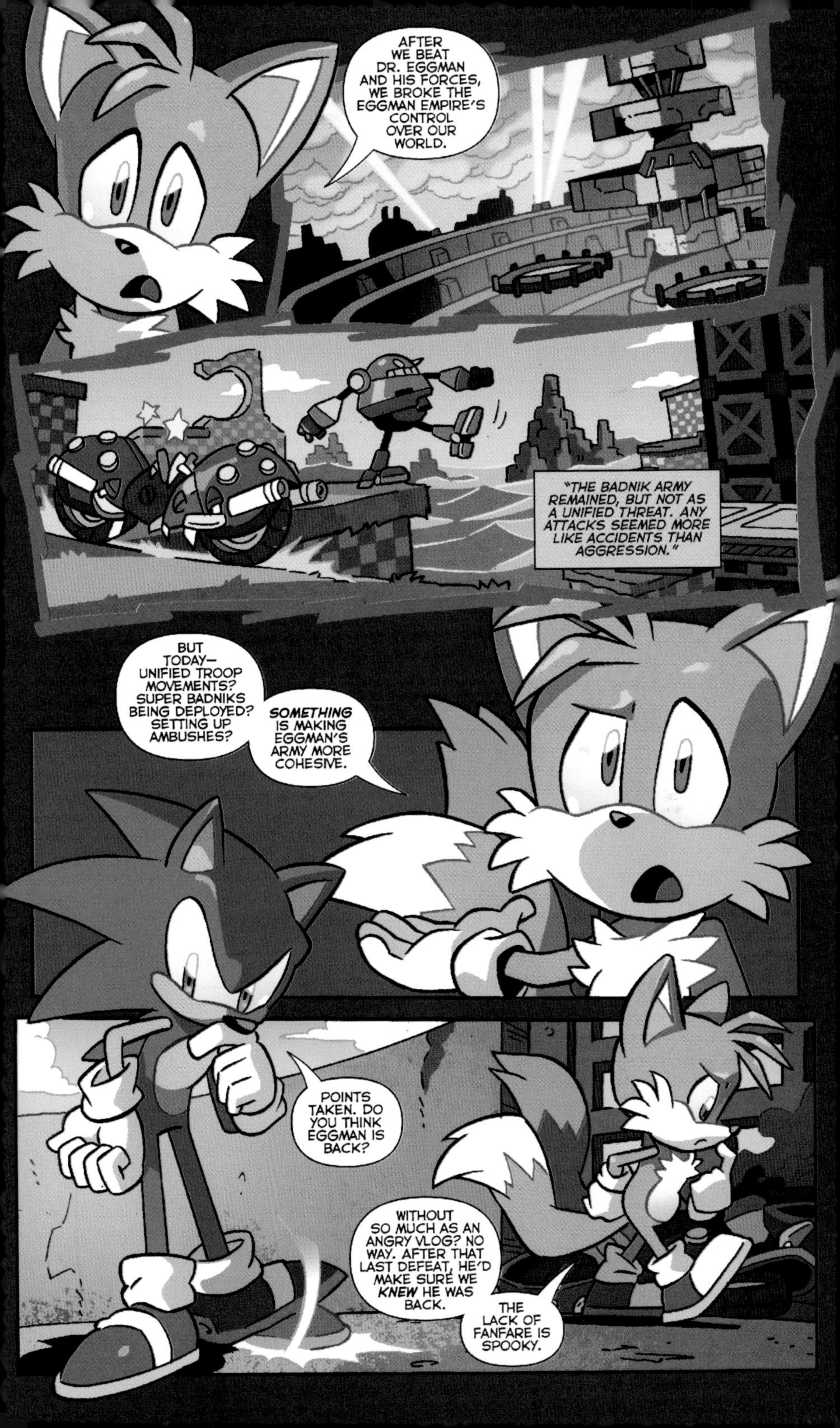
AFTER WE BEAT DR. EGGMAN AND HIS FORCES, WE BROKE THE EGGMAN EMPIRE'S CONTROL OVER OUR WORLD.
"THE BADNIK ARMY REMAINED, BUT NOT AS A UNIFIED THREAT. ANY ATTACKS SEEMED MORE LIKE ACCIDENTS THAN AGGRESSION."
BUT TODAY— UNIFIED TROOP MOVEMENTS? SUPER BADNIKS BEING DEPLOYED? SETTING UP AMBUSHES?
SOMETHING IS MAKING EGGMAN'S ARMY MORE COHESIVE.
POINTS TAKEN. DO YOU THINK EGGMAN IS BACK?
WITHOUT SO MUCH AS AN ANGRY VLOG? NO WAY. AFTER THAT LAST DEFEAT, HE'D MAKE SURE WE *KNEW* HE WAS BACK.
THE LACK OF FANFARE IS SPOOKY.

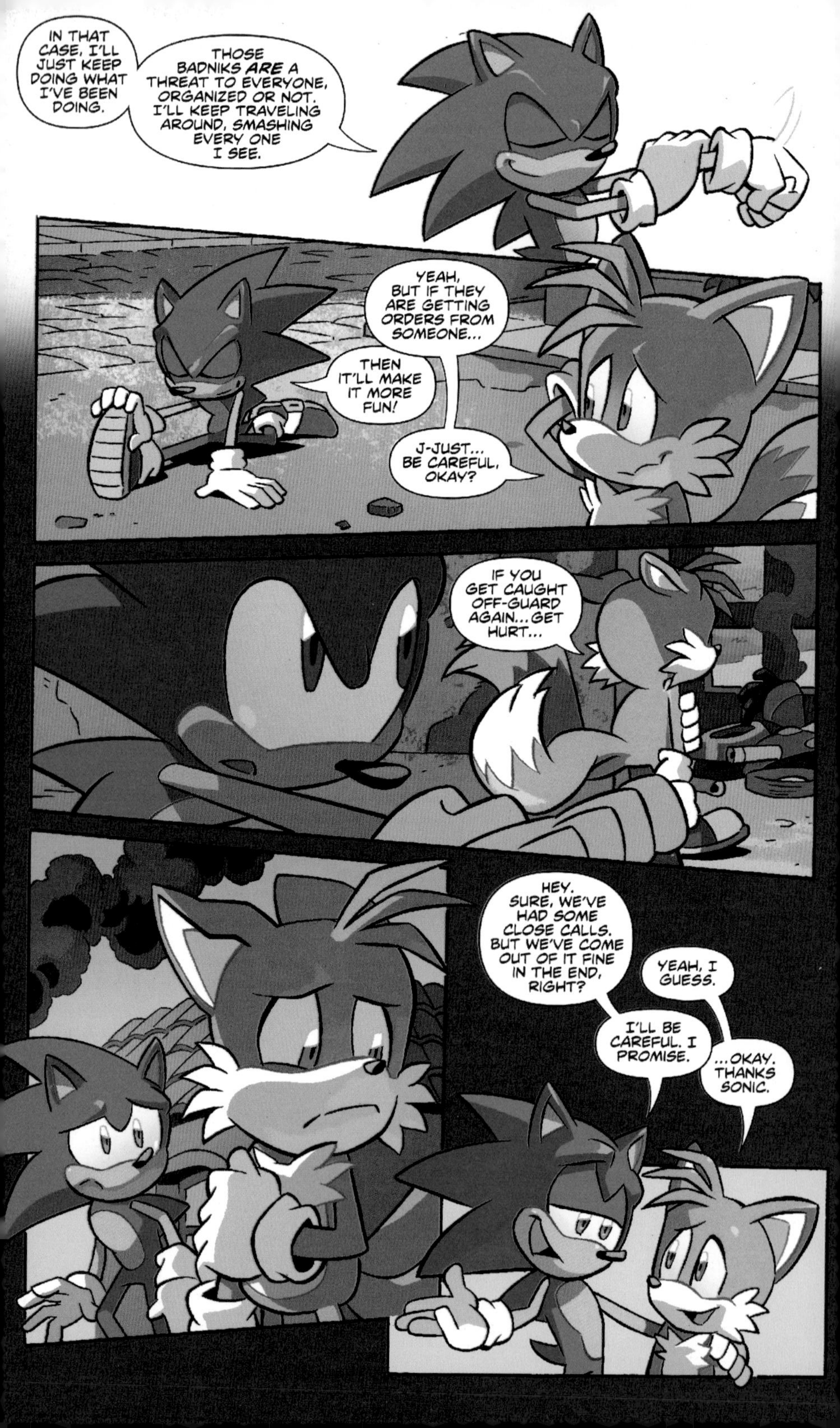

IN THAT CASE, I'LL JUST KEEP DOING WHAT I'VE BEEN DOING.
THOSE BADNIKS ARE A THREAT TO EVERYONE, ORGANIZED OR NOT. I'LL KEEP TRAVELING AROUND, SMASHING EVERY ONE I SEE.
YEAH, BUT IF THEY ARE GETTING ORDERS FROM SOMEONE...
THEN IT'LL MAKE IT MORE FUN!
J-JUST... BE CAREFUL, OKAY?
IF YOU GET CAUGHT OFF-GUARD AGAIN... GET HURT...
HEY. SURE, WE'VE HAD SOME CLOSE CALLS. BUT WE'VE COME OUT OF IT FINE IN THE END, RIGHT?
YEAH, I GUESS.
I'LL BE CAREFUL. I PROMISE.
...OKAY. THANKS SONIC.

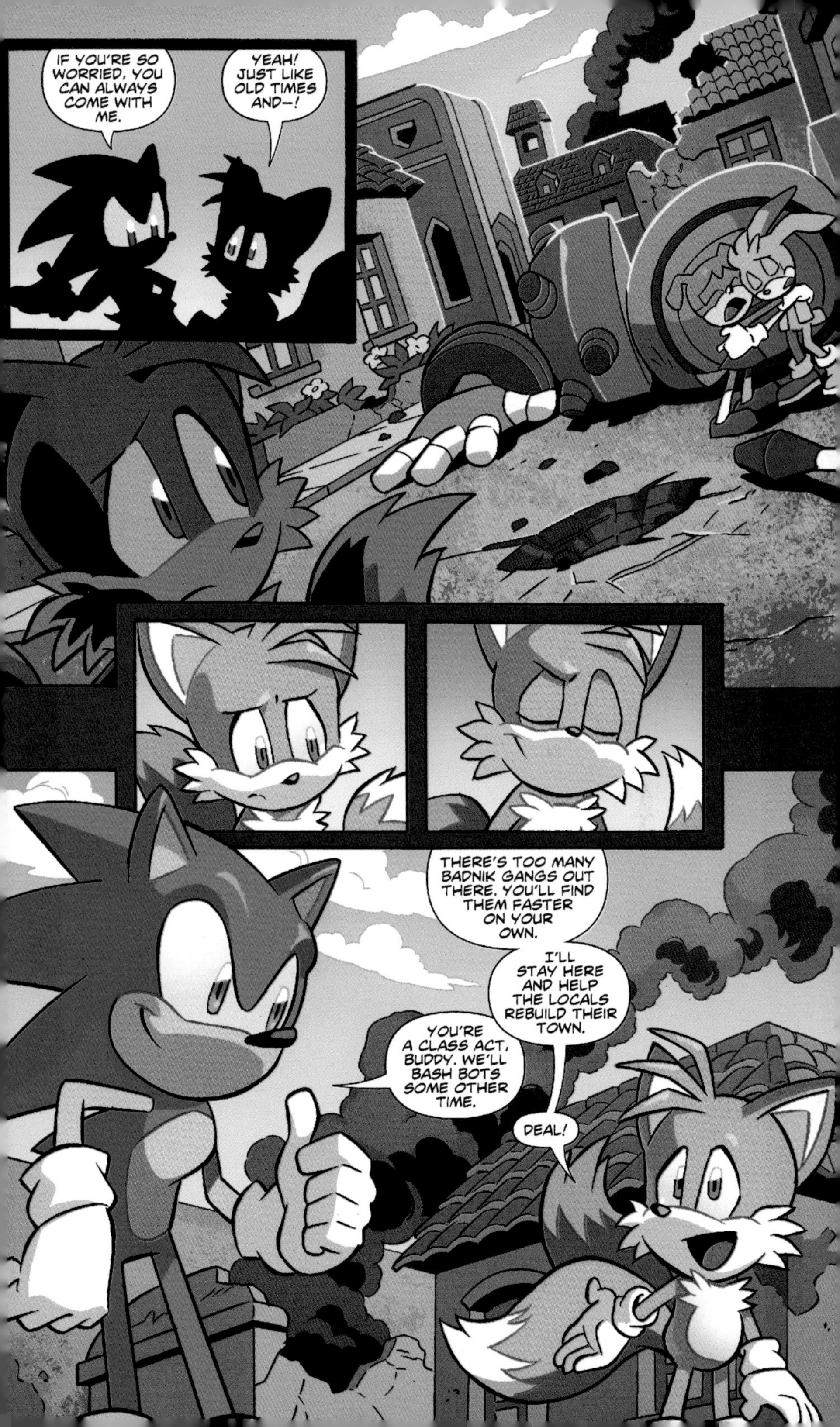
IF YOU'RE SO WORRIED, YOU CAN ALWAYS COME WITH ME.
YEAH! JUST LIKE OLD TIMES AND--!
THERE'S TOO MANY BADNIK GANGS OUT THERE. YOU'LL FIND THEM FASTER ON YOUR OWN.
I'LL STAY HERE AND HELP THE LOCALS REBUILD THEIR TOWN.
YOU'RE A CLASS ACT, BUDDY. WE'LL BASH BOTS SOME OTHER TIME.
DEAL!

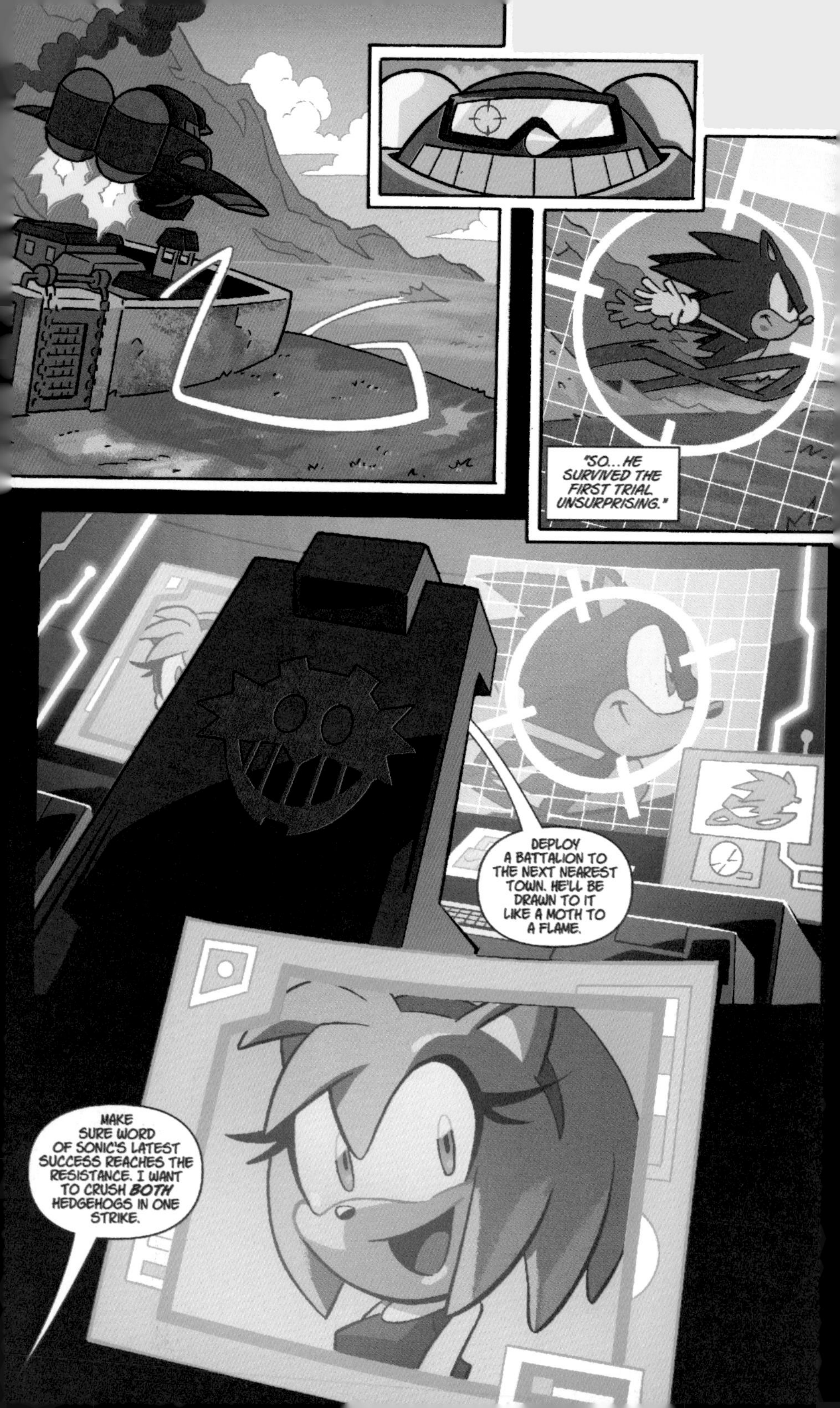
"SO... HE SURVIVED THE FIRST TRIAL. UNSURPRISING."
DEPLOY A BATTALION TO THE NEXT NEAREST TOWN. HE'LL BE DRAWN TO IT LIKE A MOTH TO A FLAME.
MAKE SURE WORD OF SONIC'S LATEST SUCCESS REACHES THE RESISTANCE. I WANT TO CRUSH *BOTH* HEDGEHOGS IN ONE STRIKE.

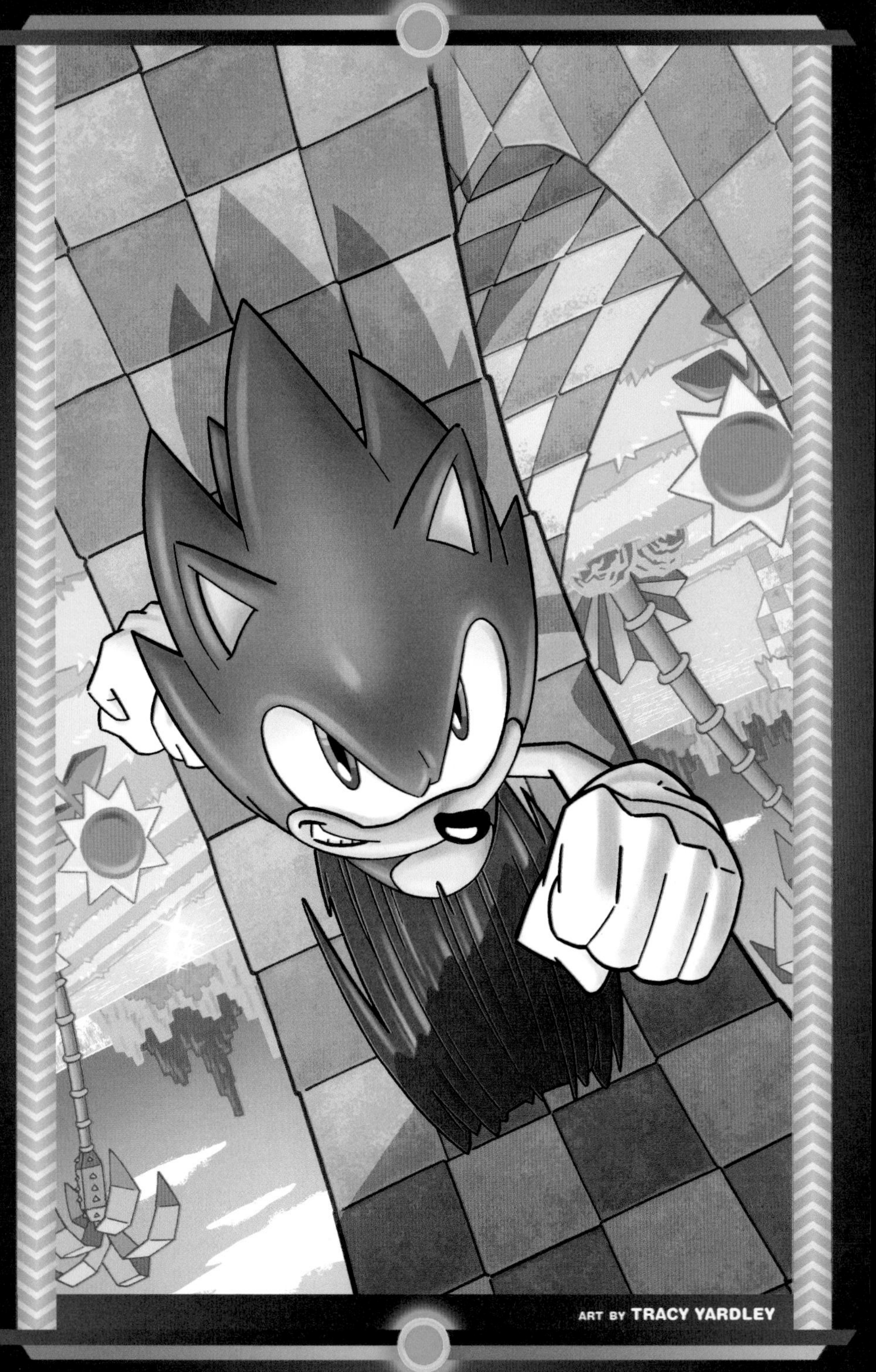

ART BY TRACY YARDLEY

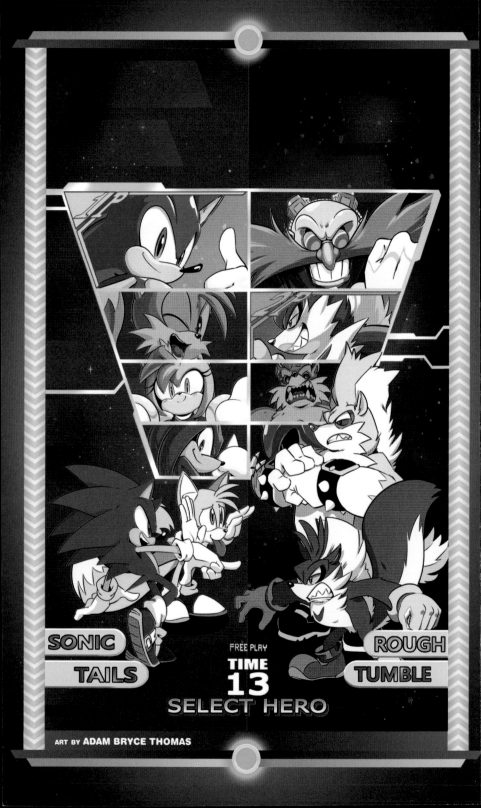

SONIC
TAILS

FREE PLAY
TIME
13
SELECT HERO

ROUGH
TUMBLE

ART BY ADAM BRYCE THOMAS

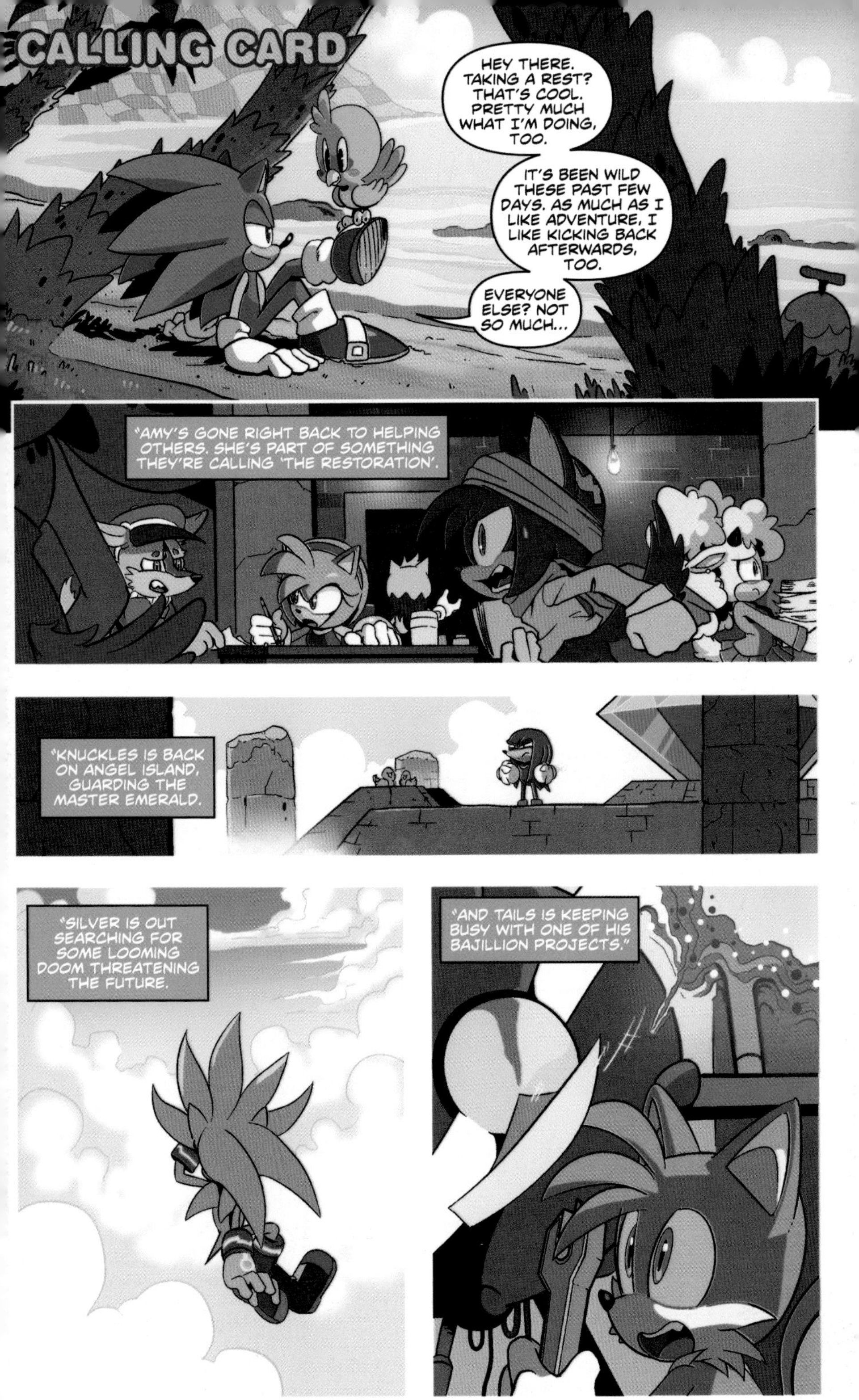
CALLING CARD
HEY THERE. TAKING A REST? THAT'S COOL. PRETTY MUCH WHAT I'M DOING, TOO.
IT'S BEEN WILD THESE PAST FEW DAYS. AS MUCH AS I LIKE ADVENTURE, I LIKE KICKING BACK AFTERWARDS, TOO.
EVERYONE ELSE? NOT SO MUCH...
"AMY'S GONE RIGHT BACK TO HELPING OTHERS. SHE'S PART OF SOMETHING THEY'RE CALLING 'THE RESTORATION'.
"KNUCKLES IS BACK ON ANGEL ISLAND, GUARDING THE MASTER EMERALD.
"SILVER IS OUT SEARCHING FOR SOME LOOMING DOOM THREATENING THE FUTURE.
"AND TAILS IS KEEPING BUSY WITH ONE OF HIS BAJILLION PROJECTS."

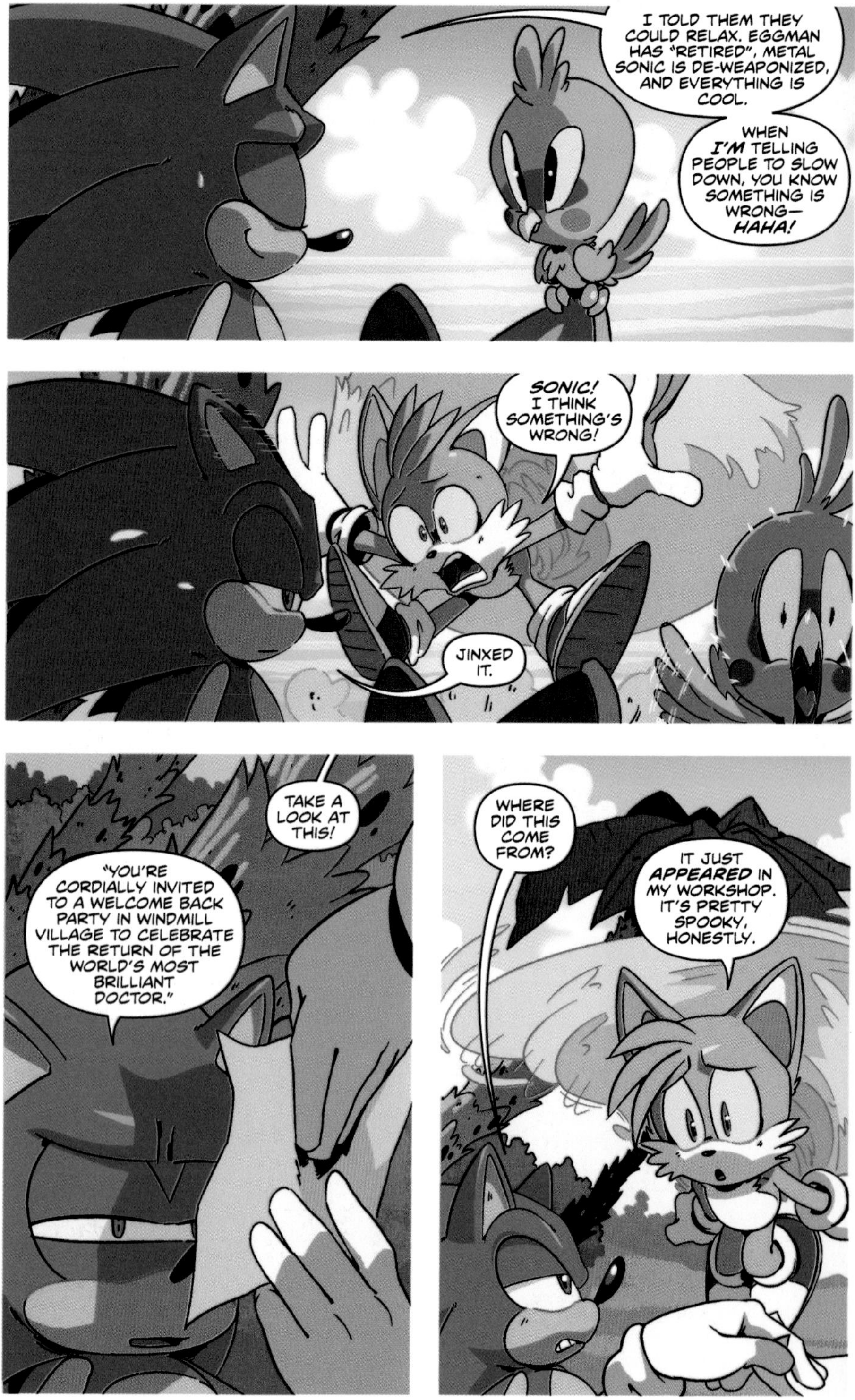
I TOLD THEM THEY COULD RELAX. EGGMAN HAS "RETIRED", METAL SONIC IS DE-WEAPONIZED, AND EVERYTHING IS COOL.
WHEN *I'M* TELLING PEOPLE TO SLOW DOWN, YOU KNOW SOMETHING IS WRONG— *HAHA!*
SONIC! I THINK SOMETHING'S WRONG!
JINXED IT.
TAKE A LOOK AT THIS!
"YOU'RE CORDIALLY INVITED TO A WELCOME BACK PARTY IN WINDMILL VILLAGE TO CELEBRATE THE RETURN OF THE WORLD'S MOST BRILLIANT DOCTOR."
WHERE DID THIS COME FROM?
IT JUST *APPEARED* IN MY WORKSHOP. IT'S PRETTY SPOOKY, HONESTLY.

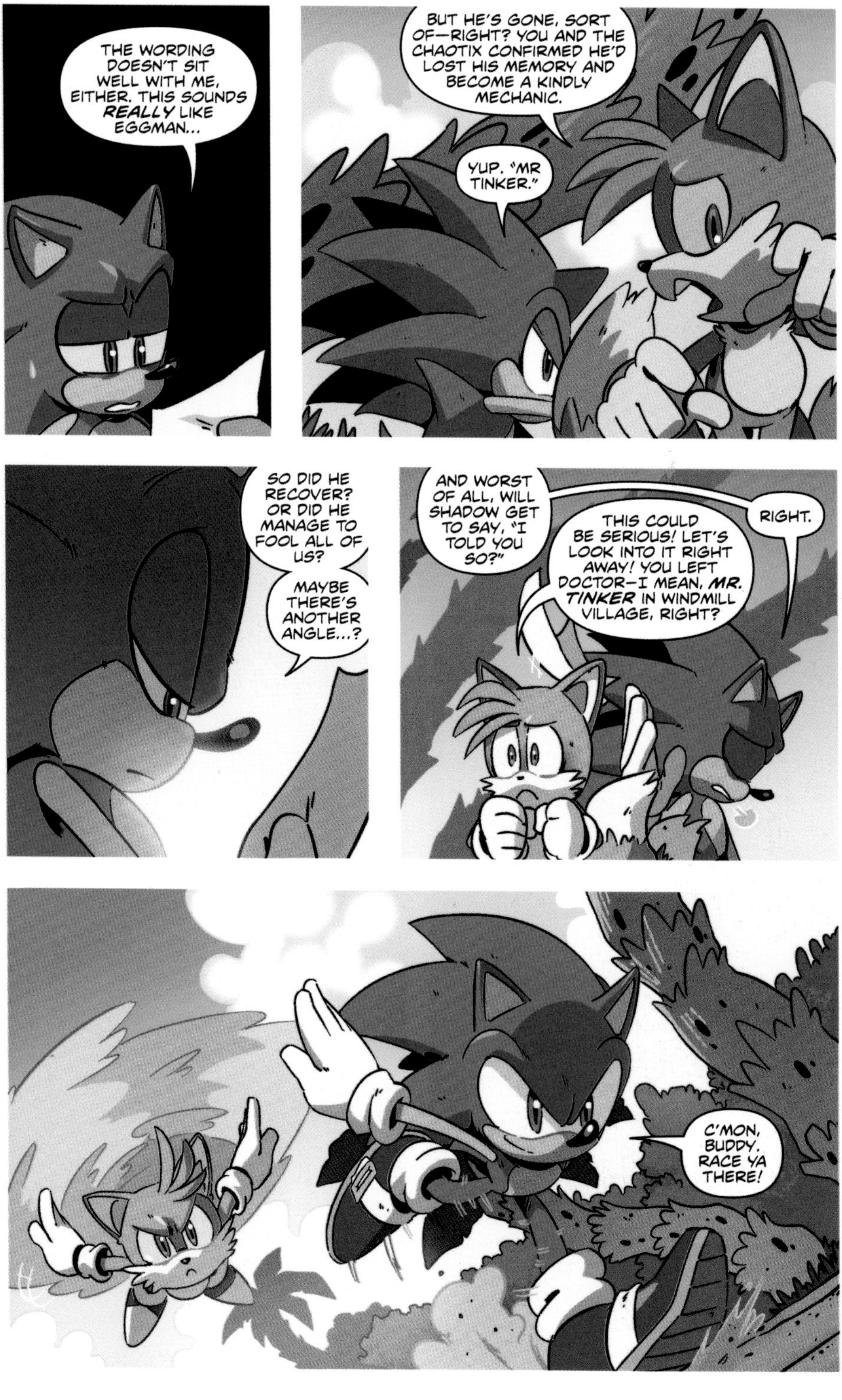
THE WORDING DOESN'T SIT WELL WITH ME, EITHER. THIS SOUNDS *REALLY* LIKE EGGMAN...
BUT HE'S GONE, SORT OF—RIGHT? YOU AND THE CHAOTIX CONFIRMED HE'D LOST HIS MEMORY AND BECOME A KINDLY MECHANIC.
YUP. "MR TINKER."
SO DID HE RECOVER? OR DID HE MANAGE TO FOOL ALL OF US?
MAYBE THERE'S ANOTHER ANGLE...?
AND WORST OF ALL, WILL SHADOW GET TO SAY, "I TOLD YOU SO?"
THIS COULD BE SERIOUS! LET'S LOOK INTO IT RIGHT AWAY! YOU LEFT DOCTOR—I MEAN, *MR. TINKER* IN WINDMILL VILLAGE, RIGHT?
RIGHT.
C'MON, BUDDY. RACE YA THERE!

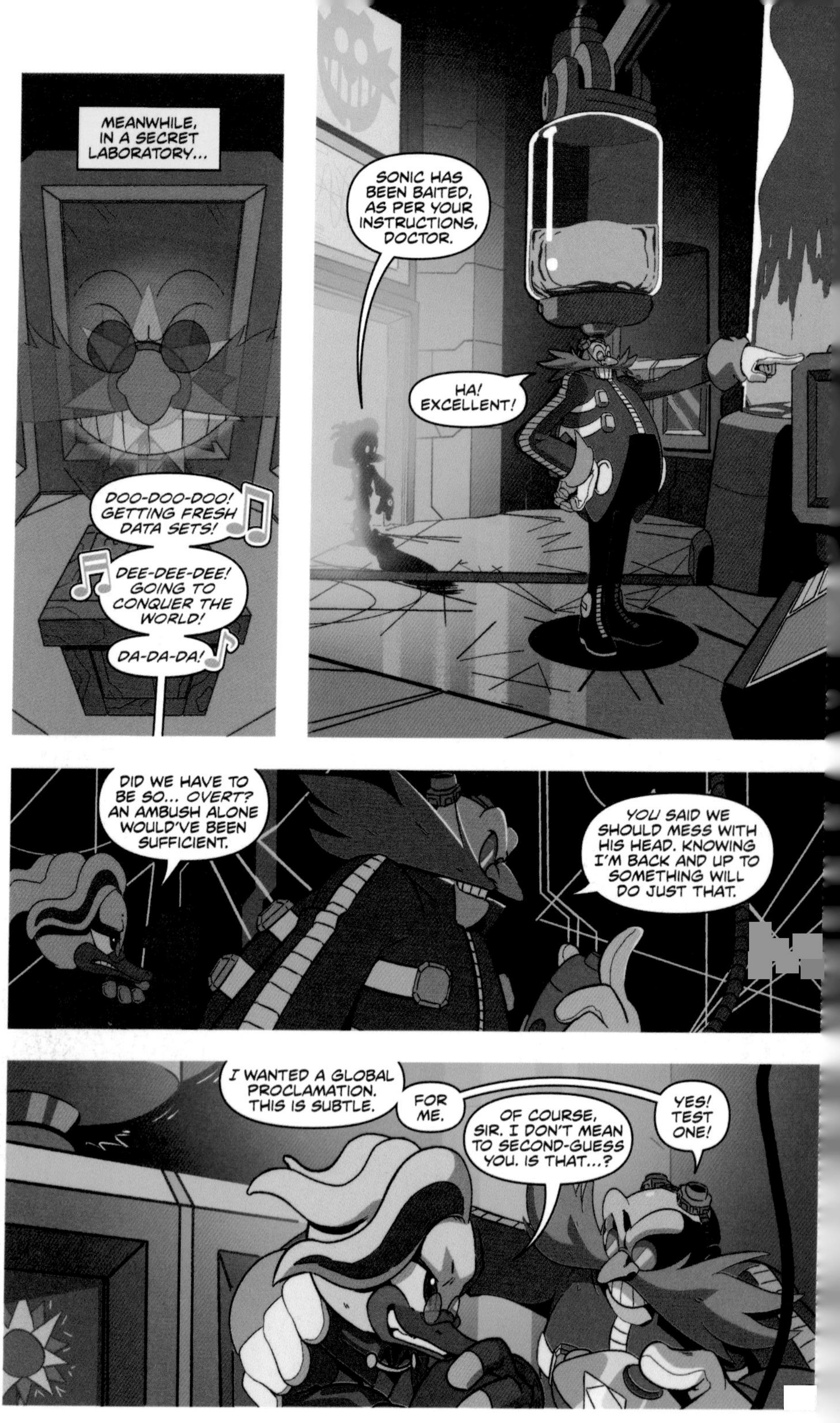

MEANWHILE, IN A SECRET LABORATORY...
DOO-DOO-DOO! GETTING FRESH DATA SETS!
DEE-DEE-DEE! GOING TO CONQUER THE WORLD!
DA-DA-DA!
SONIC HAS BEEN BAITED, AS PER YOUR INSTRUCTIONS, DOCTOR.
HA! EXCELLENT!
DID WE HAVE TO BE SO... OVERT? AN AMBUSH ALONE WOULD'VE BEEN SUFFICIENT.
YOU SAID WE SHOULD MESS WITH HIS HEAD. KNOWING I'M BACK AND UP TO SOMETHING WILL DO JUST THAT.
I WANTED A GLOBAL PROCLAMATION. THIS IS SUBTLE.
FOR ME.
OF COURSE, SIR. I DON'T MEAN TO SECOND-GUESS YOU. IS THAT...?
YES! TEST ONE!

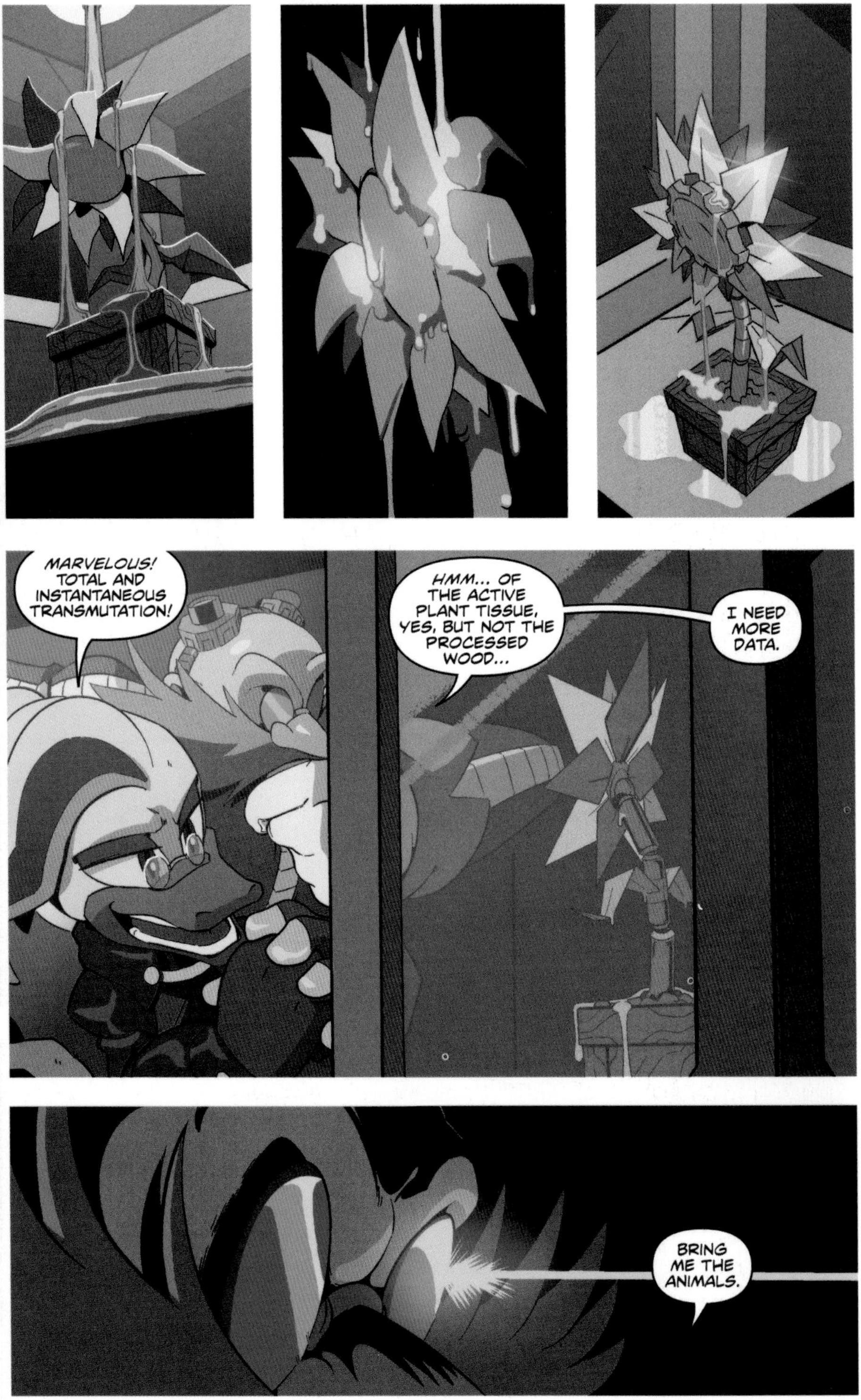

MARVELOUS! TOTAL AND INSTANTANEOUS TRANSMUTATION!
HMM... OF THE ACTIVE PLANT TISSUE, YES, BUT NOT THE PROCESSED WOOD...
I NEED MORE DATA.
BRING ME THE ANIMALS.

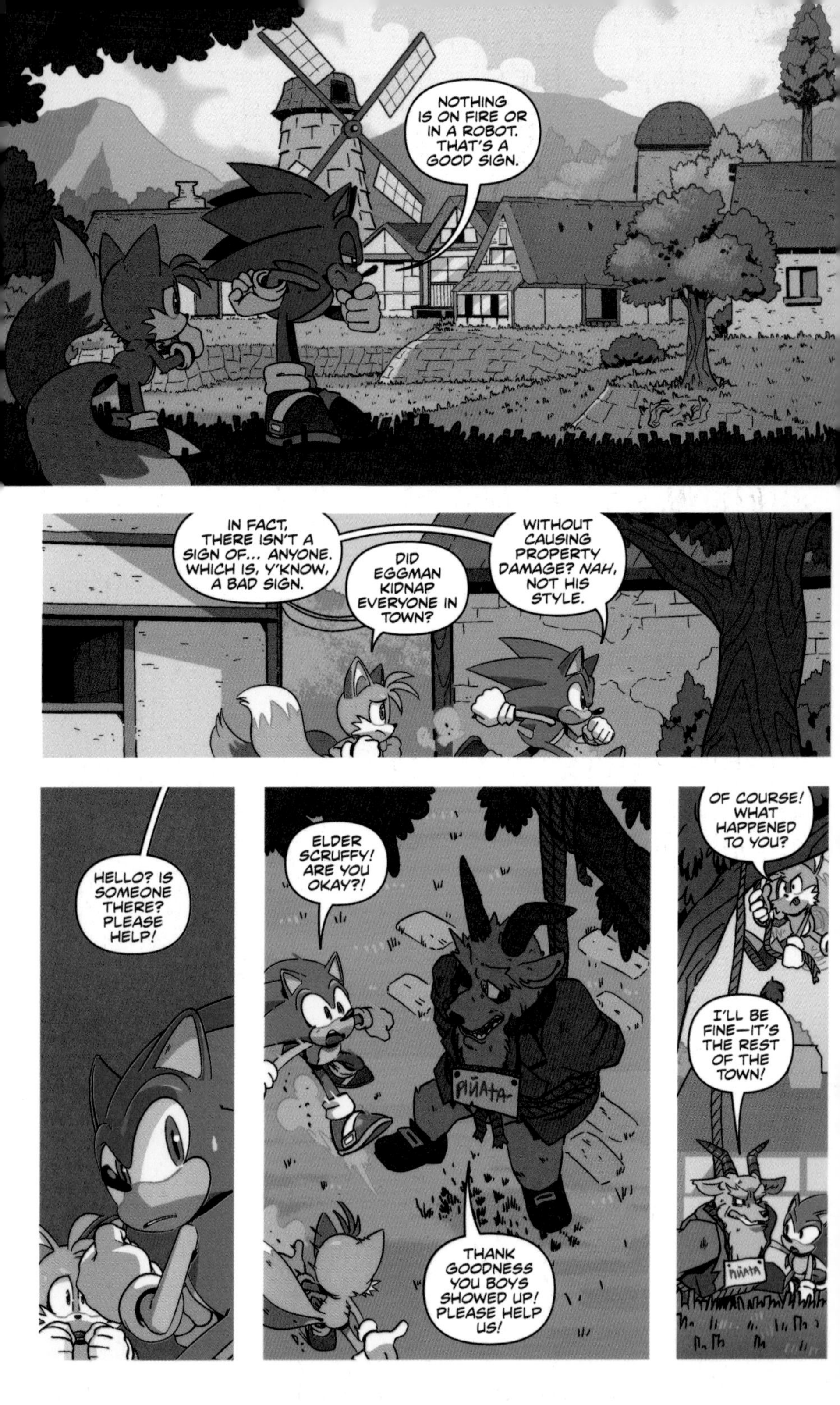
NOTHING IS ON FIRE OR IN A ROBOT. THAT'S A GOOD SIGN.
IN FACT, THERE ISN'T A SIGN OF... ANYONE. WHICH IS, Y'KNOW, A BAD SIGN.
DID EGGMAN KIDNAP EVERYONE IN TOWN?
WITHOUT CAUSING PROPERTY DAMAGE? *NAH,* NOT HIS STYLE.
HELLO? IS SOMEONE THERE? PLEASE HELP!
ELDER SCRUFFY! ARE YOU OKAY?!
PIÑATA
THANK GOODNESS YOU BOYS SHOWED UP! PLEASE HELP US!
OF COURSE! WHAT HAPPENED TO YOU?
I'LL BE FINE—IT'S THE REST OF THE TOWN!
PIÑATA

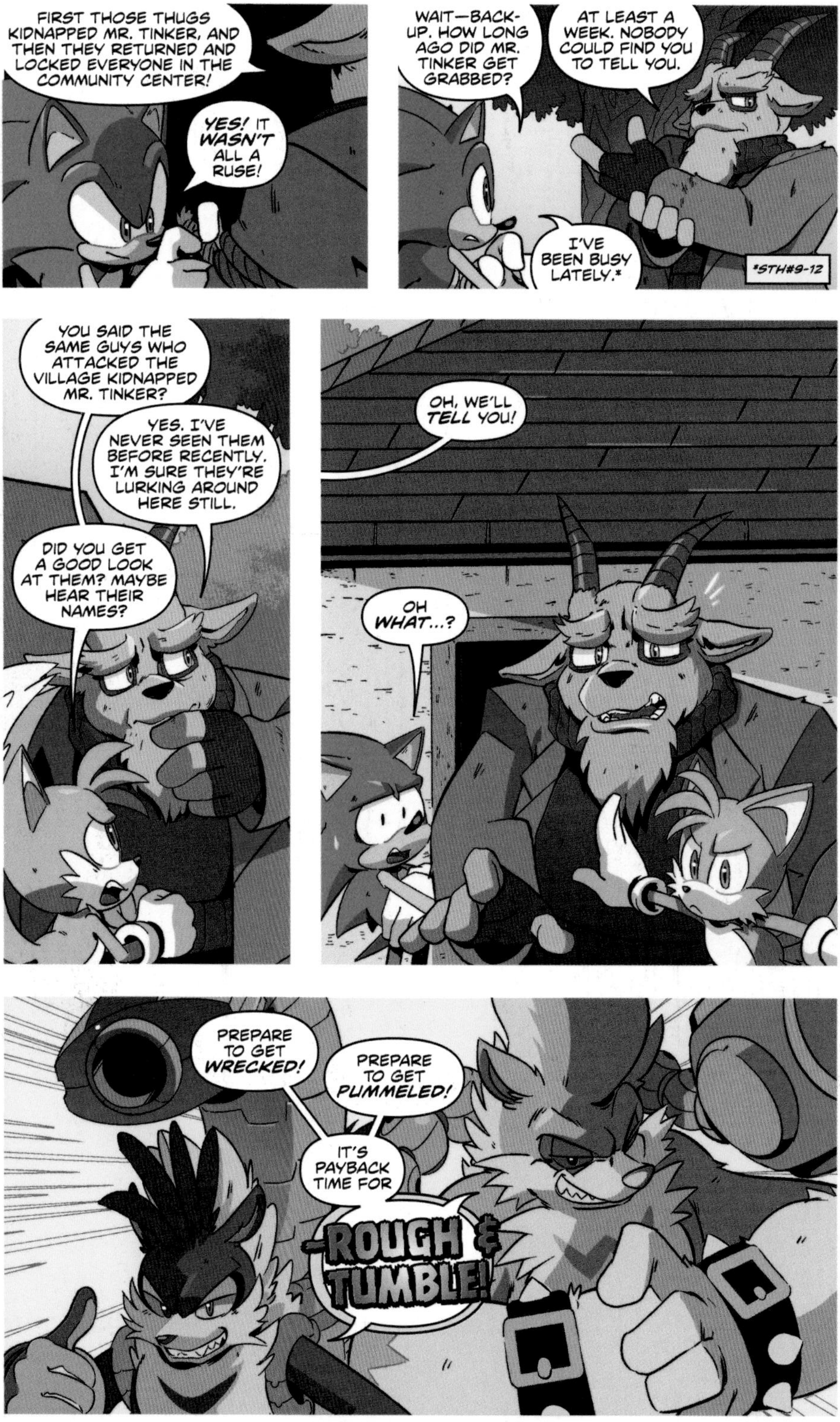
FIRST THOSE THUGS KIDNAPPED MR. TINKER, AND THEN THEY RETURNED AND LOCKED EVERYONE IN THE COMMUNITY CENTER!
YES! IT WASN'T ALL A RUSE!
WAIT—BACK-UP. HOW LONG AGO DID MR. TINKER GET GRABBED?
AT LEAST A WEEK. NOBODY COULD FIND YOU TO TELL YOU.
I'VE BEEN BUSY LATELY.*
*STH#9-12
YOU SAID THE SAME GUYS WHO ATTACKED THE VILLAGE KIDNAPPED MR. TINKER?
YES. I'VE NEVER SEEN THEM BEFORE RECENTLY. I'M SURE THEY'RE LURKING AROUND HERE STILL.
DID YOU GET A GOOD LOOK AT THEM? MAYBE HEAR THEIR NAMES?
OH, WE'LL TELL YOU!
OH WHAT...?
PREPARE TO GET WRECKED!
PREPARE TO GET PUMMELED!
IT'S PAYBACK TIME FOR
ROUGH & TUMBLE!

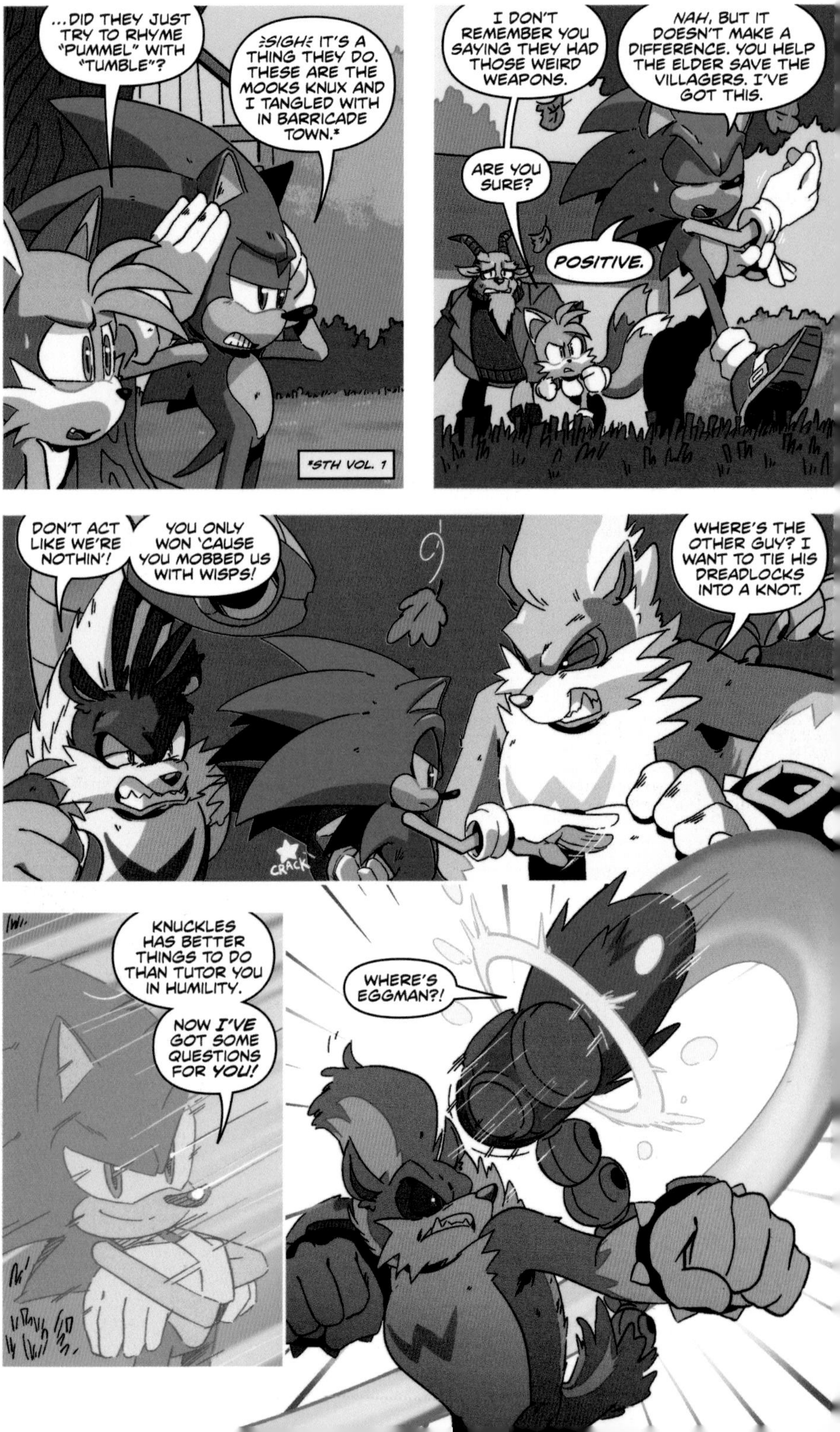
...DID THEY JUST TRY TO RHYME "PUMMEL" WITH "TUMBLE"?
SIGH IT'S A THING THEY DO. THESE ARE THE MOOKS KNUX AND I TANGLED WITH IN BARRICADE TOWN.*
*STH VOL. 1
I DON'T REMEMBER YOU SAYING THEY HAD THOSE WEIRD WEAPONS.
NAH, BUT IT DOESN'T MAKE A DIFFERENCE. YOU HELP THE ELDER SAVE THE VILLAGERS. I'VE GOT THIS.
ARE YOU SURE?
POSITIVE.
DON'T ACT LIKE WE'RE NOTHIN'!
YOU ONLY WON 'CAUSE YOU MOBBED US WITH WISPS!
WHERE'S THE OTHER GUY? I WANT TO TIE HIS DREADLOCKS INTO A KNOT.
CRACK
KNUCKLES HAS BETTER THINGS TO DO THAN TUTOR YOU IN HUMILITY.
NOW I'VE GOT SOME QUESTIONS FOR YOU!
WHERE'S EGGMAN?!

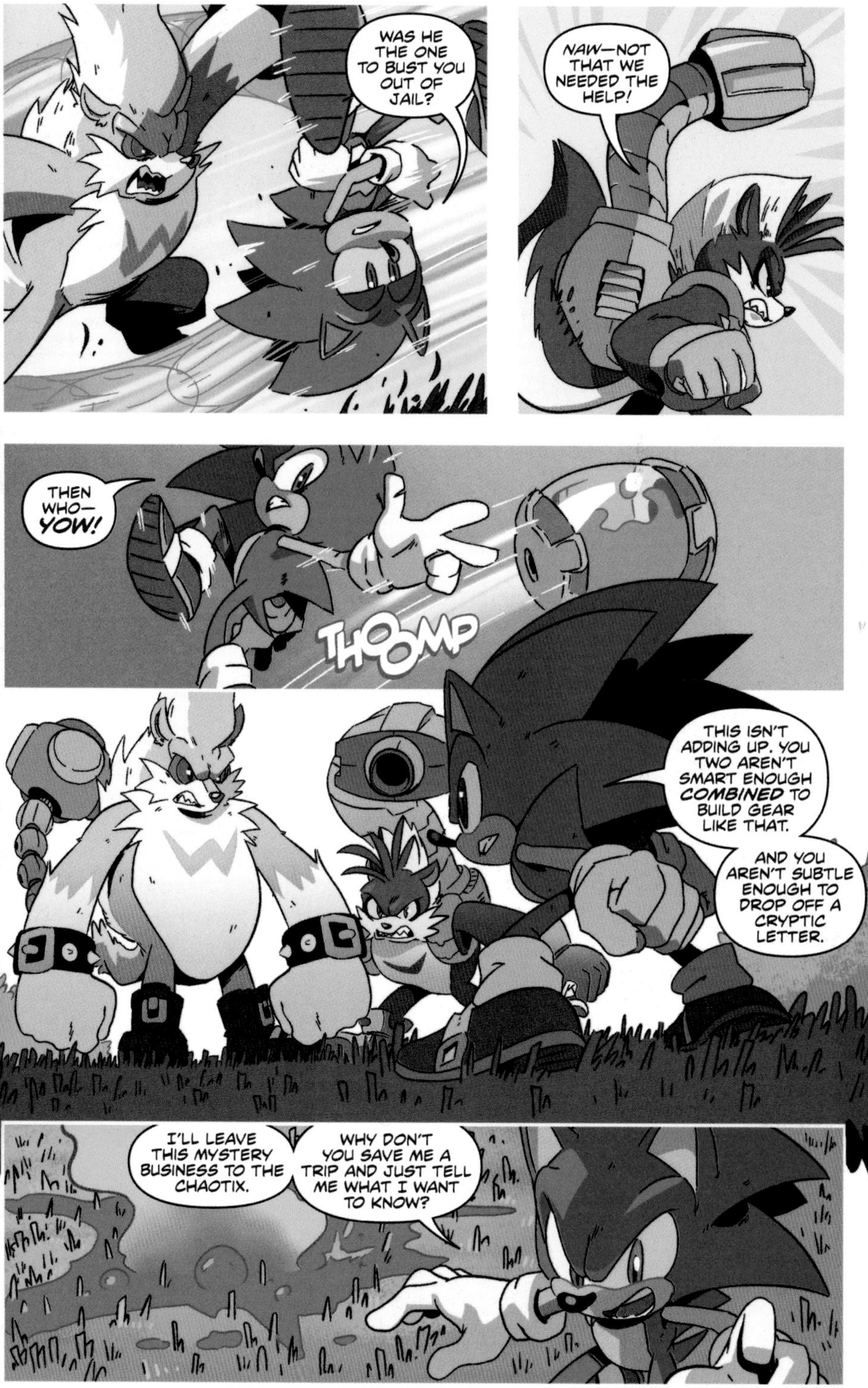
WAS HE THE ONE TO BUST YOU OUT OF JAIL?
NAW—NOT THAT WE NEEDED THE HELP!
THEN WHO— YOW!
THOOMP
THIS ISN'T ADDING UP. YOU TWO AREN'T SMART ENOUGH COMBINED TO BUILD GEAR LIKE THAT.
AND YOU AREN'T SUBTLE ENOUGH TO DROP OFF A CRYPTIC LETTER.
I'LL LEAVE THIS MYSTERY BUSINESS TO THE CHAOTIX.
WHY DON'T YOU SAVE ME A TRIP AND JUST TELL ME WHAT I WANT TO KNOW?

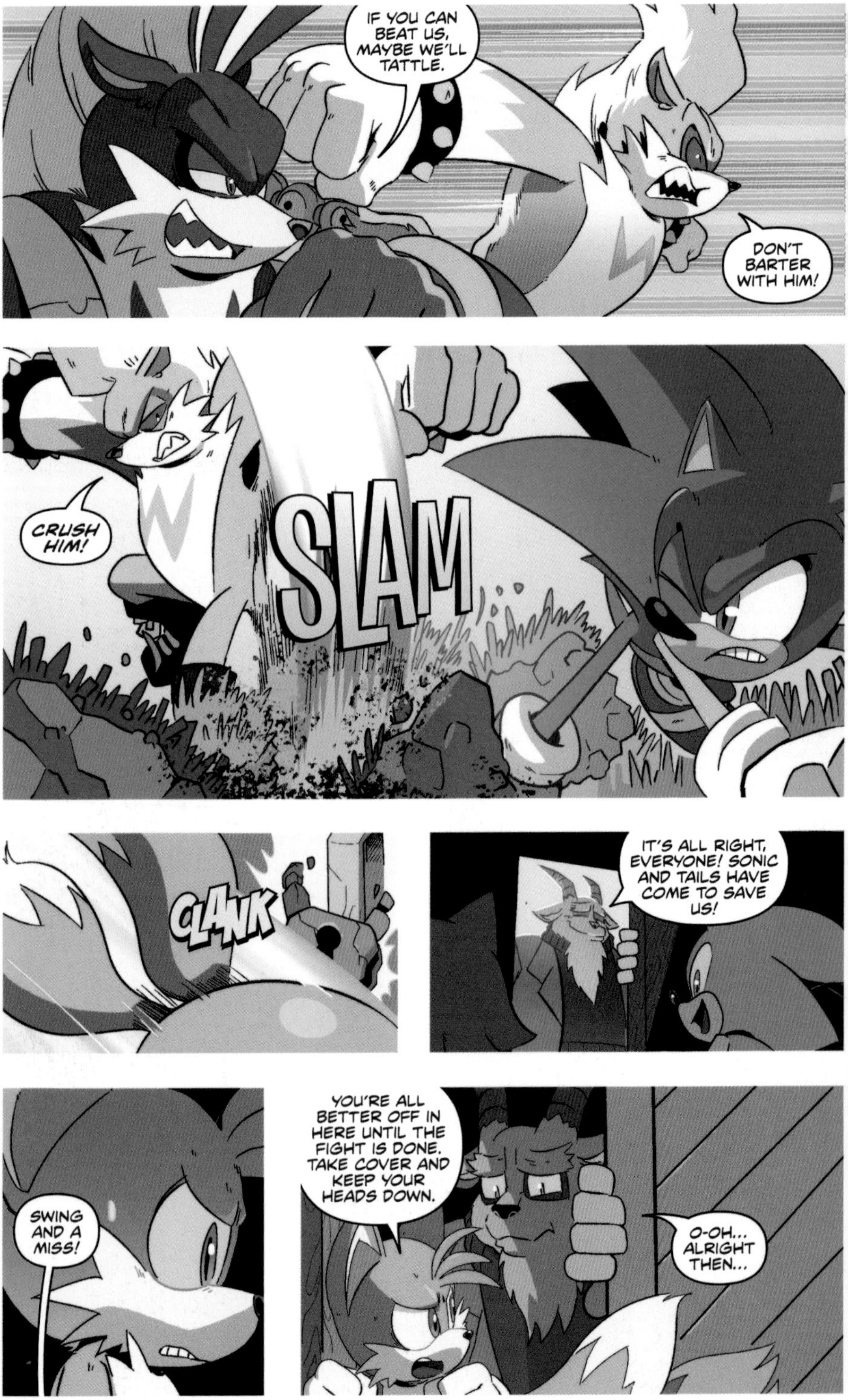
IF YOU CAN BEAT US, MAYBE WE'LL TATTLE.
DON'T BARTER WITH HIM!
CRUSH HIM!
SLAM
CLANK
IT'S ALL RIGHT, EVERYONE! SONIC AND TAILS HAVE COME TO SAVE US!
SWING AND A MISS!
YOU'RE ALL BETTER OFF IN HERE UNTIL THE FIGHT IS DONE. TAKE COVER AND KEEP YOUR HEADS DOWN.
O-OH... ALRIGHT THEN...

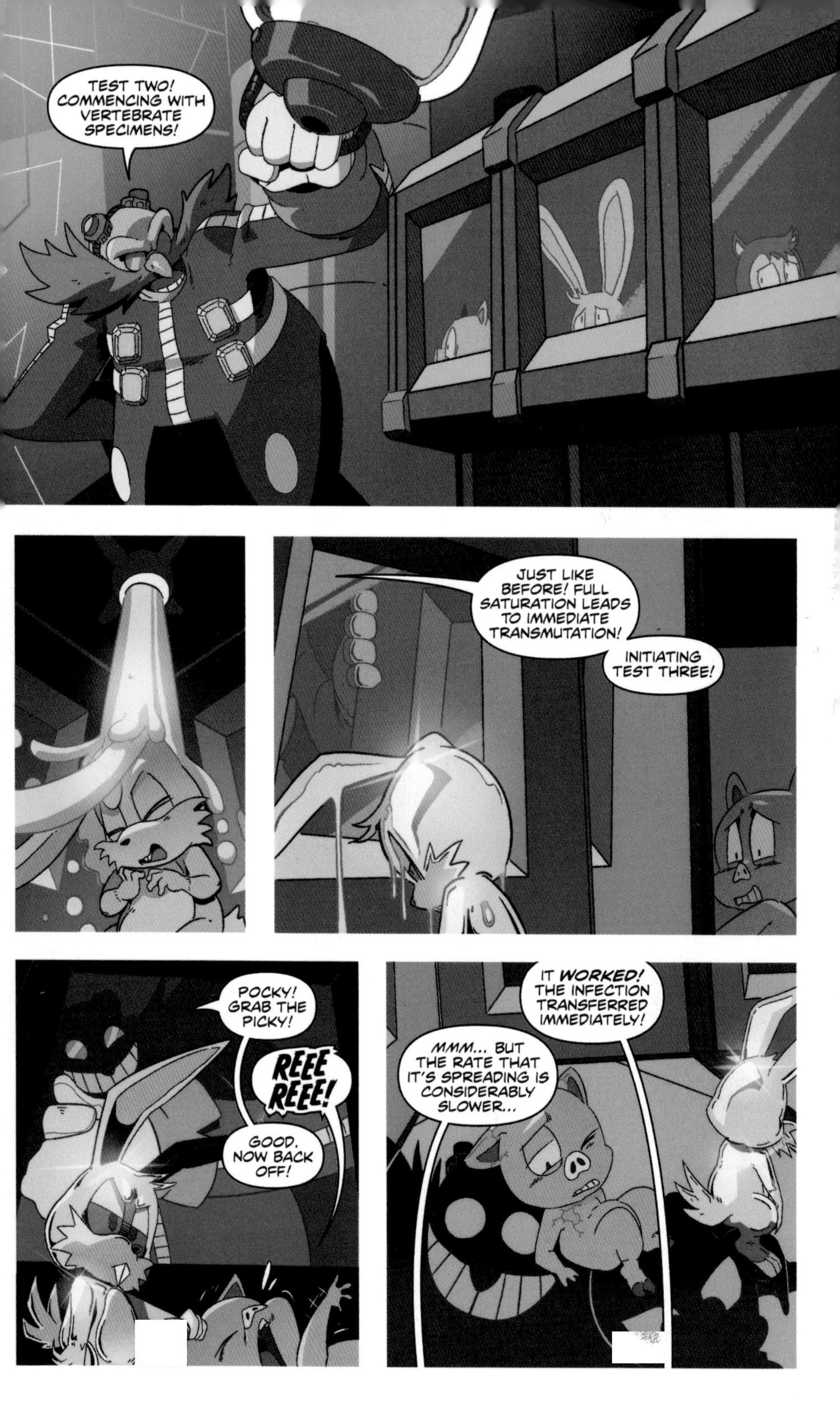
TEST TWO! COMMENCING WITH VERTEBRATE SPECIMENS!
JUST LIKE BEFORE! FULL SATURATION LEADS TO IMMEDIATE TRANSMUTATION!
INITIATING TEST THREE!
POCKY! GRAB THE PICKY!
REEE REEE!
GOOD. NOW BACK OFF!
IT WORKED! THE INFECTION TRANSFERRED IMMEDIATELY!
MMM... BUT THE RATE THAT IT'S SPREADING IS CONSIDERABLY SLOWER...

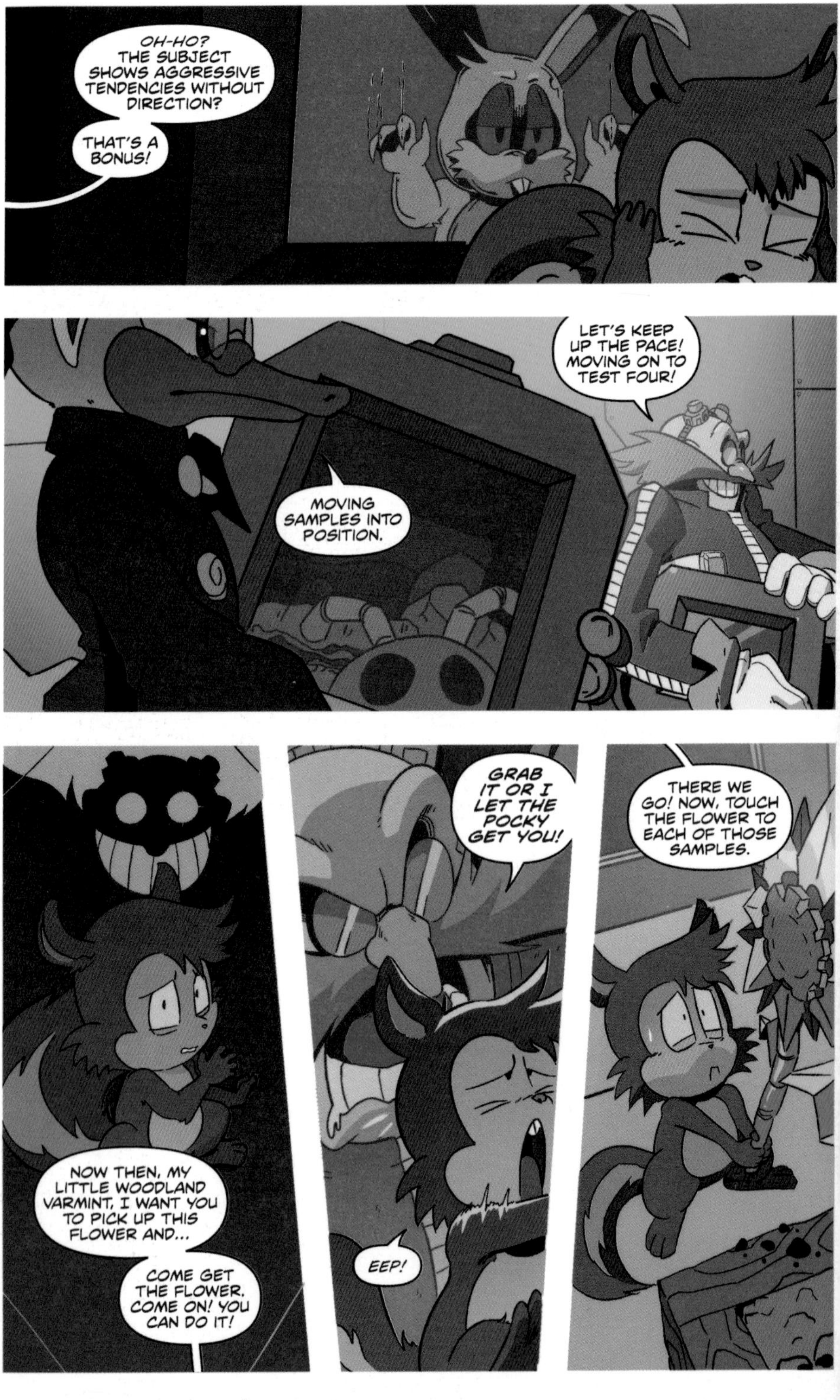
OH-HO? THE SUBJECT SHOWS AGGRESSIVE TENDENCIES WITHOUT DIRECTION?
THAT'S A BONUS!
LET'S KEEP UP THE PACE! MOVING ON TO TEST FOUR!
MOVING SAMPLES INTO POSITION.
NOW THEN, MY LITTLE WOODLAND VARMINT, I WANT YOU TO PICK UP THIS FLOWER AND...
COME GET THE FLOWER. COME ON! YOU CAN DO IT!
GRAB IT OR I LET THE POCKY GET YOU!
EEP!
THERE WE GO! NOW, TOUCH THE FLOWER TO EACH OF THOSE SAMPLES.

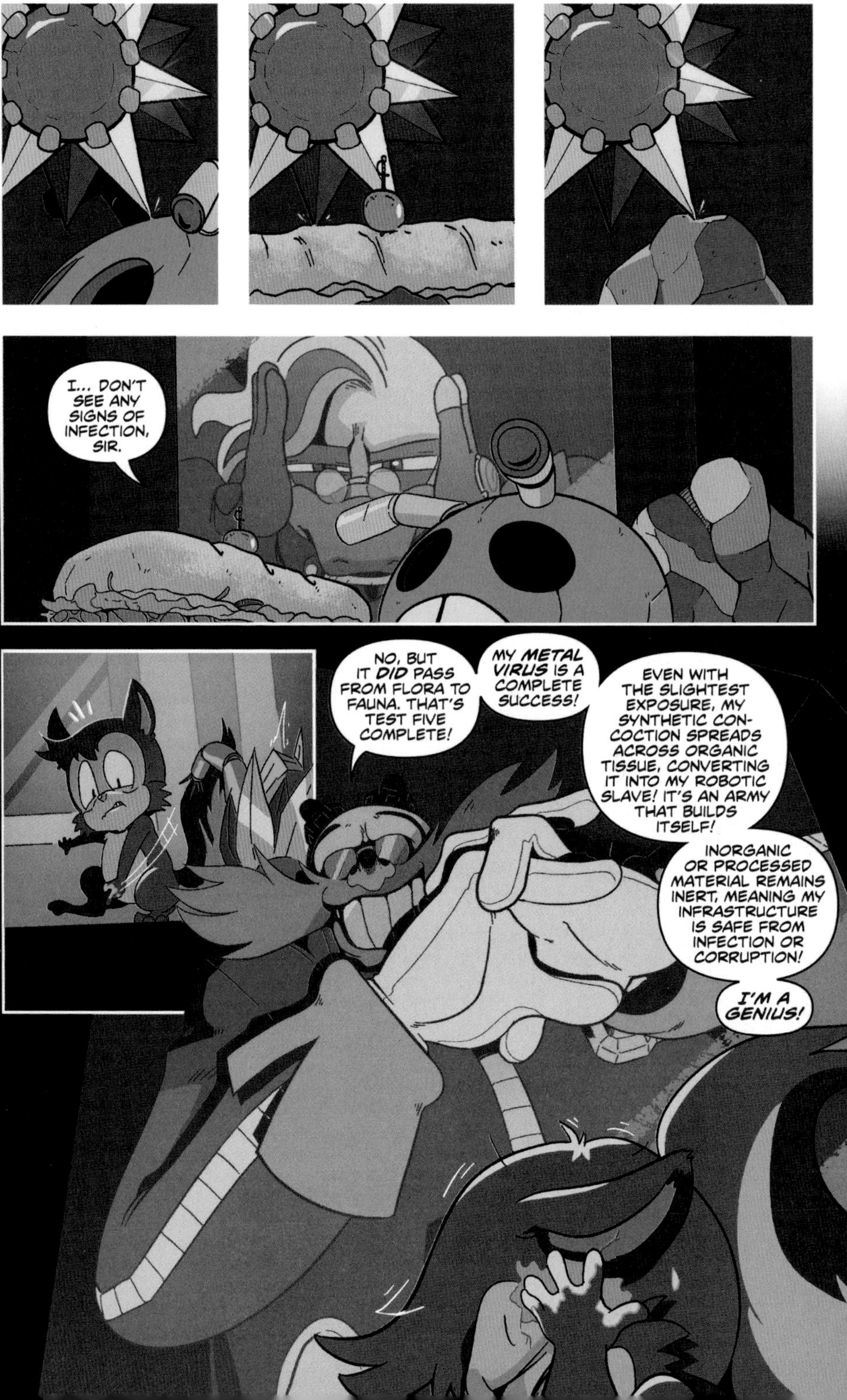
I... DON'T SEE ANY SIGNS OF INFECTION, SIR.
NO, BUT IT DID PASS FROM FLORA TO FAUNA. THAT'S TEST FIVE COMPLETE!
MY METAL VIRUS IS A COMPLETE SUCCESS!
EVEN WITH THE SLIGHTEST EXPOSURE, MY SYNTHETIC CON-COCTION SPREADS ACROSS ORGANIC TISSUE, CONVERTING IT INTO MY ROBOTIC SLAVE! IT'S AN ARMY THAT BUILDS ITSELF!
INORGANIC OR PROCESSED MATERIAL REMAINS INERT, MEANING MY INFRASTRUCTURE IS SAFE FROM INFECTION OR CORRUPTION!
I'M A GENIUS!

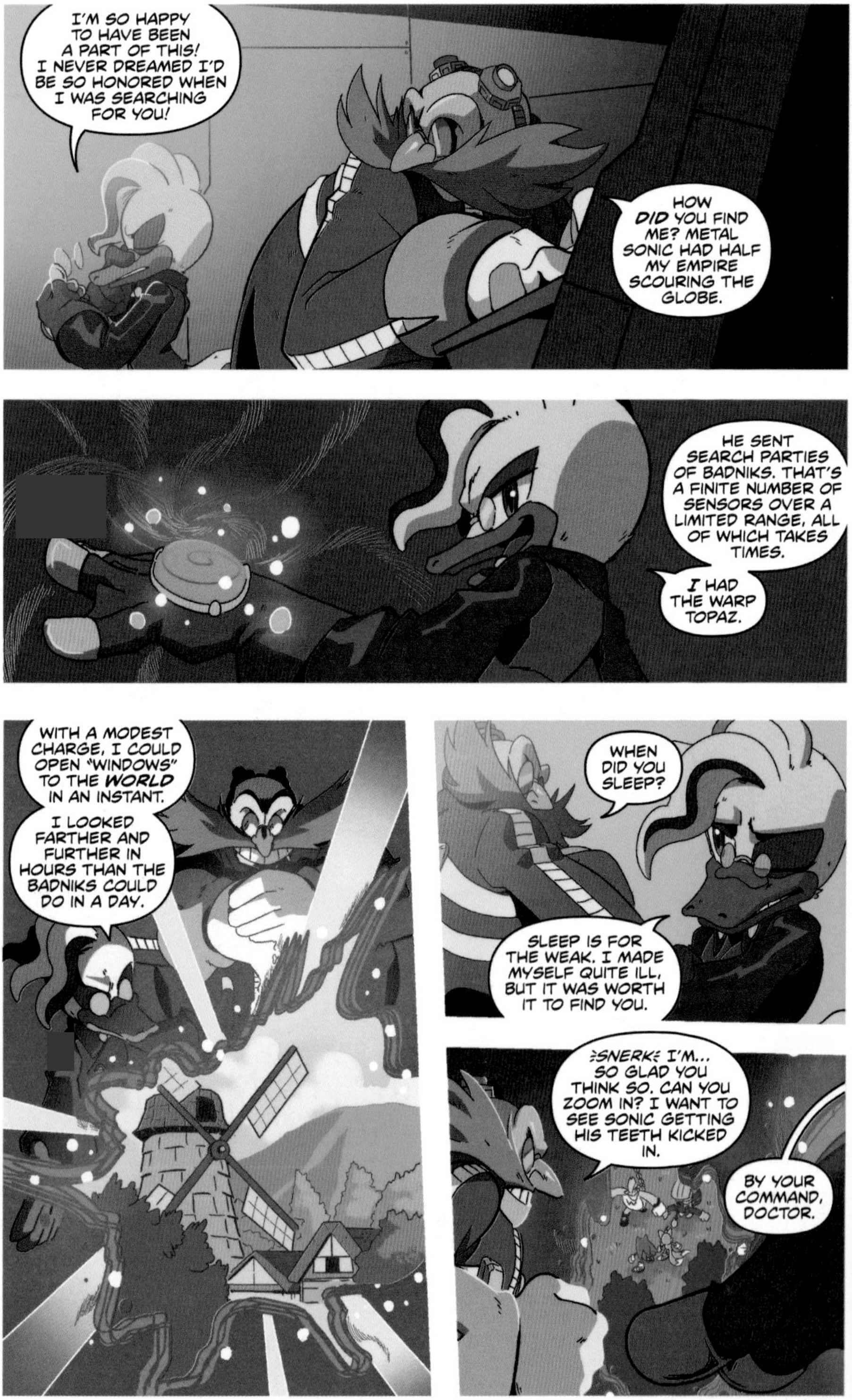
I'M SO HAPPY TO HAVE BEEN A PART OF THIS! I NEVER DREAMED I'D BE SO HONORED WHEN I WAS SEARCHING FOR YOU!
HOW *DID* YOU FIND ME? METAL SONIC HAD HALF MY EMPIRE SCOURING THE GLOBE.
HE SENT SEARCH PARTIES OF BADNIKS. THAT'S A FINITE NUMBER OF SENSORS OVER A LIMITED RANGE, ALL OF WHICH TAKES TIMES.
I HAD THE WARP TOPAZ.
WITH A MODEST CHARGE, I COULD OPEN "WINDOWS" TO THE *WORLD* IN AN INSTANT.
I LOOKED FARTHER AND FURTHER IN HOURS THAN THE BADNIKS COULD DO IN A DAY.
WHEN DID YOU SLEEP?
SLEEP IS FOR THE WEAK. I MADE MYSELF QUITE ILL, BUT IT WAS WORTH IT TO FIND YOU.
SNERK I'M... SO GLAD YOU THINK SO. CAN YOU ZOOM IN? I WANT TO SEE SONIC GETTING HIS TEETH KICKED IN.
BY YOUR COMMAND, DOCTOR.

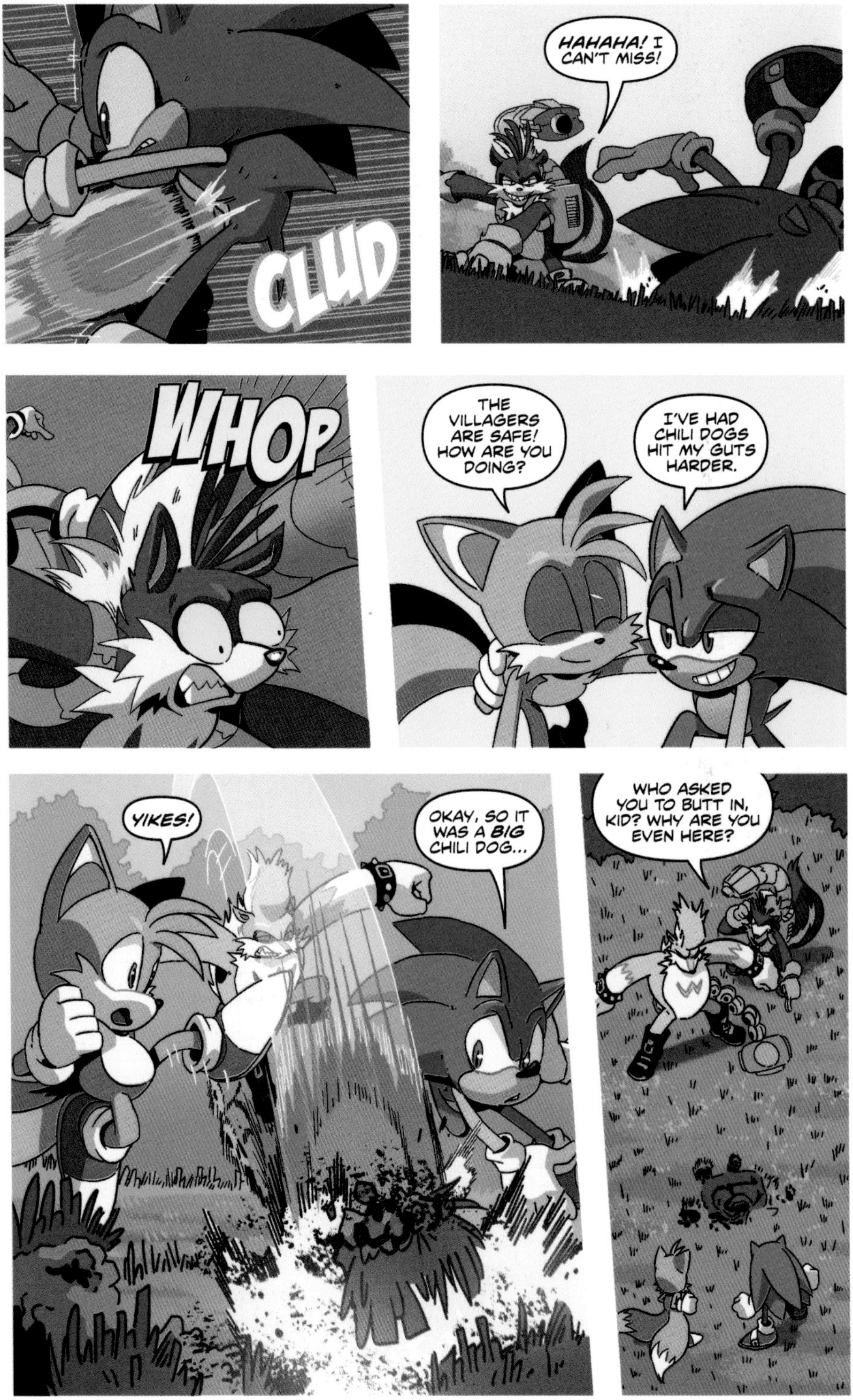
CLUD
HAHAHA! I CAN'T MISS!
WHOP
THE VILLAGERS ARE SAFE! HOW ARE YOU DOING?
I'VE HAD CHILI DOGS HIT MY GUTS HARDER.
YIKES!
OKAY, SO IT WAS A *BIG* CHILI DOG...
WHO ASKED YOU TO BUTT IN, KID? WHY ARE YOU EVEN HERE?

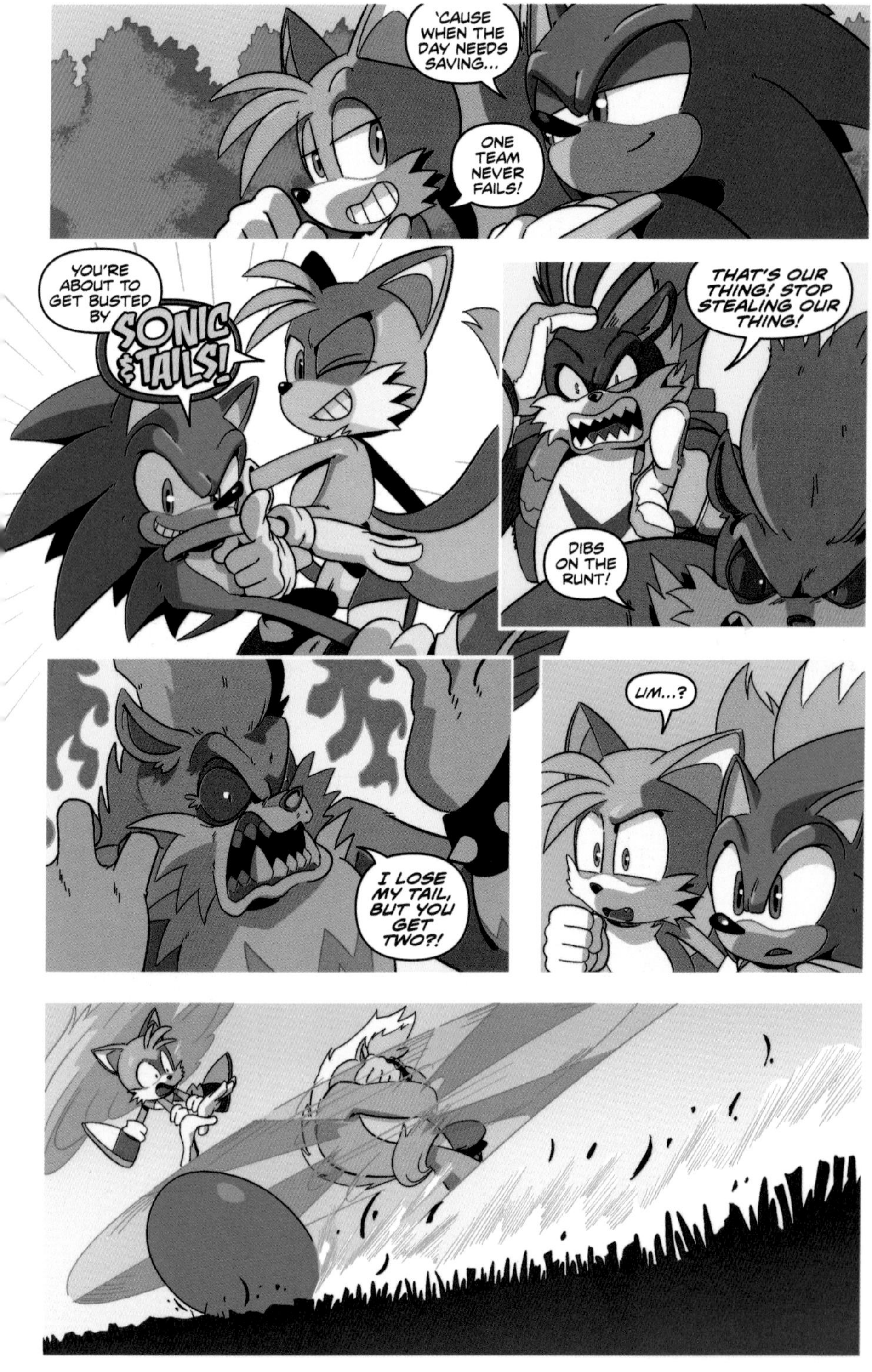
'CAUSE WHEN THE DAY NEEDS SAVING...
ONE TEAM NEVER FAILS!
YOU'RE ABOUT TO GET BUSTED BY
SONIC & TAILS!
THAT'S OUR THING! STOP STEALING OUR THING!
DIBS ON THE RUNT!
I LOSE MY TAIL, BUT YOU GET TWO?!
UM...?

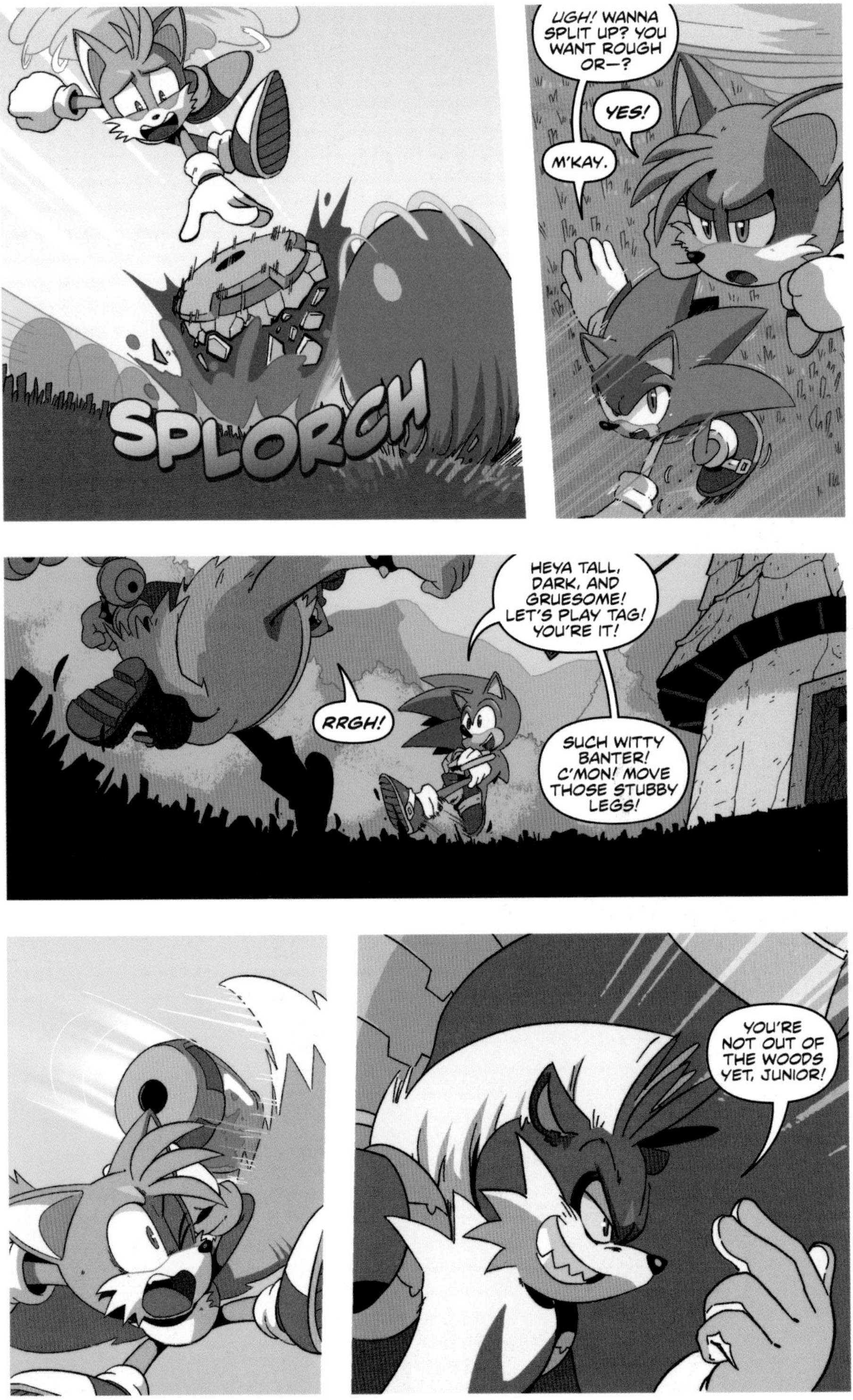
SPLORCH
UGH! WANNA SPLIT UP? YOU WANT ROUGH OR—?
YES!
M'KAY.
HEYA TALL, DARK, AND GRUESOME! LET'S PLAY TAG! YOU'RE IT!
RRGH!
SUCH WITTY BANTER! C'MON! MOVE THOSE STUBBY LEGS!
YOU'RE NOT OUT OF THE WOODS YET, JUNIOR!

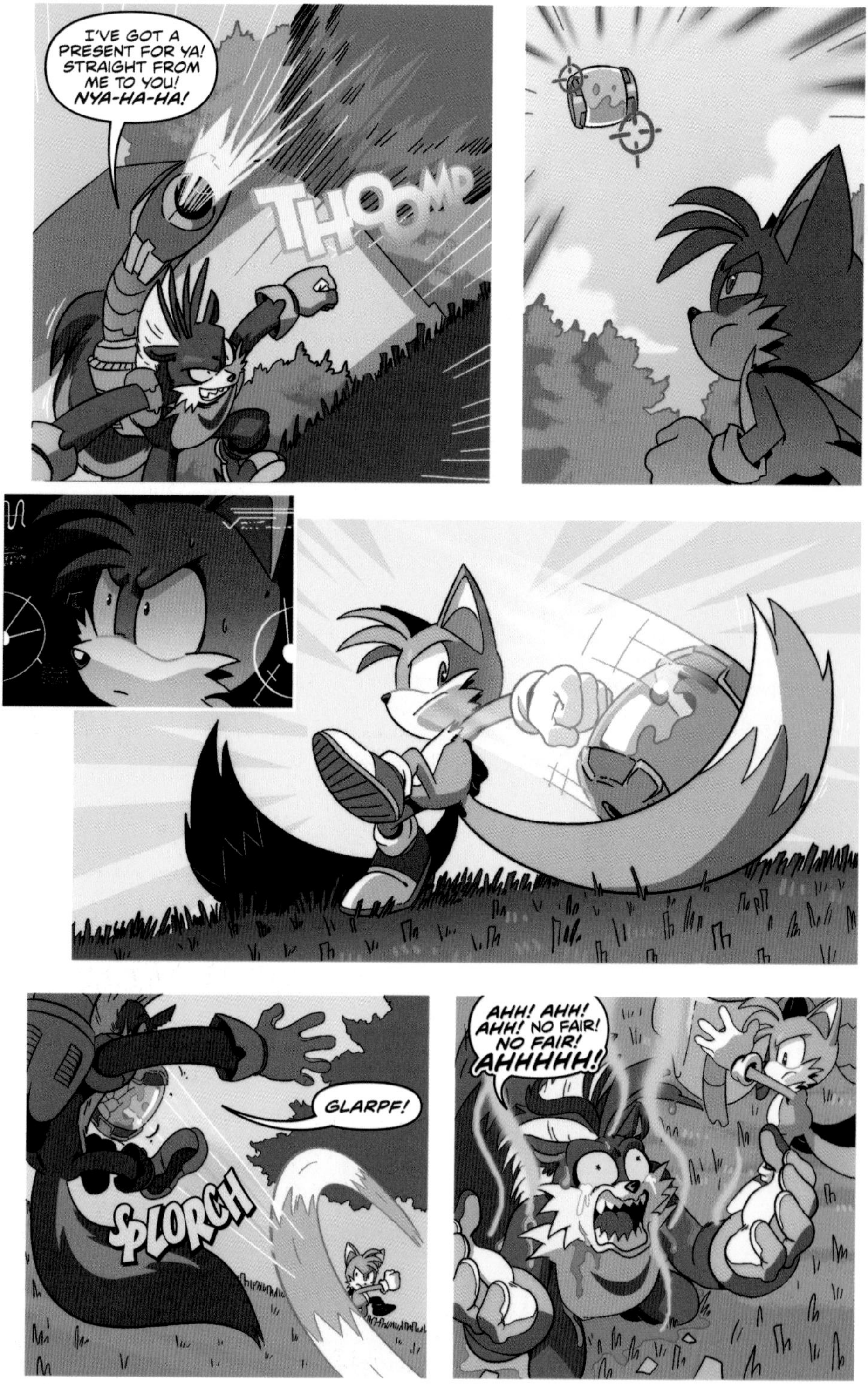

I'VE GOT A PRESENT FOR YA! STRAIGHT FROM ME TO YOU! NYA-HA-HA!
THOOMP
GLARPF!
SPLORCH
AHH! AHH! AHH! NO FAIR! NO FAIR! AHHHHH!

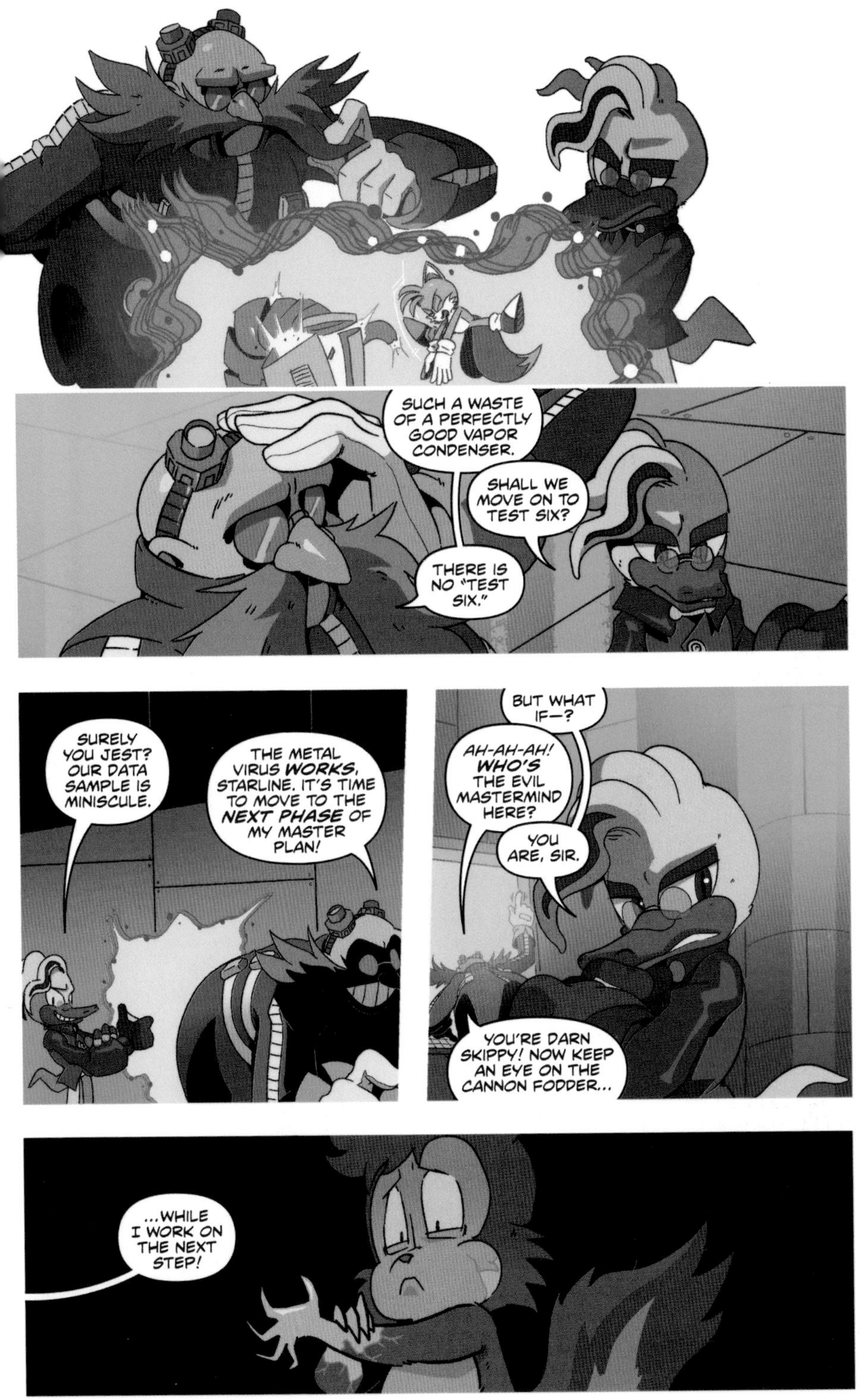
SUCH A WASTE OF A PERFECTLY GOOD VAPOR CONDENSER.
SHALL WE MOVE ON TO TEST SIX?
THERE IS NO "TEST SIX."
SURELY YOU JEST? OUR DATA SAMPLE IS MINISCULE.
THE METAL VIRUS WORKS, STARLINE. IT'S TIME TO MOVE TO THE NEXT PHASE OF MY MASTER PLAN!
BUT WHAT IF—?
AH-AH-AH! WHO'S THE EVIL MASTERMIND HERE?
YOU ARE, SIR.
YOU'RE DARN SKIPPY! NOW KEEP AN EYE ON THE CANNON FODDER...
...WHILE I WORK ON THE NEXT STEP!

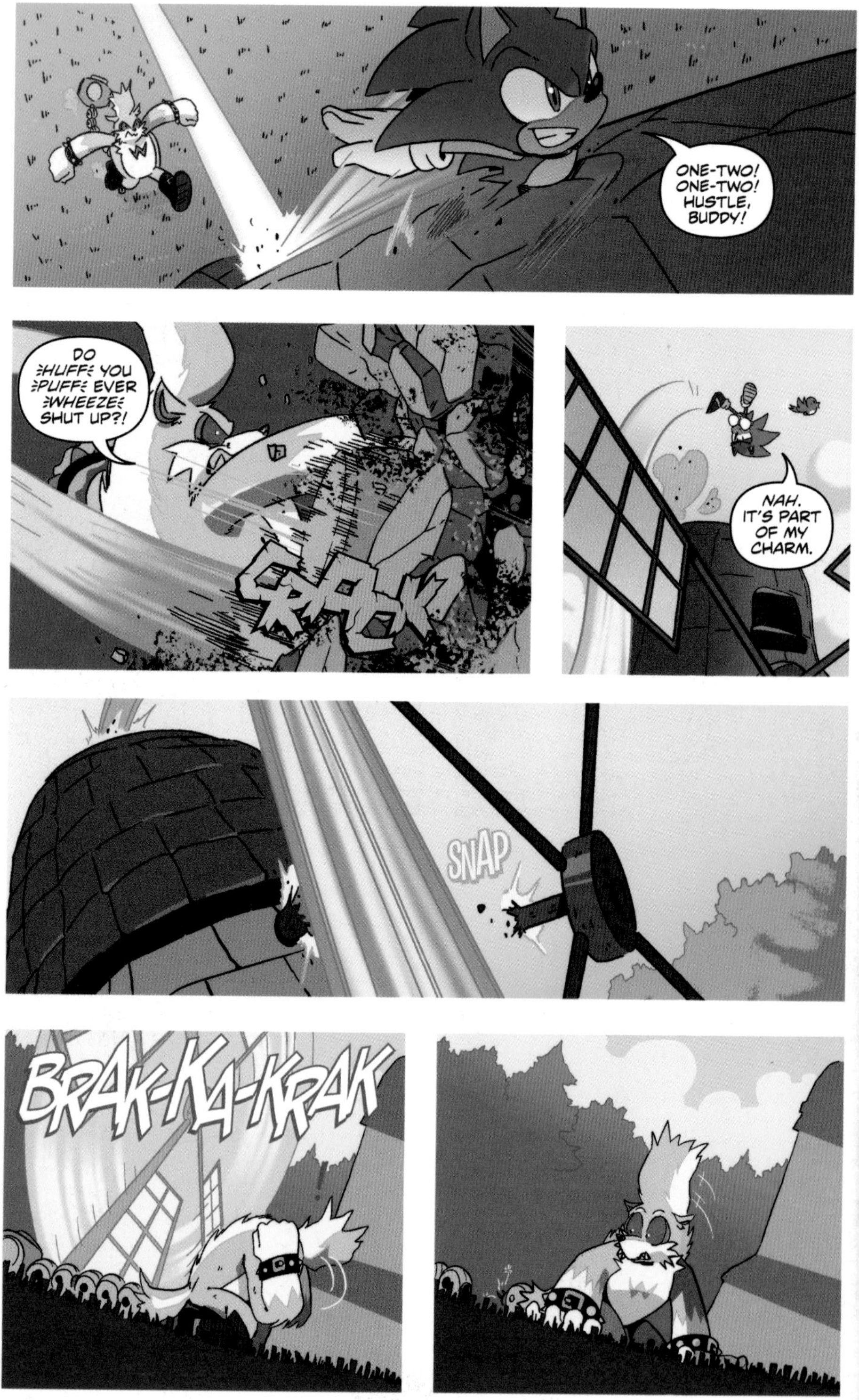
ONE-TWO! ONE-TWO! HUSTLE, BUDDY!
DO *HUFF* YOU *PUFF* EVER *WHEEZE* SHUT UP?!
KRAK
NAH. IT'S PART OF MY CHARM.
SNAP
BRAK-KA-KRAK

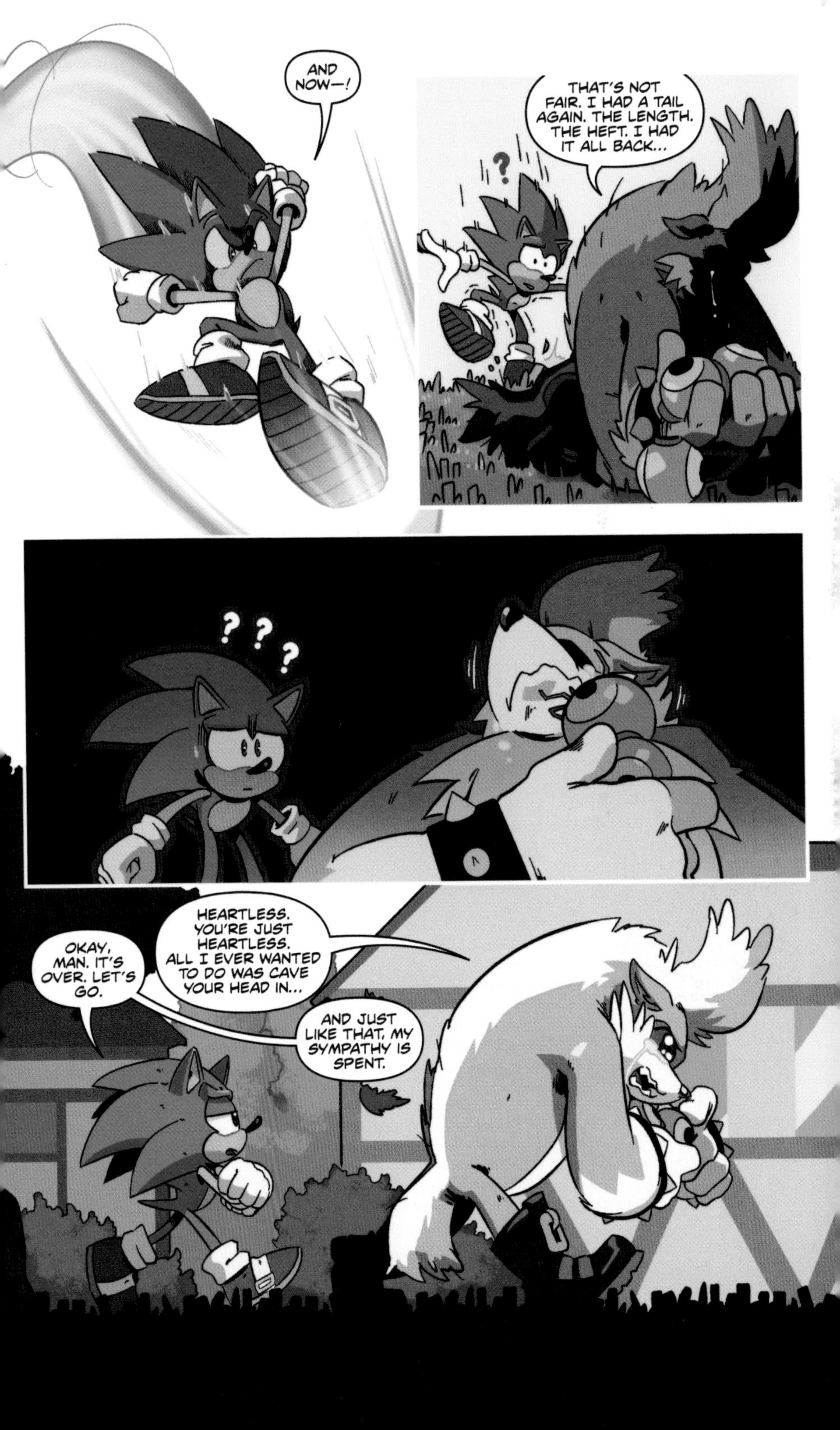
AND NOW—!
THAT'S NOT FAIR. I HAD A TAIL AGAIN. THE LENGTH. THE HEFT. I HAD IT ALL BACK...
?
? ? ?
OKAY, MAN. IT'S OVER. LET'S GO.
HEARTLESS. YOU'RE JUST HEARTLESS. ALL I EVER WANTED TO DO WAS CAVE YOUR HEAD IN...
AND JUST LIKE THAT, MY SYMPATHY IS SPENT.

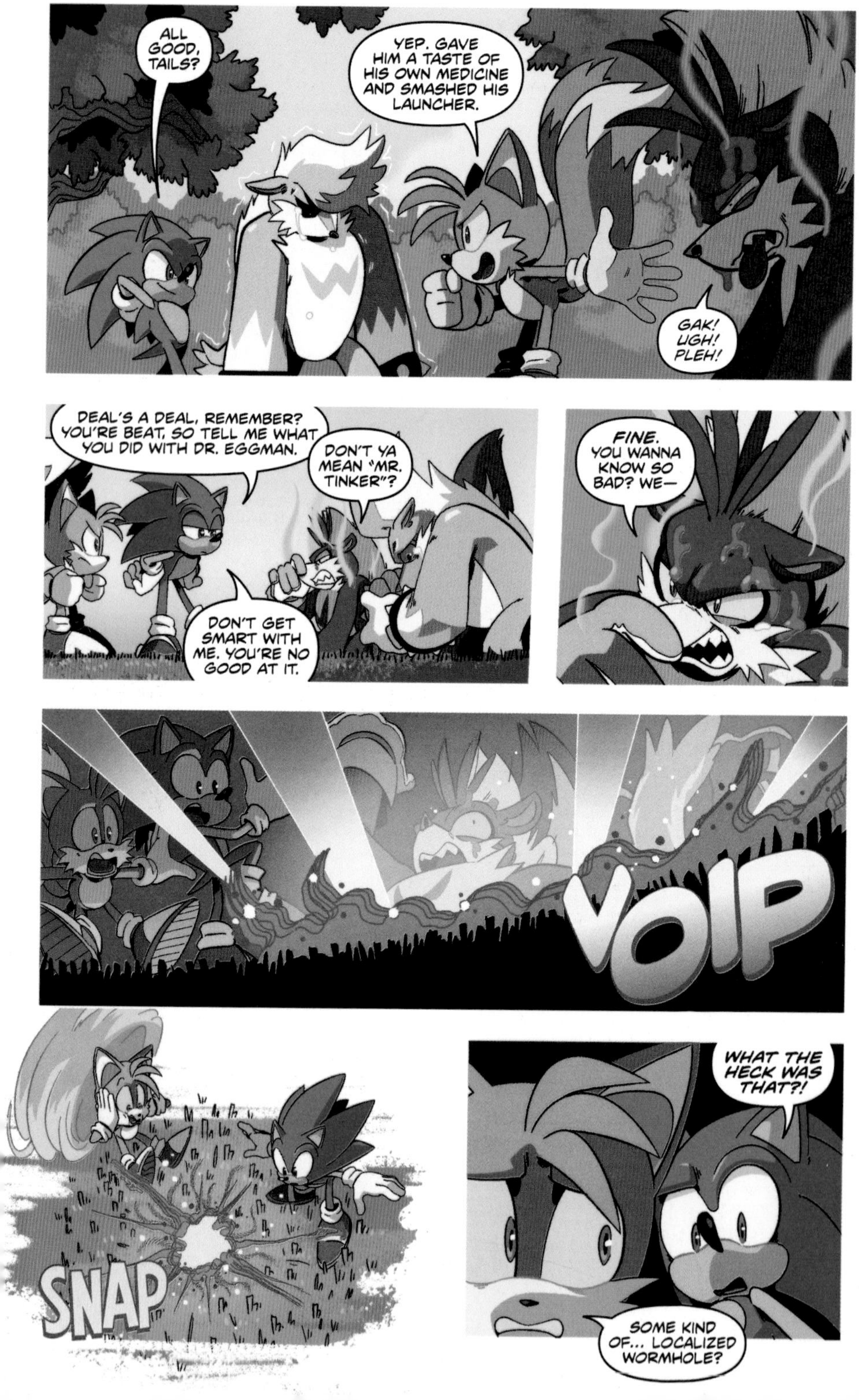
ALL GOOD, TAILS?
YEP. GAVE HIM A TASTE OF HIS OWN MEDICINE AND SMASHED HIS LAUNCHER.
GAK! UGH! PLEH!
DEAL'S A DEAL, REMEMBER? YOU'RE BEAT, SO TELL ME WHAT YOU DID WITH DR. EGGMAN.
DON'T YA MEAN "MR. TINKER"?
DON'T GET SMART WITH ME. YOU'RE NO GOOD AT IT.
FINE. YOU WANNA KNOW SO BAD? WE—
VOIP
SNAP
WHAT THE HECK WAS THAT?!
SOME KIND OF... LOCALIZED WORMHOLE?

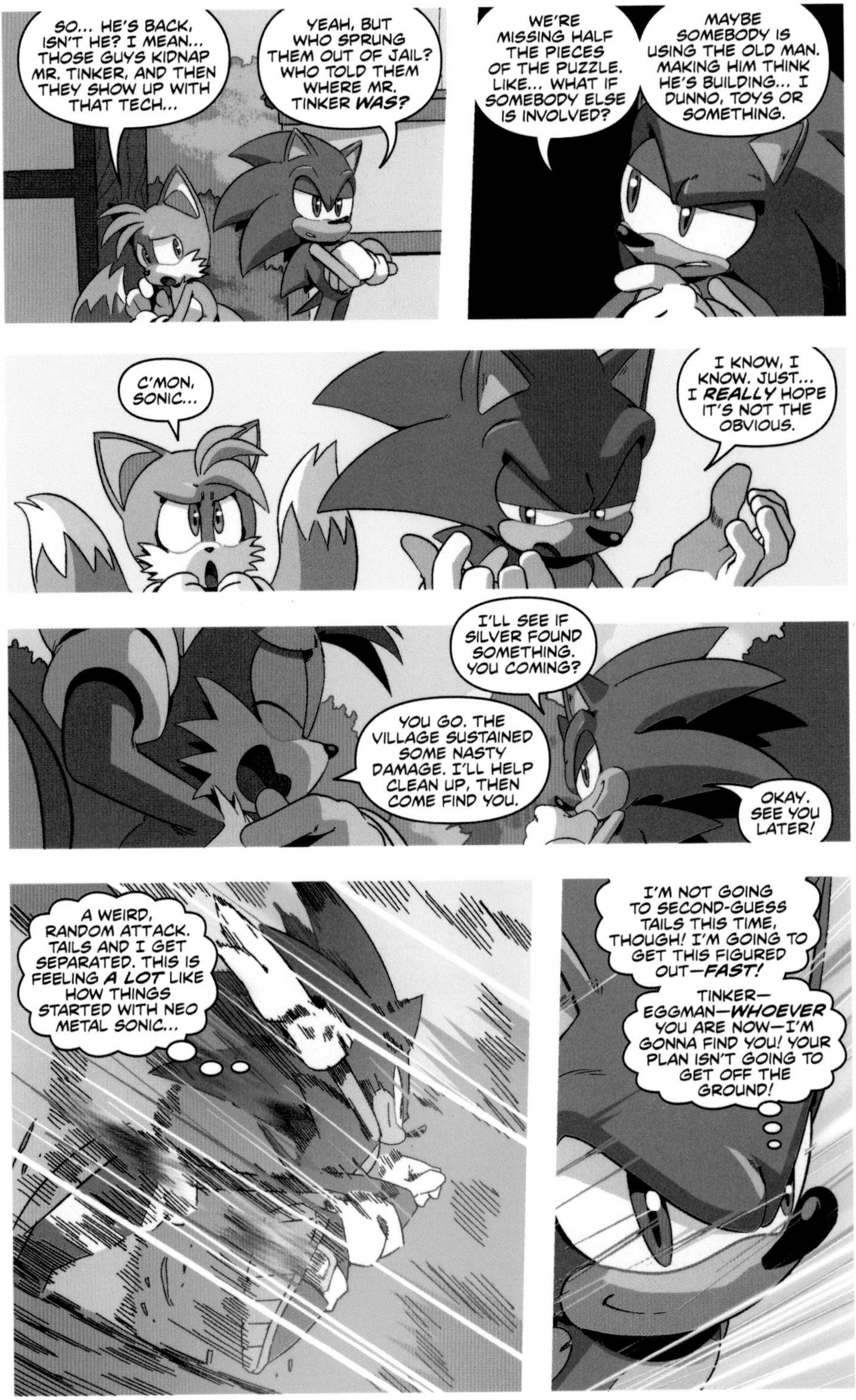
SO... HE'S BACK, ISN'T HE? I MEAN... THOSE GUYS KIDNAP MR. TINKER, AND THEN THEY SHOW UP WITH THAT TECH...
YEAH, BUT WHO SPRUNG THEM OUT OF JAIL? WHO TOLD THEM WHERE MR. TINKER *WAS?*
WE'RE MISSING HALF THE PIECES OF THE PUZZLE. LIKE... WHAT IF SOMEBODY ELSE IS INVOLVED?
MAYBE SOMEBODY IS USING THE OLD MAN. MAKING HIM THINK HE'S BUILDING... I DUNNO, TOYS OR SOMETHING.
C'MON, SONIC...
I KNOW, I KNOW. JUST... I *REALLY* HOPE IT'S NOT THE OBVIOUS.
I'LL SEE IF SILVER FOUND SOMETHING. YOU COMING?
YOU GO. THE VILLAGE SUSTAINED SOME NASTY DAMAGE. I'LL HELP CLEAN UP, THEN COME FIND YOU.
OKAY. SEE YOU LATER!
A WEIRD, RANDOM ATTACK. TAILS AND I GET SEPARATED. THIS IS FEELING *A LOT* LIKE HOW THINGS STARTED WITH NEO METAL SONIC...
I'M NOT GOING TO SECOND-GUESS TAILS THIS TIME, THOUGH! I'M GOING TO GET THIS FIGURED OUT—*FAST!*
TINKER—EGGMAN—*WHOEVER* YOU ARE NOW—I'M GONNA FIND YOU! YOUR PLAN ISN'T GOING TO GET OFF THE GROUND!

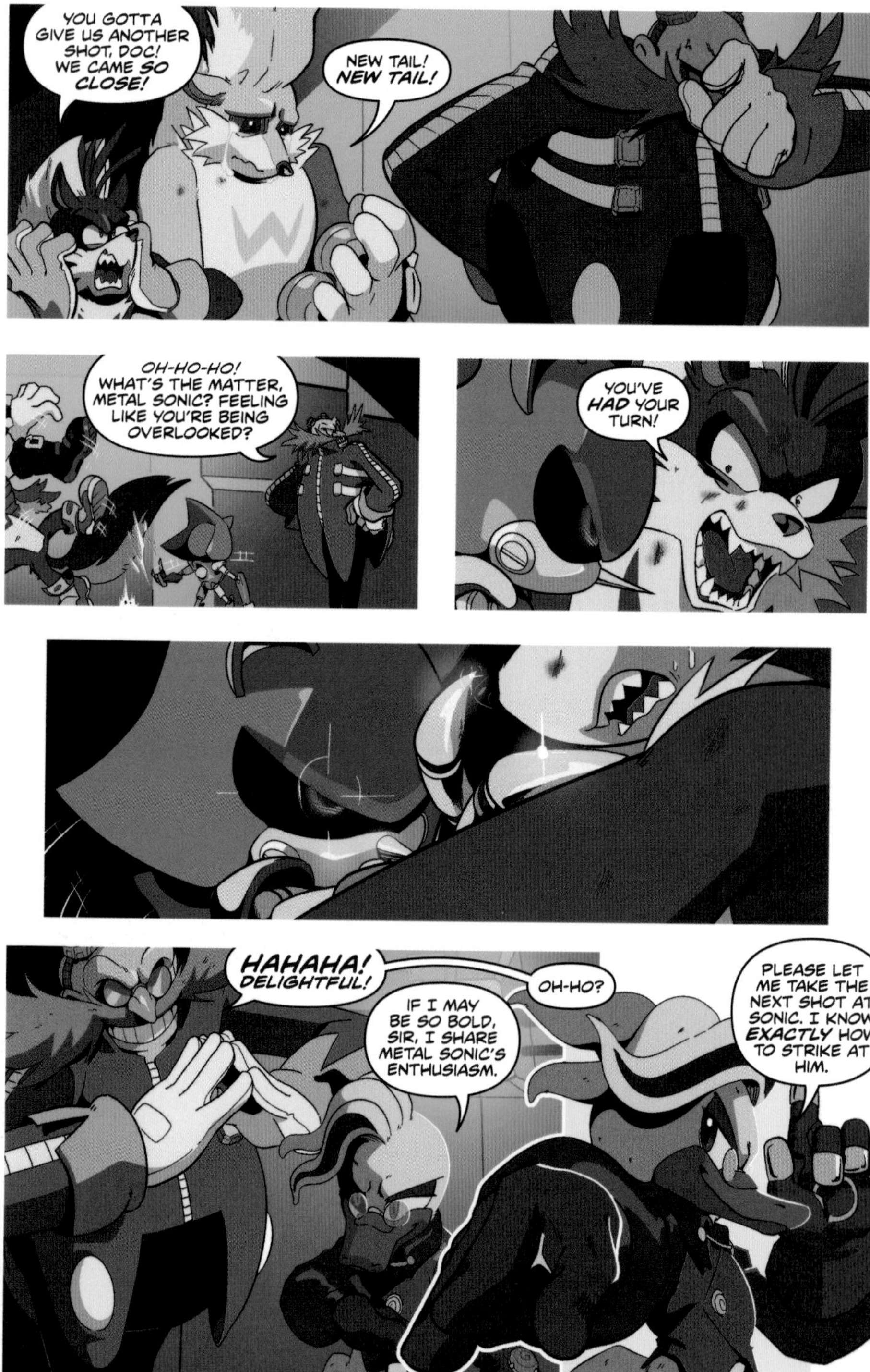
YOU GOTTA GIVE US ANOTHER SHOT, DOC! WE CAME SO CLOSE!
NEW TAIL! NEW TAIL!
OH-HO-HO! WHAT'S THE MATTER, METAL SONIC? FEELING LIKE YOU'RE BEING OVERLOOKED?
YOU'VE HAD YOUR TURN!
HAHAHA! DELIGHTFUL!
OH-HO?
IF I MAY BE SO BOLD, SIR, I SHARE METAL SONIC'S ENTHUSIASM.
PLEASE LET ME TAKE THE NEXT SHOT AT SONIC. I KNOW EXACTLY HOW TO STRIKE AT HIM.

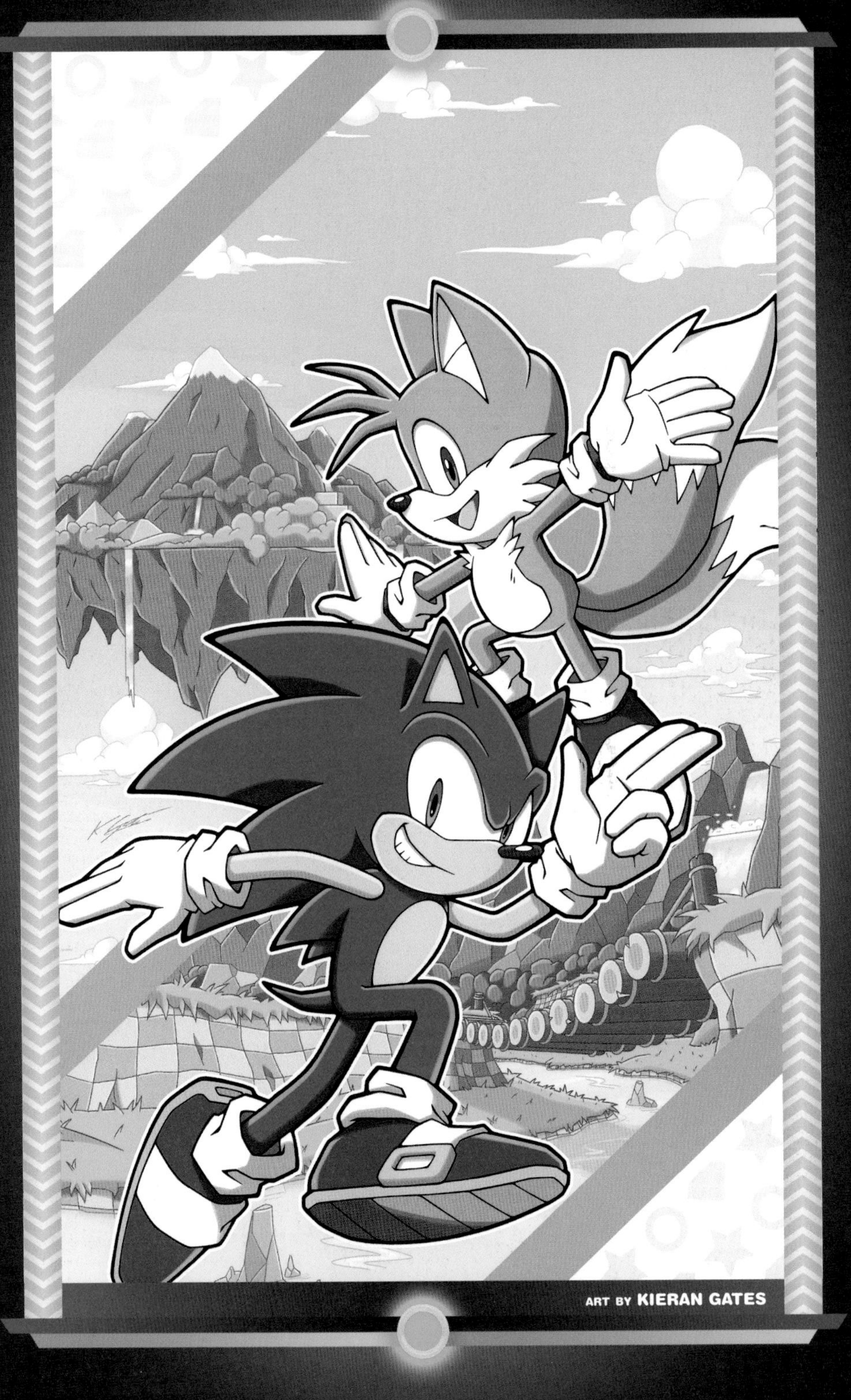

ART BY KIERAN GATES

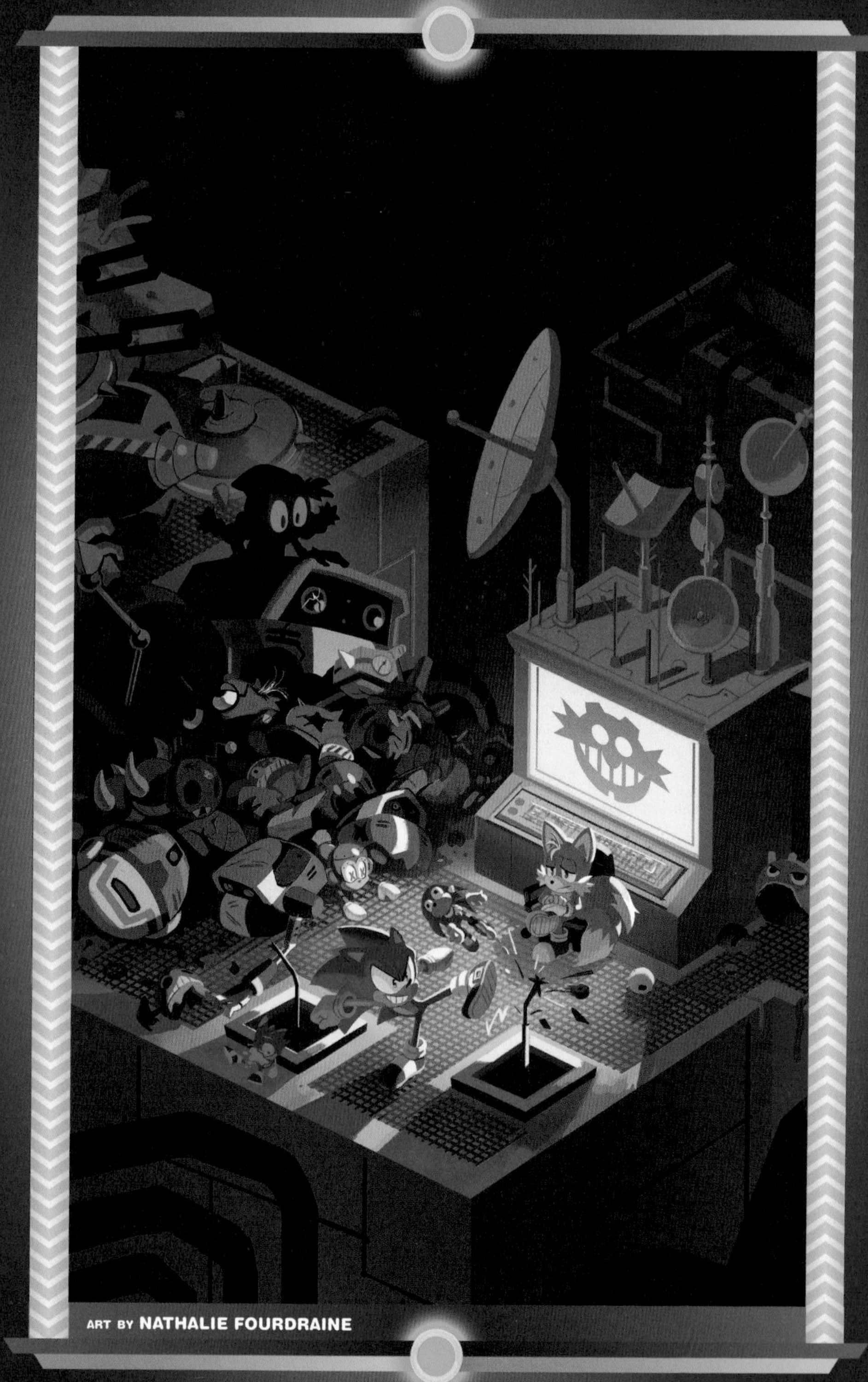

ART BY NATHALIE FOURDRAINE

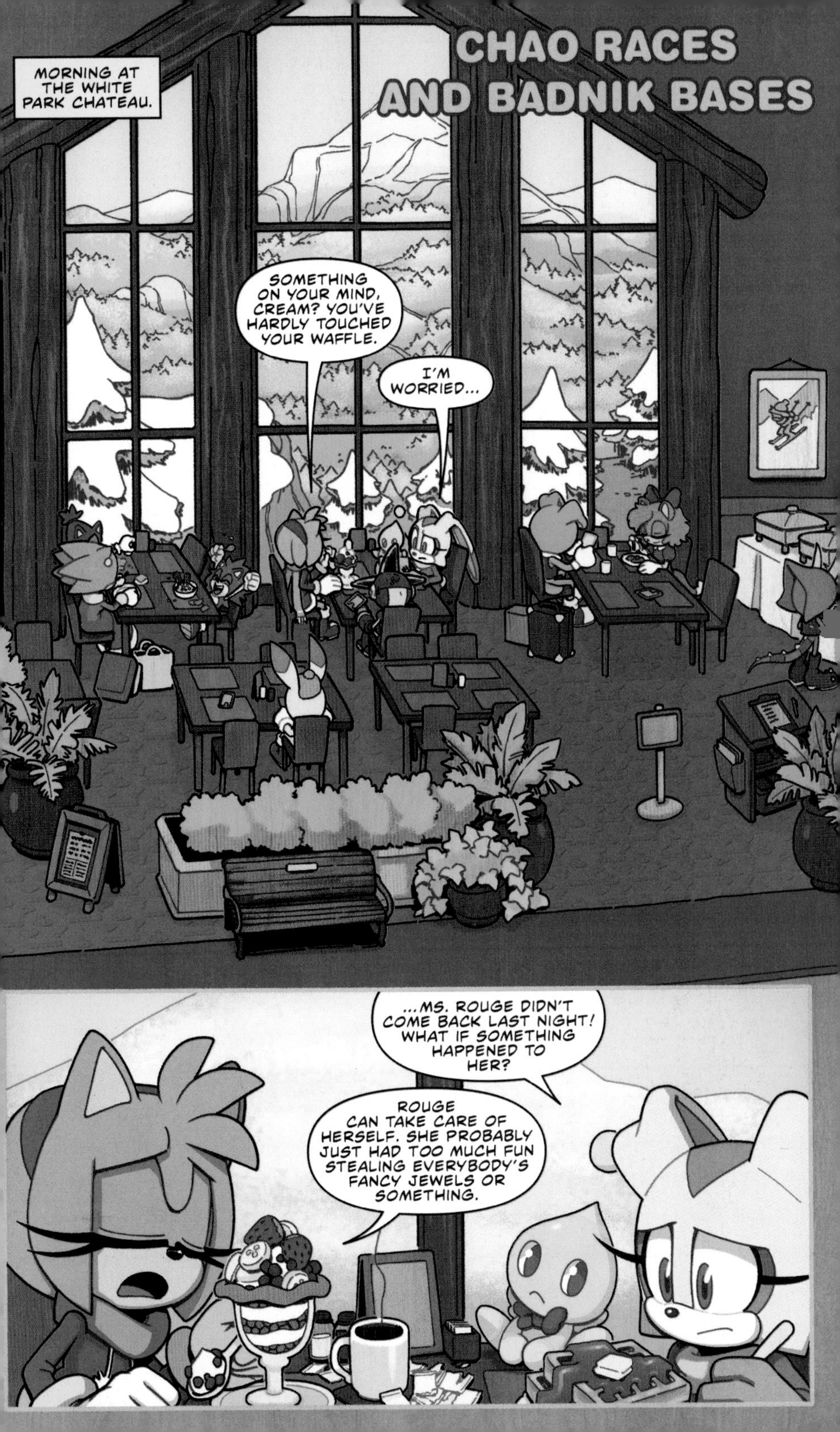
CHAO RACES AND BADNIK BASES
MORNING AT THE WHITE PARK CHATEAU.
SOMETHING ON YOUR MIND, CREAM? YOU'VE HARDLY TOUCHED YOUR WAFFLE.
I'M WORRIED...
...MS. ROUGE DIDN'T COME BACK LAST NIGHT! WHAT IF SOMETHING HAPPENED TO HER?
ROUGE CAN TAKE CARE OF HERSELF. SHE PROBABLY JUST HAD TOO MUCH FUN STEALING EVERYBODY'S FANCY JEWELS OR SOMETHING.

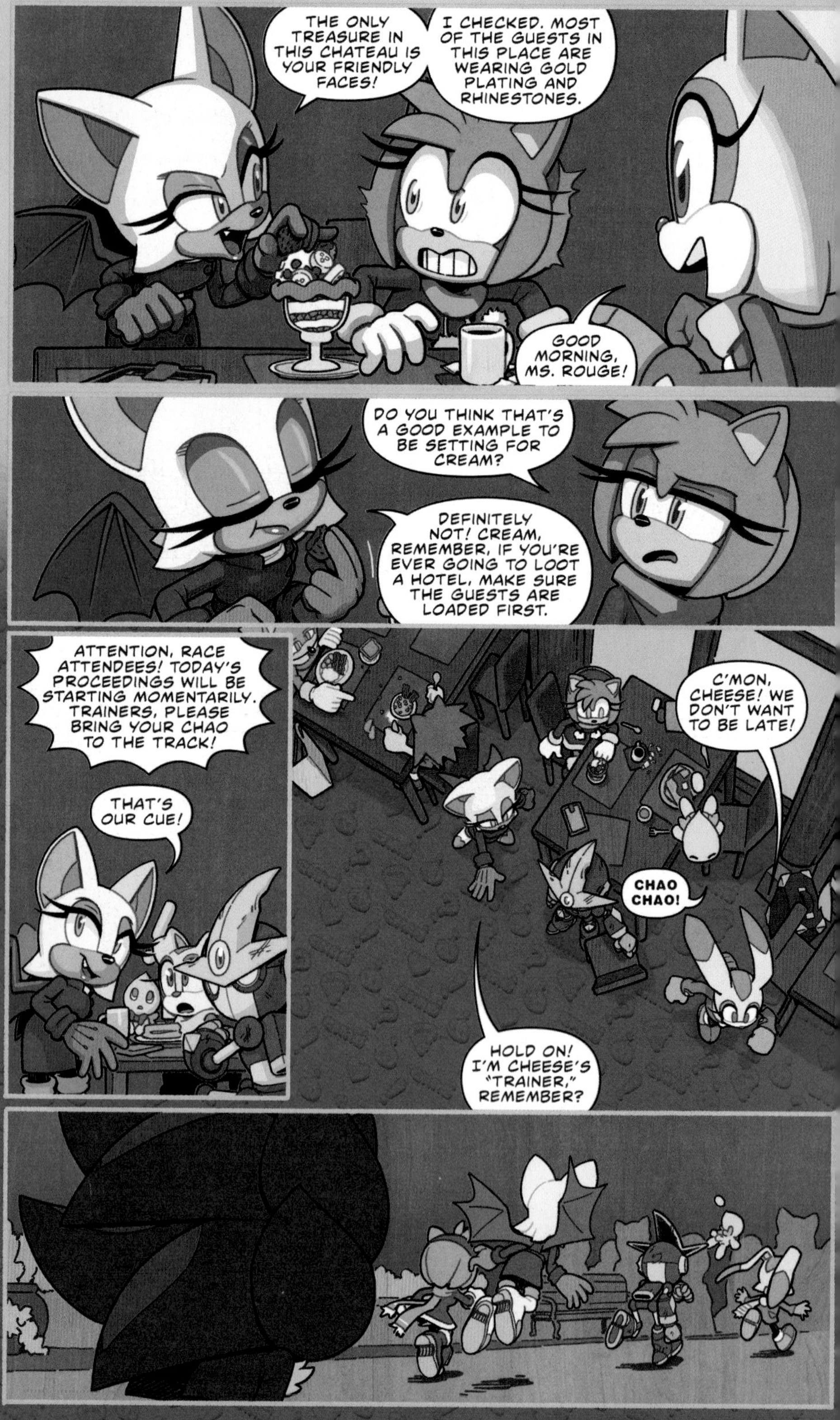
THE ONLY TREASURE IN THIS CHATEAU IS YOUR FRIENDLY FACES!
I CHECKED. MOST OF THE GUESTS IN THIS PLACE ARE WEARING GOLD PLATING AND RHINESTONES.
GOOD MORNING, MS. ROUGE!
DO YOU THINK THAT'S A GOOD EXAMPLE TO BE SETTING FOR CREAM?
DEFINITELY NOT! CREAM, REMEMBER, IF YOU'RE EVER GOING TO LOOT A HOTEL, MAKE SURE THE GUESTS ARE LOADED FIRST.
ATTENTION, RACE ATTENDEES! TODAY'S PROCEEDINGS WILL BE STARTING MOMENTARILY. TRAINERS, PLEASE BRING YOUR CHAO TO THE TRACK!
THAT'S OUR CUE!
C'MON, CHEESE! WE DON'T WANT TO BE LATE!
CHAO CHAO!
HOLD ON! I'M CHEESE'S "TRAINER," REMEMBER?

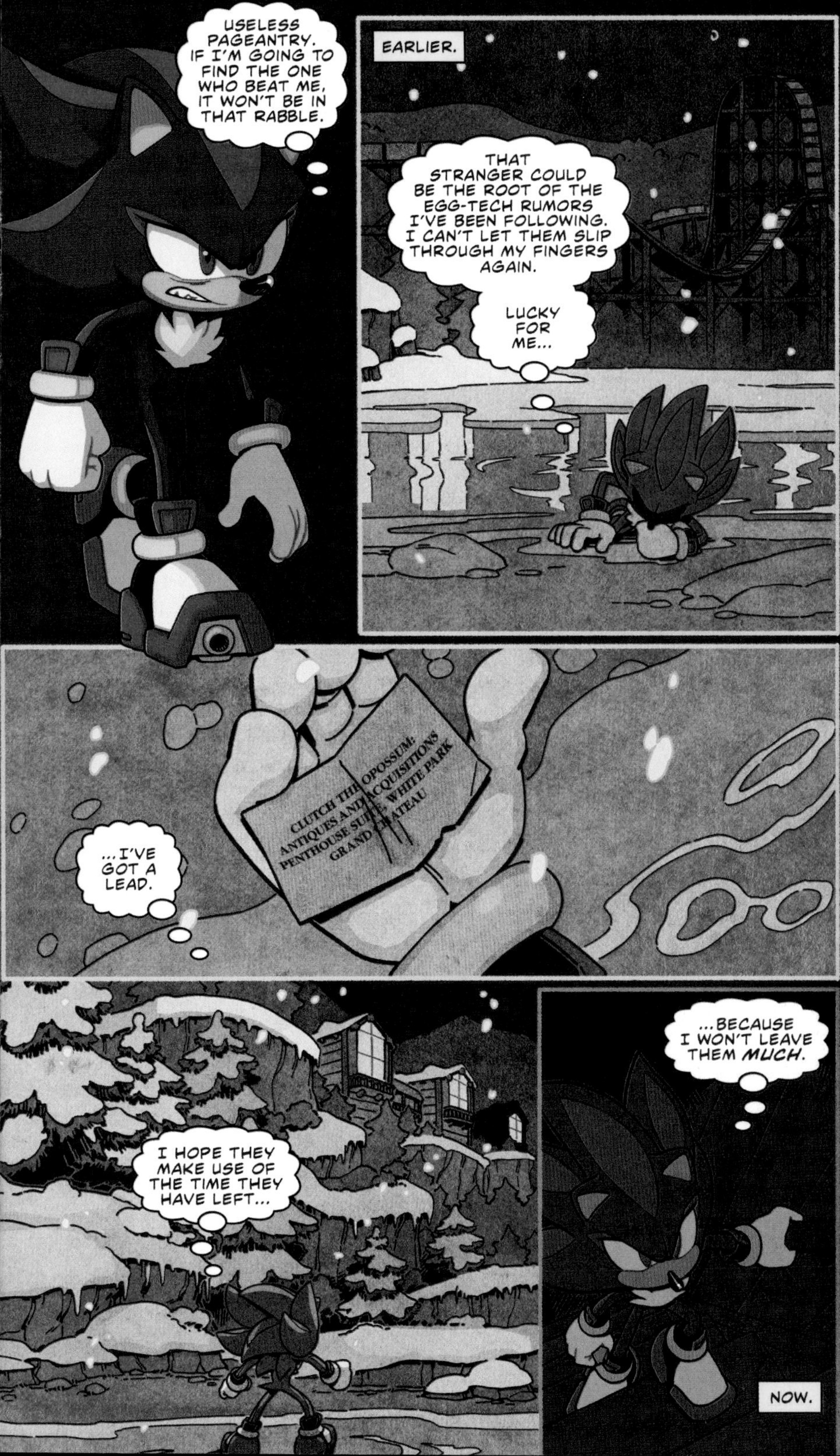
USELESS PAGEANTRY. IF I'M GOING TO FIND THE ONE WHO BEAT ME, IT WON'T BE IN THAT RABBLE.
EARLIER.
THAT STRANGER COULD BE THE ROOT OF THE EGG-TECH RUMORS I'VE BEEN FOLLOWING. I CAN'T LET THEM SLIP THROUGH MY FINGERS AGAIN.
LUCKY FOR ME...
CLUTCH THE OPOSSUM:
ANTIQUES AND ACQUISITIONS
PENTHOUSE SUITE, WHITE PARK
GRAND CHATEAU
...I'VE GOT A LEAD.
I HOPE THEY MAKE USE OF THE TIME THEY HAVE LEFT...
...BECAUSE I WON'T LEAVE THEM *MUCH*.
NOW.

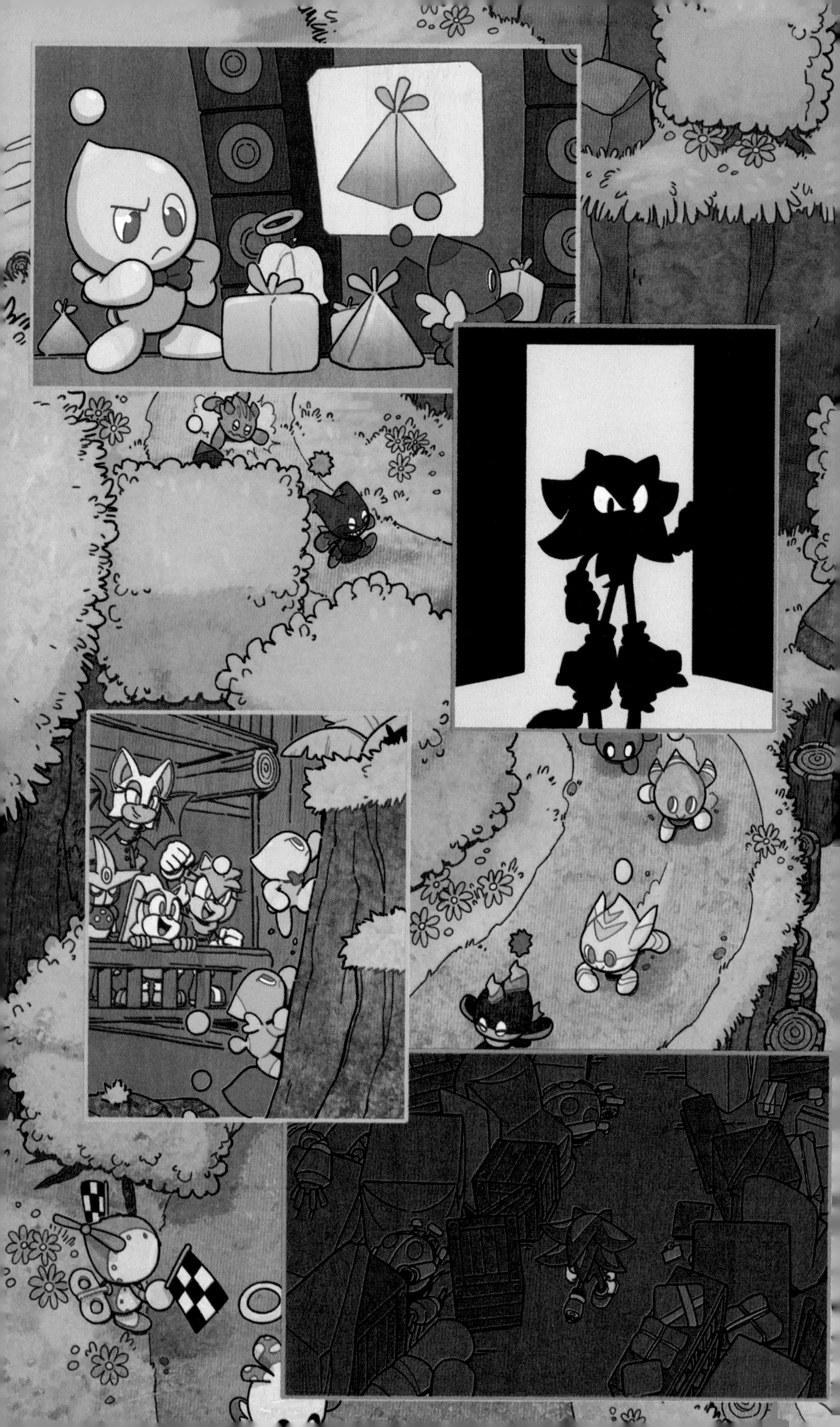

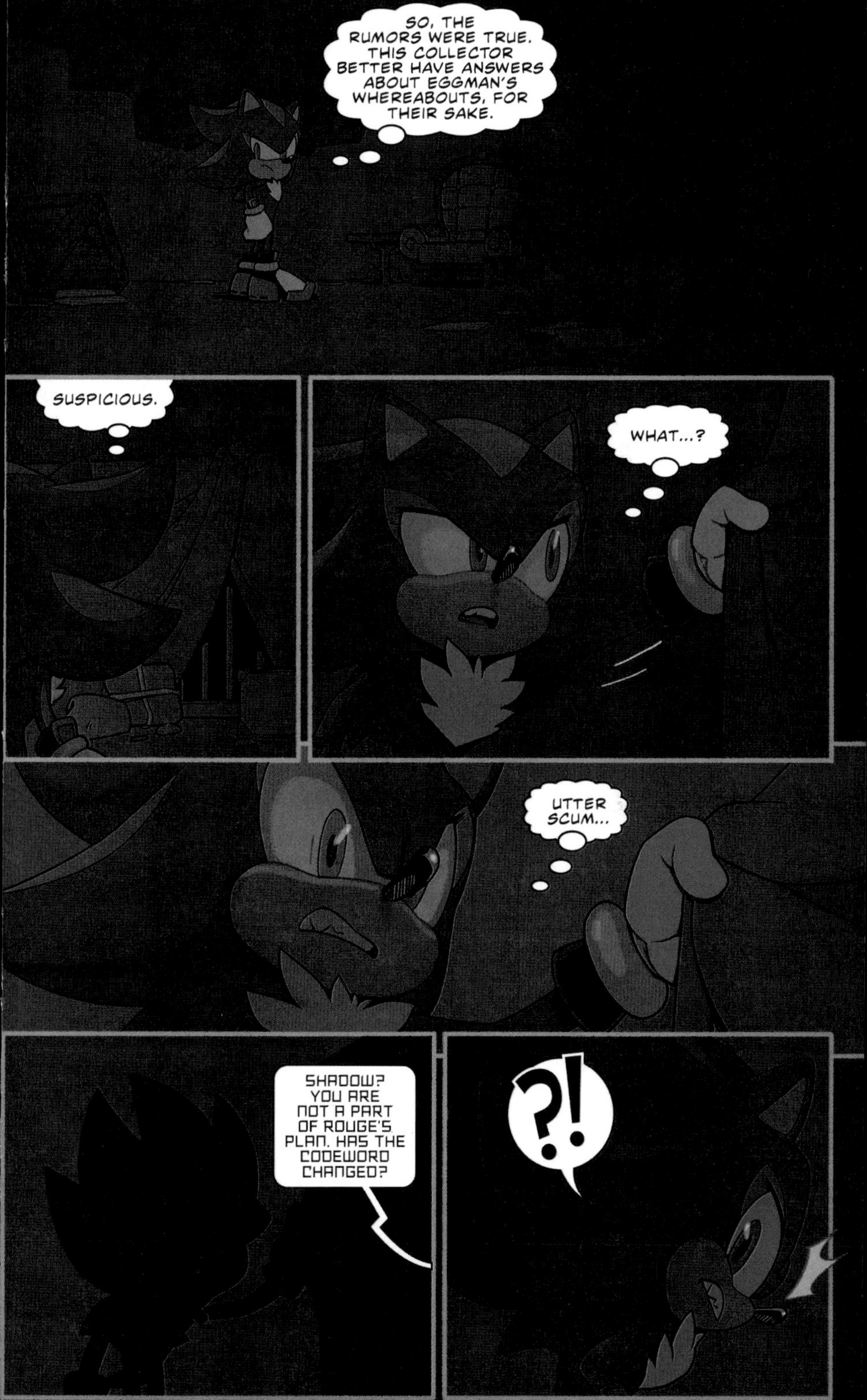
SO, THE RUMORS WERE TRUE. THIS COLLECTOR BETTER HAVE ANSWERS ABOUT EGGMAN'S WHEREABOUTS, FOR THEIR SAKE.
SUSPICIOUS.
WHAT...?
UTTER SCUM...
SHADOW? YOU ARE NOT A PART OF ROUGE'S PLAN. HAS THE CODEWORD CHANGED?
?!

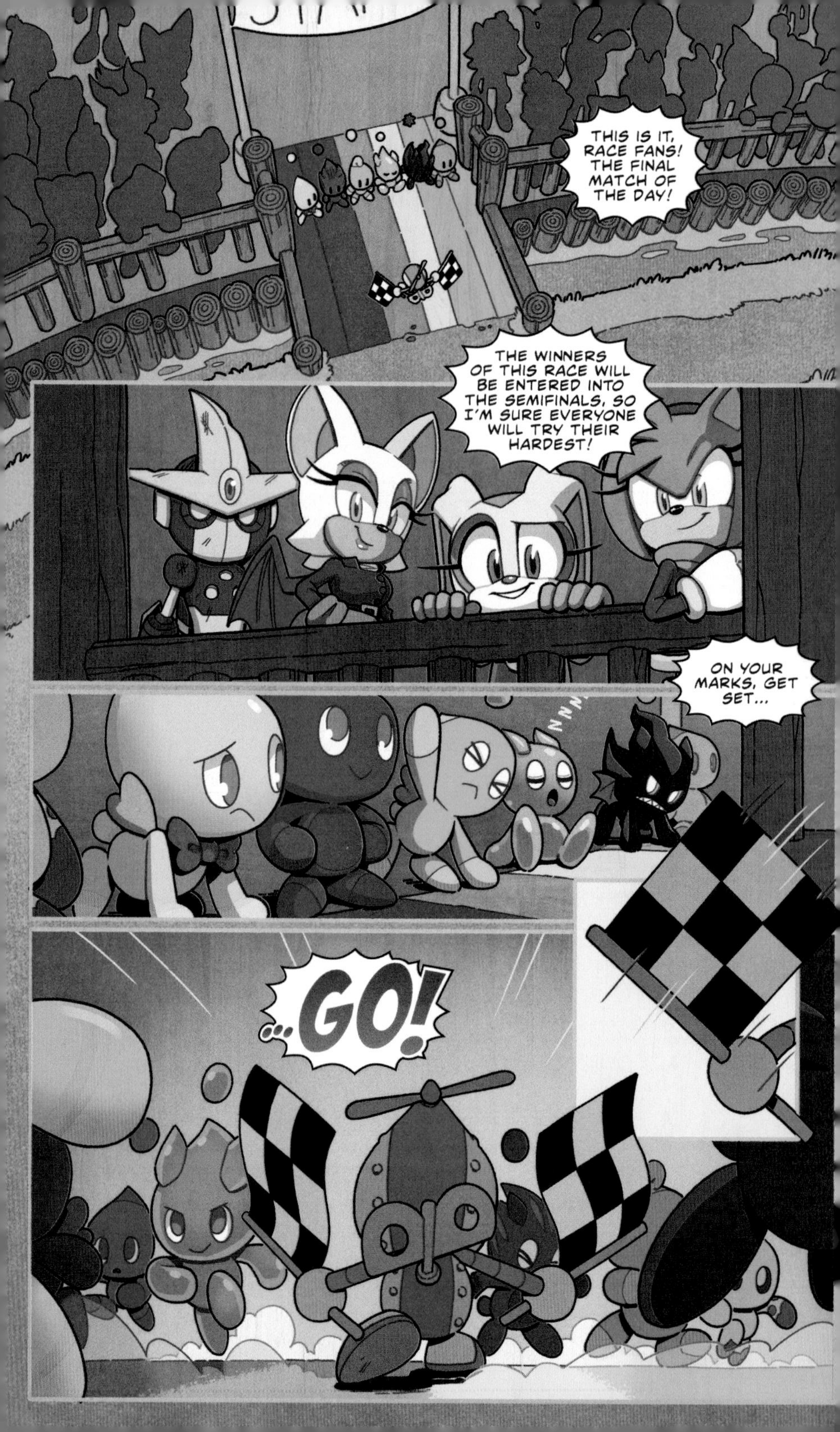
THIS IS IT, RACE FANS! THE FINAL MATCH OF THE DAY!
THE WINNERS OF THIS RACE WILL BE ENTERED INTO THE SEMIFINALS, SO I'M SURE EVERYONE WILL TRY THEIR HARDEST!
ON YOUR MARKS, GET SET...
NNN
...GO!

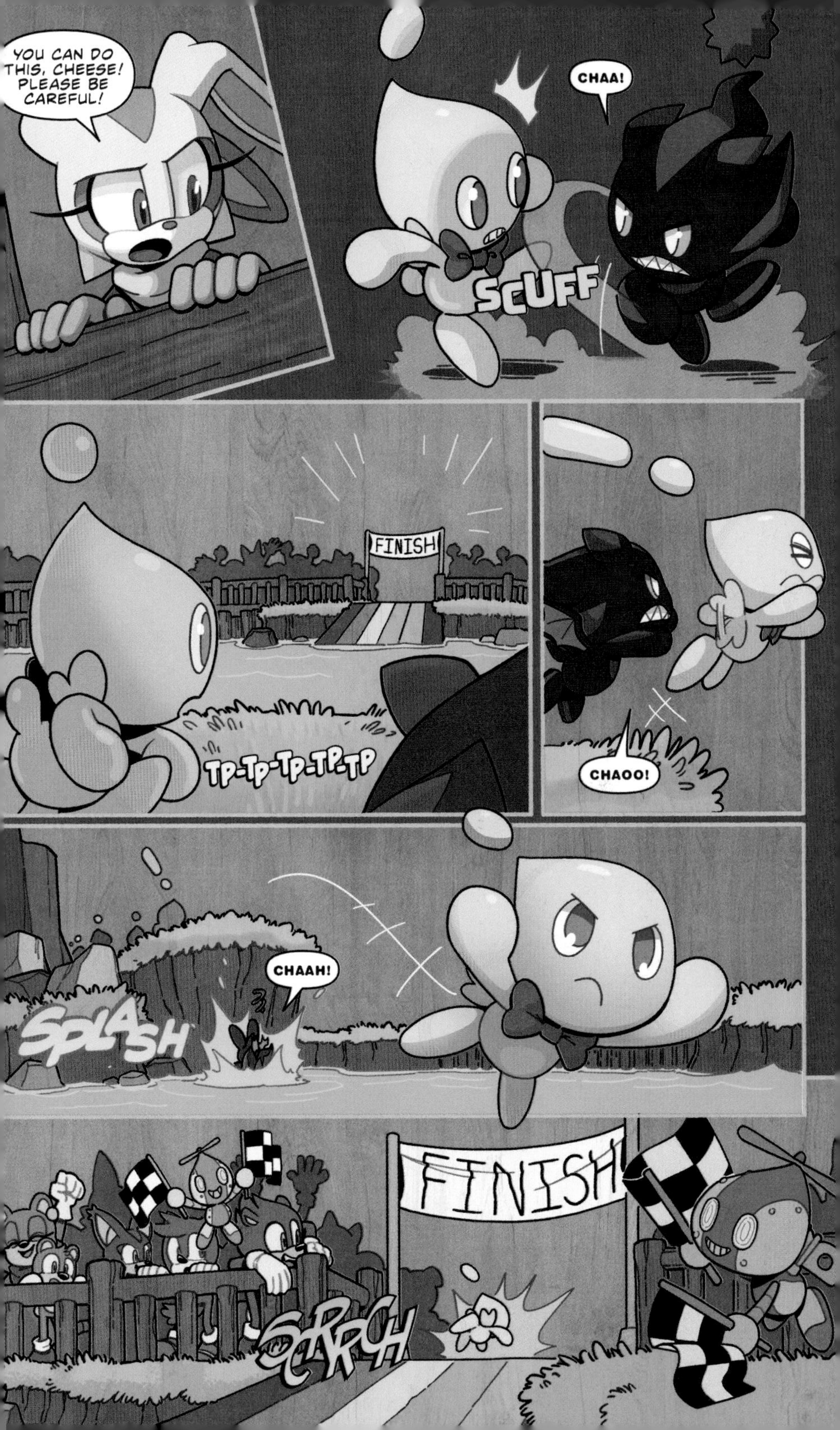
YOU CAN DO THIS, CHEESE! PLEASE BE CAREFUL!
CHAA!
SCUFF
FINISH
TP-TP-TP-TP-TP
CHAOO!
CHAAH!
SPLASH
FINISH
SCRRCH

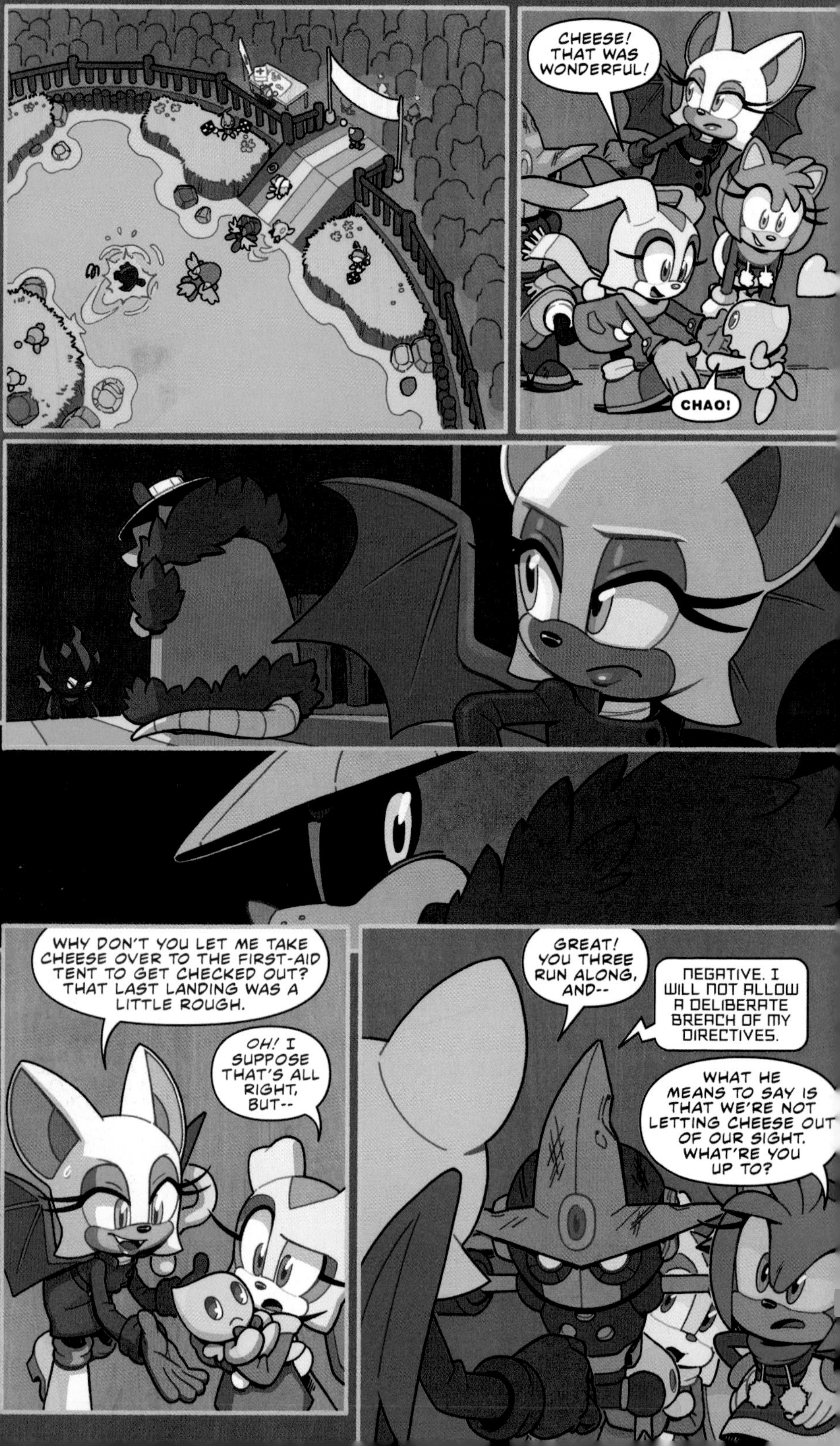
CHEESE! THAT WAS WONDERFUL!
CHAO!
WHY DON'T YOU LET ME TAKE CHEESE OVER TO THE FIRST-AID TENT TO GET CHECKED OUT? THAT LAST LANDING WAS A LITTLE ROUGH.
OH! I SUPPOSE THAT'S ALL RIGHT, BUT--
GREAT! YOU THREE RUN ALONG, AND--
NEGATIVE. I WILL NOT ALLOW A DELIBERATE BREACH OF MY DIRECTIVES.
WHAT HE MEANS TO SAY IS THAT WE'RE NOT LETTING CHEESE OUT OF OUR SIGHT. WHAT'RE YOU UP TO?

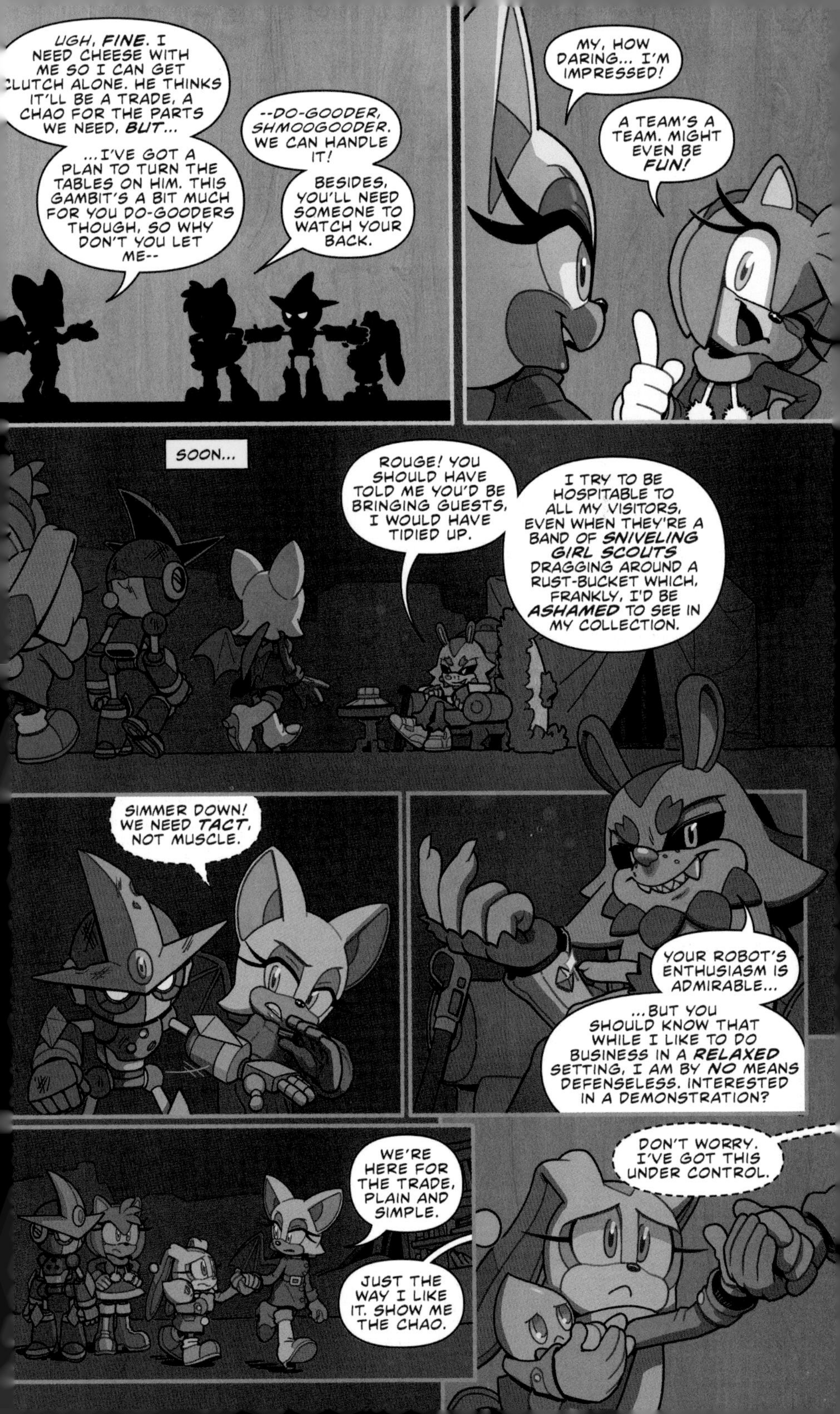
UGH, FINE. I NEED CHEESE WITH ME SO I CAN GET CLUTCH ALONE. HE THINKS IT'LL BE A TRADE, A CHAO FOR THE PARTS WE NEED, BUT...
...I'VE GOT A PLAN TO TURN THE TABLES ON HIM. THIS GAMBIT'S A BIT MUCH FOR YOU DO-GOODERS THOUGH, SO WHY DON'T YOU LET ME--
--DO-GOODER, SHMOOGOODER. WE CAN HANDLE IT!
BESIDES, YOU'LL NEED SOMEONE TO WATCH YOUR BACK.
MY, HOW DARING... I'M IMPRESSED!
A TEAM'S A TEAM. MIGHT EVEN BE FUN!
SOON...
ROUGE! YOU SHOULD HAVE TOLD ME YOU'D BE BRINGING GUESTS, I WOULD HAVE TIDIED UP.
I TRY TO BE HOSPITABLE TO ALL MY VISITORS, EVEN WHEN THEY'RE A BAND OF SNIVELING GIRL SCOUTS DRAGGING AROUND A RUST-BUCKET WHICH, FRANKLY, I'D BE ASHAMED TO SEE IN MY COLLECTION.
SIMMER DOWN! WE NEED TACT, NOT MUSCLE.
YOUR ROBOT'S ENTHUSIASM IS ADMIRABLE...
...BUT YOU SHOULD KNOW THAT WHILE I LIKE TO DO BUSINESS IN A RELAXED SETTING, I AM BY NO MEANS DEFENSELESS. INTERESTED IN A DEMONSTRATION?
WE'RE HERE FOR THE TRADE, PLAIN AND SIMPLE.
JUST THE WAY I LIKE IT. SHOW ME THE CHAO.
DON'T WORRY. I'VE GOT THIS UNDER CONTROL.

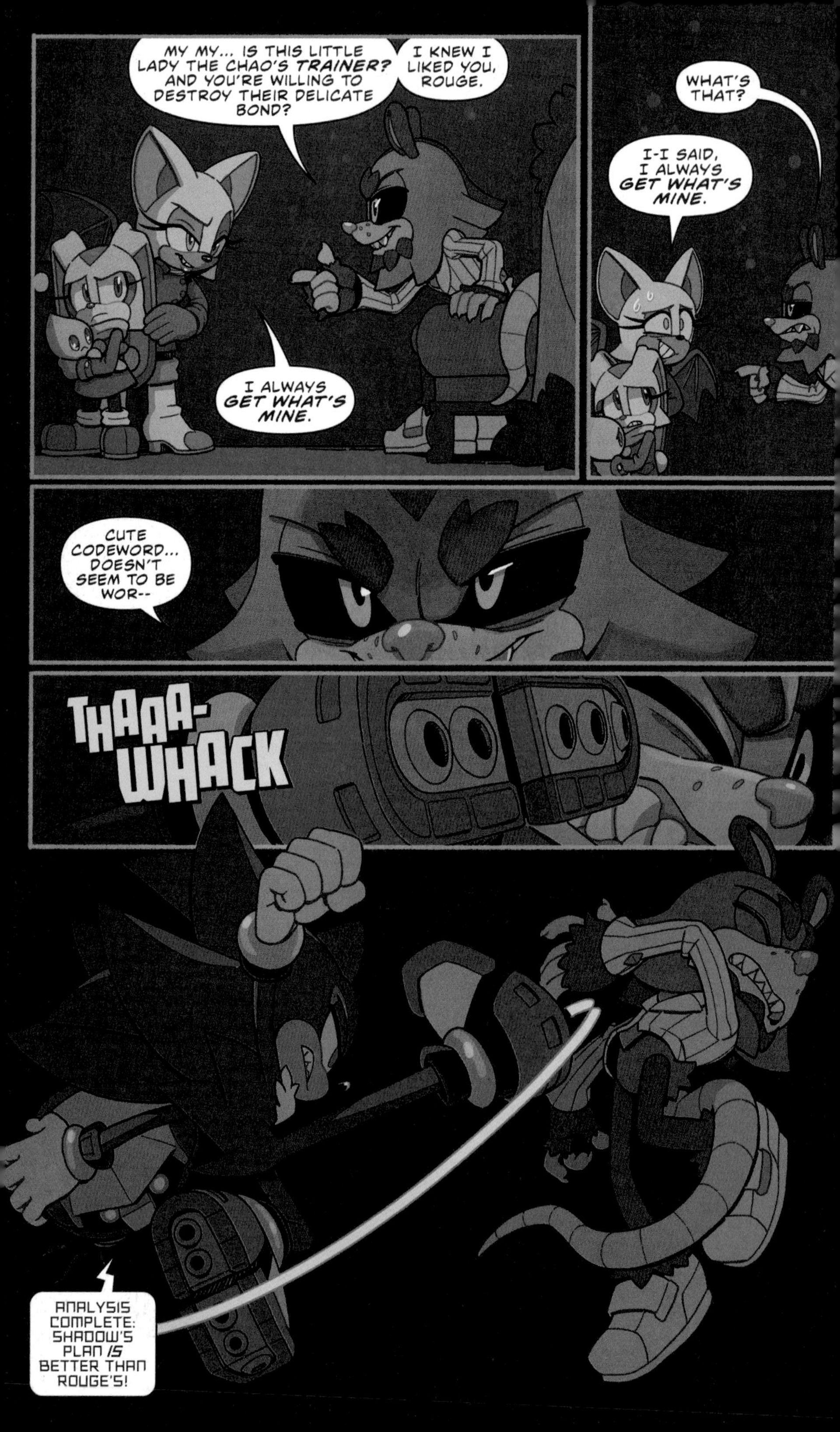

MY MY... IS THIS LITTLE LADY THE CHAO'S *TRAINER?* AND YOU'RE WILLING TO DESTROY THEIR DELICATE BOND?
I KNEW I LIKED YOU, ROUGE.
I ALWAYS **GET WHAT'S MINE**.
WHAT'S THAT?
I-I SAID, I ALWAYS **GET WHAT'S MINE**.
CUTE CODEWORD... DOESN'T SEEM TO BE WOR--
THAAA-WHACK
ANALYSIS COMPLETE: SHADOW'S PLAN *IS* BETTER THAN ROUGE'S!

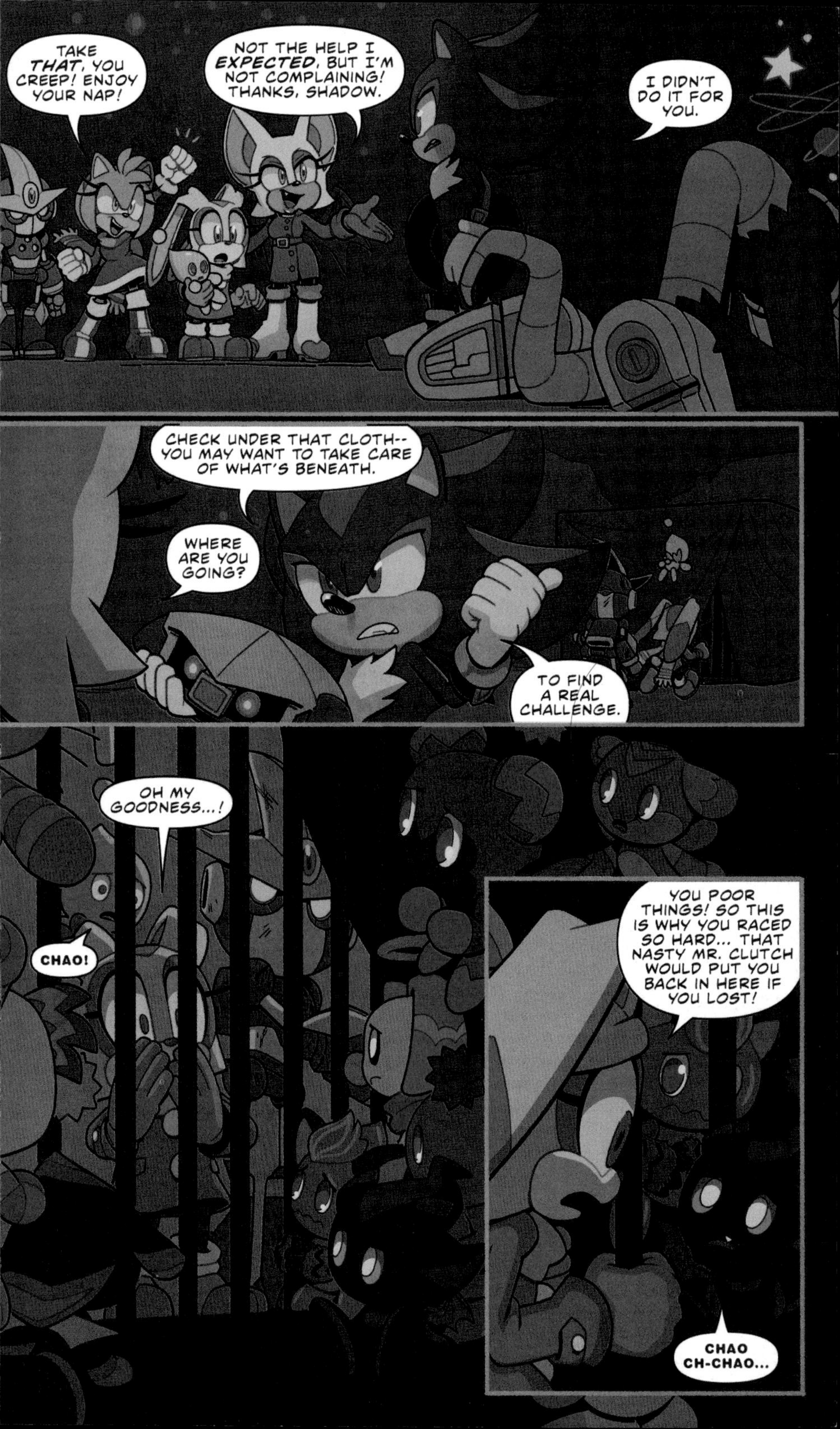
TAKE THAT, YOU CREEP! ENJOY YOUR NAP!
NOT THE HELP I EXPECTED, BUT I'M NOT COMPLAINING! THANKS, SHADOW.
I DIDN'T DO IT FOR YOU.
CHECK UNDER THAT CLOTH-- YOU MAY WANT TO TAKE CARE OF WHAT'S BENEATH.
WHERE ARE YOU GOING?
TO FIND A REAL CHALLENGE.
OH MY GOODNESS...!
CHAO!
YOU POOR THINGS! SO THIS IS WHY YOU RACED SO HARD... THAT NASTY MR. CLUTCH WOULD PUT YOU BACK IN HERE IF YOU LOST!
CHAO CH-CHAO...

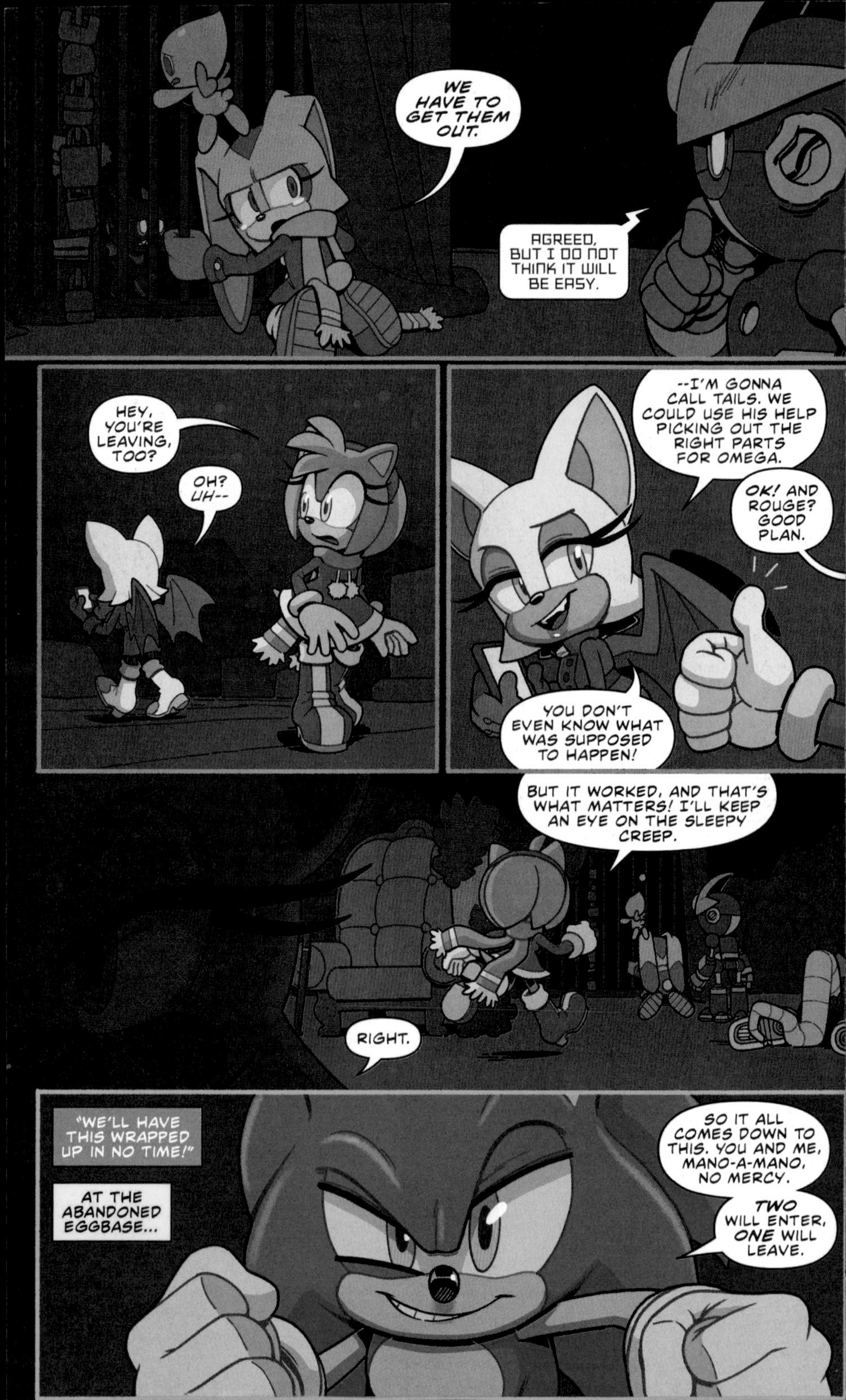
WE HAVE TO GET THEM OUT.
AGREED, BUT I DO NOT THINK IT WILL BE EASY.
HEY, YOU'RE LEAVING, TOO?
OH? UH--
--I'M GONNA CALL TAILS. WE COULD USE HIS HELP PICKING OUT THE RIGHT PARTS FOR OMEGA.
OK! AND ROUGE? GOOD PLAN.
YOU DON'T EVEN KNOW WHAT WAS SUPPOSED TO HAPPEN!
BUT IT WORKED, AND THAT'S WHAT MATTERS! I'LL KEEP AN EYE ON THE SLEEPY CREEP.
RIGHT.
"WE'LL HAVE THIS WRAPPED UP IN NO TIME!"
AT THE ABANDONED EGGBASE...
SO IT ALL COMES DOWN TO THIS. YOU AND ME, MANO-A-MANO, NO MERCY.
TWO WILL ENTER, ONE WILL LEAVE.

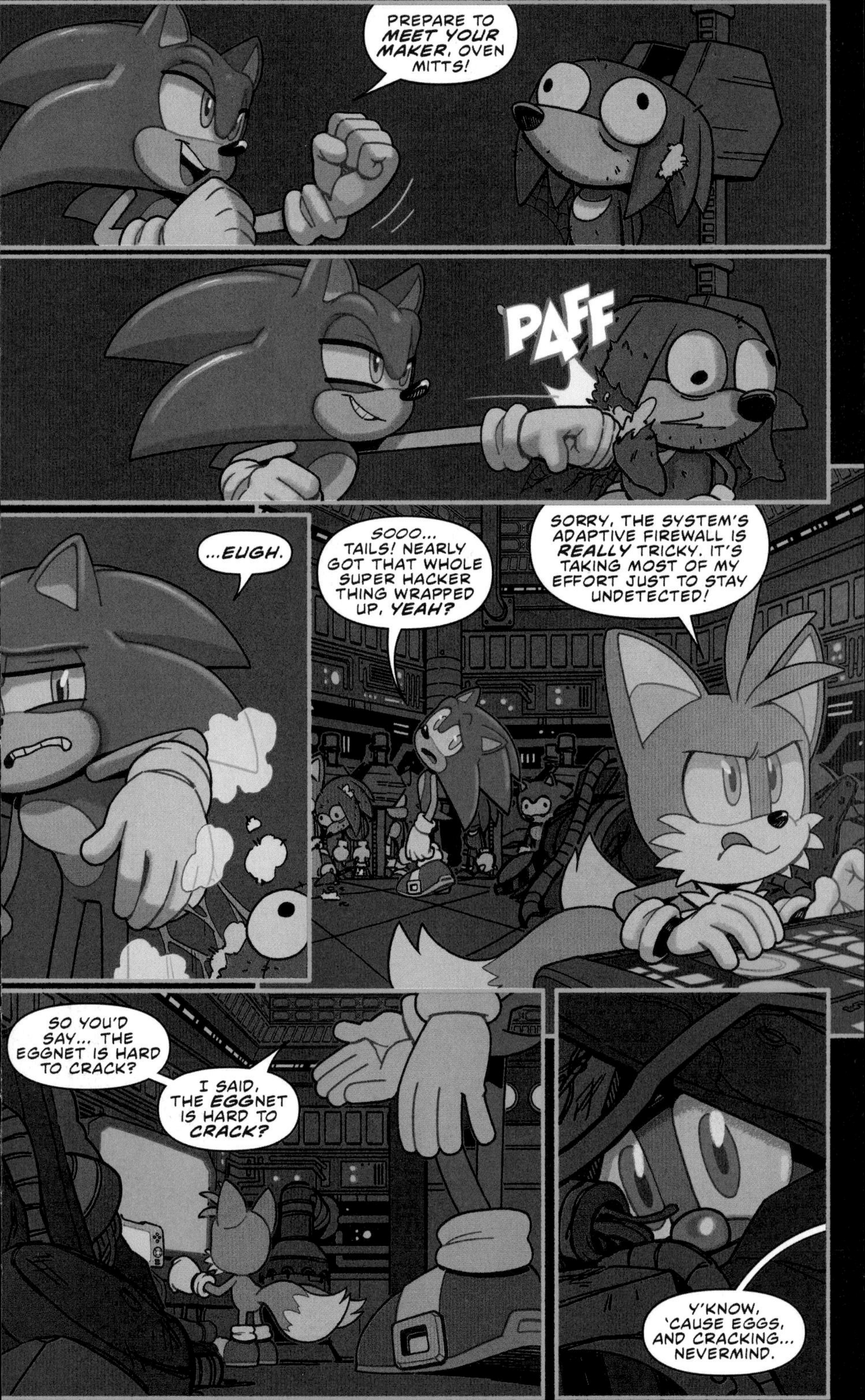
PREPARE TO MEET YOUR MAKER, OVEN MITTS!
PAFF
...EUGH.
SOOO... TAILS! NEARLY GOT THAT WHOLE SUPER HACKER THING WRAPPED UP, YEAH?
SORRY, THE SYSTEM'S ADAPTIVE FIREWALL IS REALLY TRICKY. IT'S TAKING MOST OF MY EFFORT JUST TO STAY UNDETECTED!
SO YOU'D SAY... THE EGGNET IS HARD TO CRACK?
I SAID, THE EGGNET IS HARD TO CRACK?
Y'KNOW, 'CAUSE EGGS, AND CRACKING... NEVERMIND.

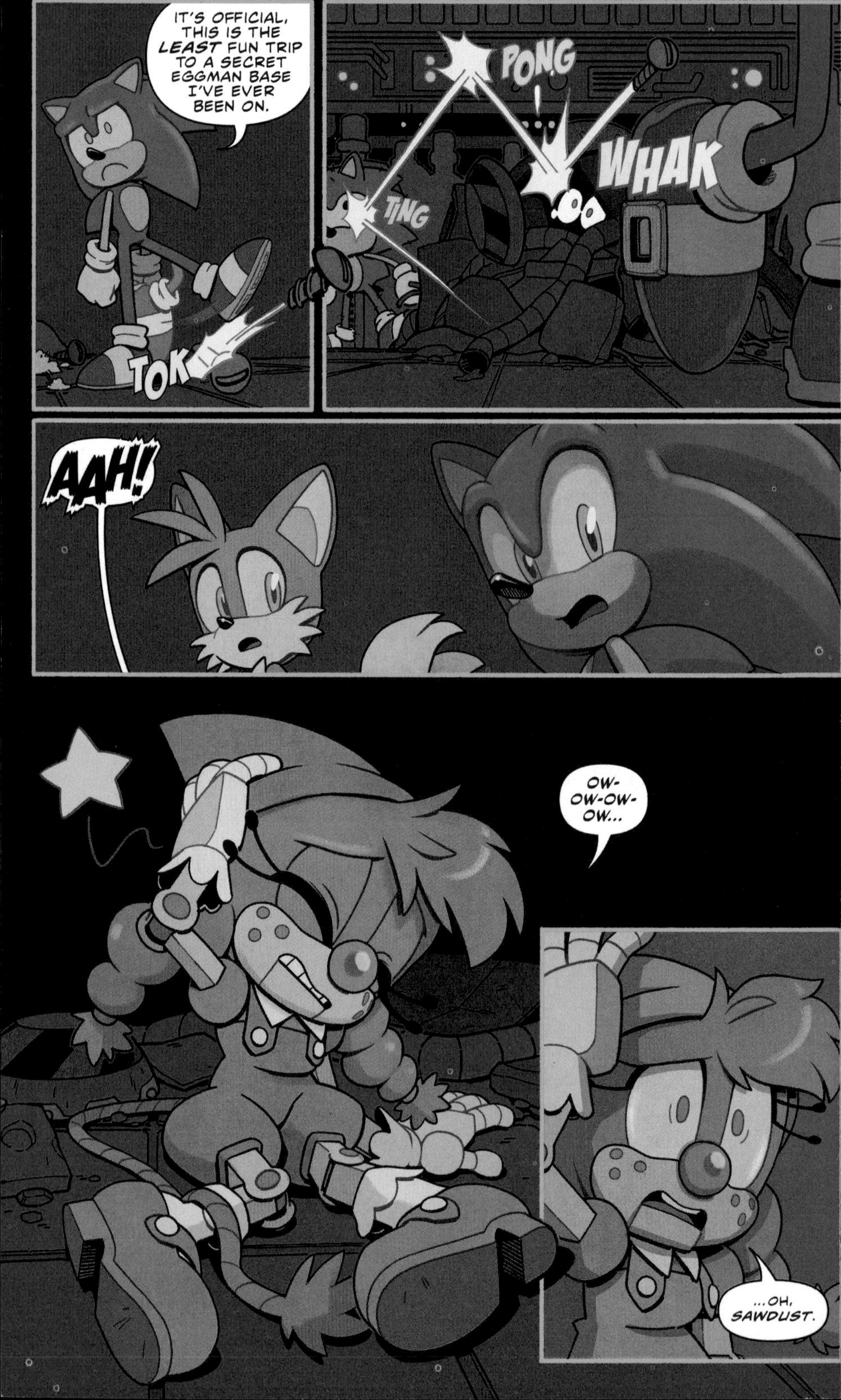
IT'S OFFICIAL, THIS IS THE LEAST FUN TRIP TO A SECRET EGGMAN BASE I'VE EVER BEEN ON.
TOK
TING
PONG
WHAK
AAH!
OW-OW-OW-OW...
...OH, SAWDUST.

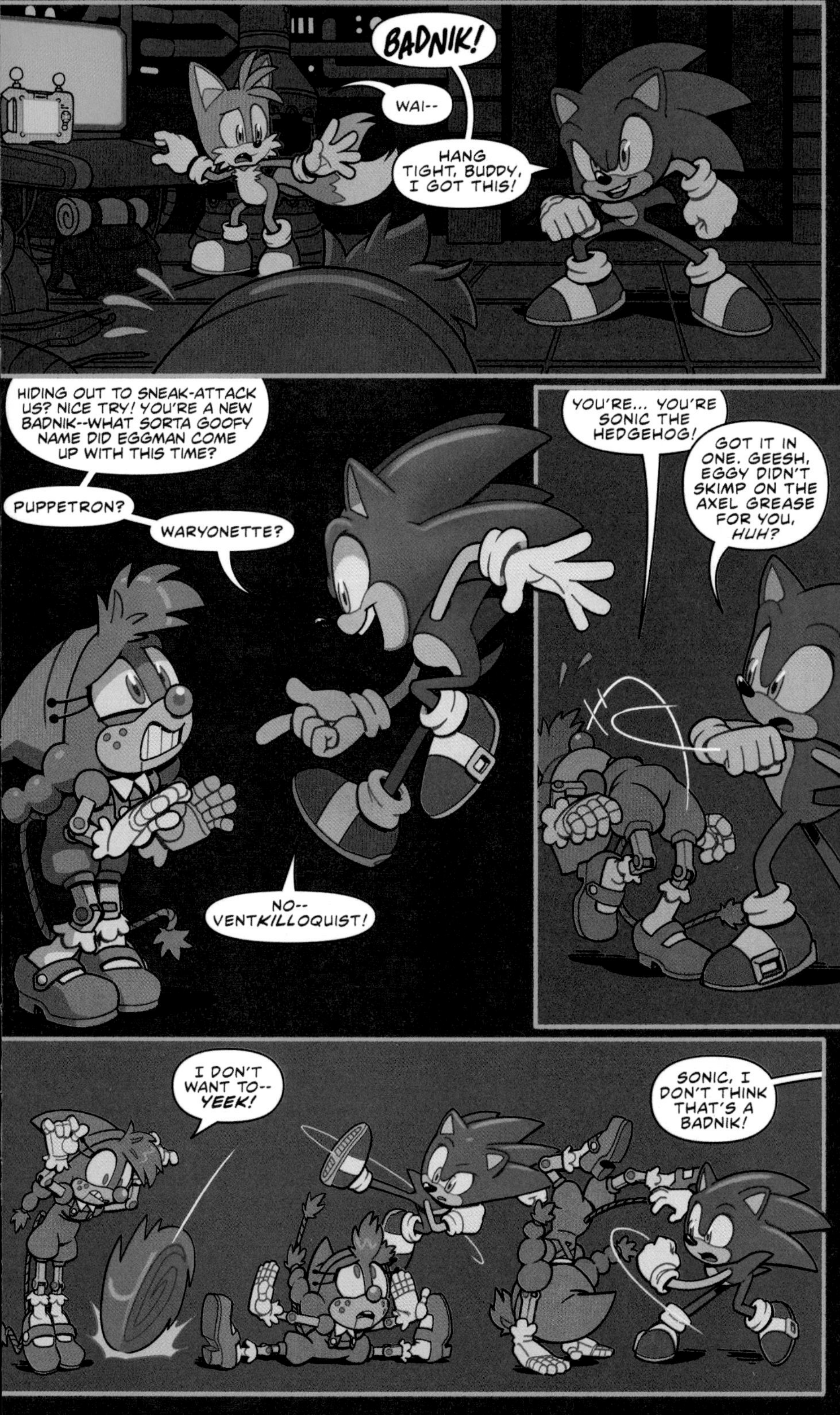
BADNIK!
WAI--
HANG TIGHT, BUDDY, I GOT THIS!
HIDING OUT TO SNEAK-ATTACK US? NICE TRY! YOU'RE A NEW BADNIK--WHAT SORTA GOOFY NAME DID EGGMAN COME UP WITH THIS TIME?
PUPPETRON?
WARYONETTE?
NO-- VENTKILLOQUIST!
YOU'RE... YOU'RE SONIC THE HEDGEHOG!
GOT IT IN ONE. GEESH, EGGY DIDN'T SKIMP ON THE AXEL GREASE FOR YOU, HUH?
I DON'T WANT TO-- YEEK!
SONIC, I DON'T THINK THAT'S A BADNIK!

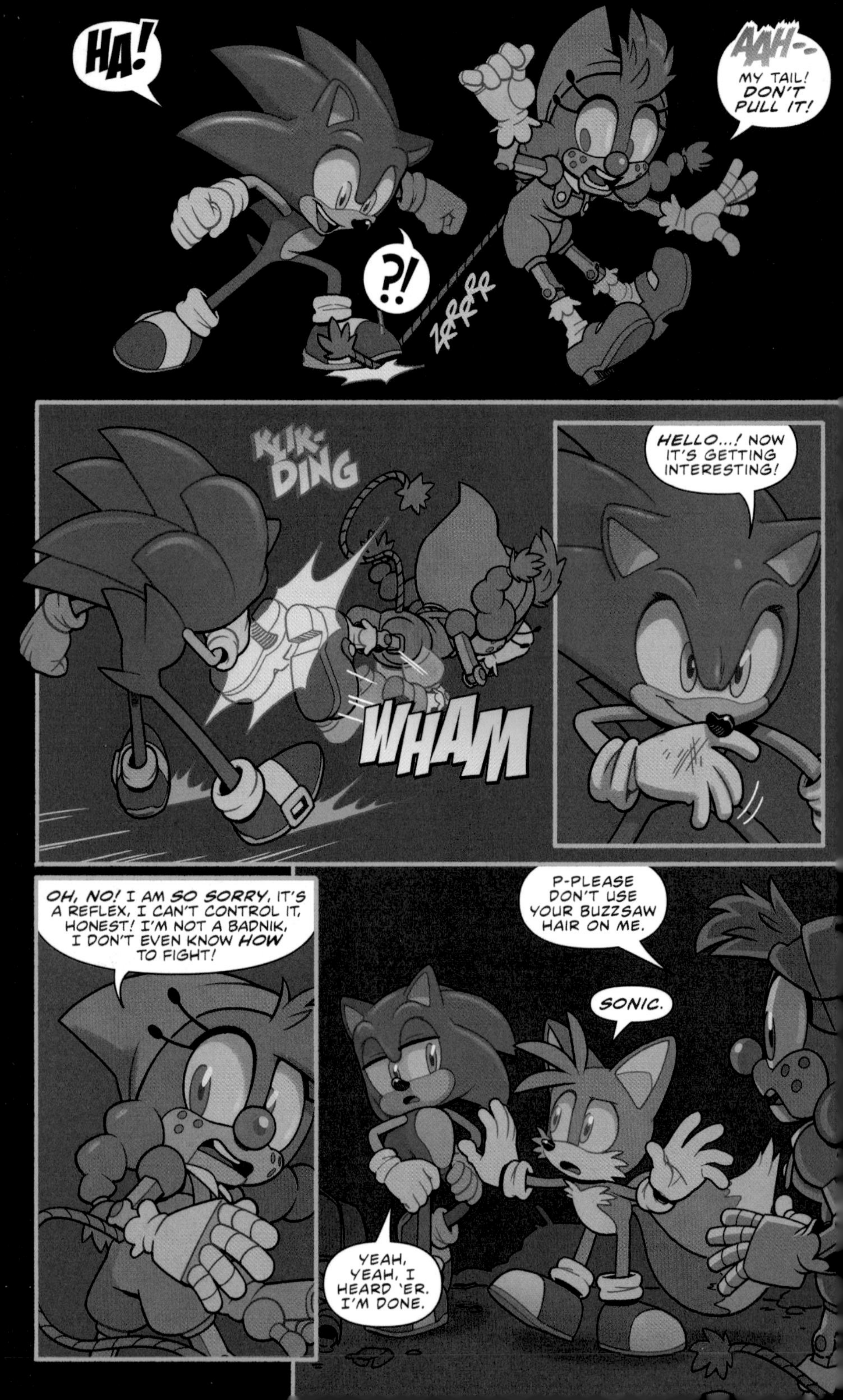
HA!
AAH--
MY TAIL! DON'T PULL IT!
?!
ZZZRRR
KLIK-DING
WHAM
HELLO...! NOW IT'S GETTING INTERESTING!
OH, NO! I AM SO SORRY, IT'S A REFLEX, I CAN'T CONTROL IT, HONEST! I'M NOT A BADNIK, I DON'T EVEN KNOW HOW TO FIGHT!
P-PLEASE DON'T USE YOUR BUZZSAW HAIR ON ME.
SONIC.
YEAH, YEAH, I HEARD 'ER. I'M DONE.

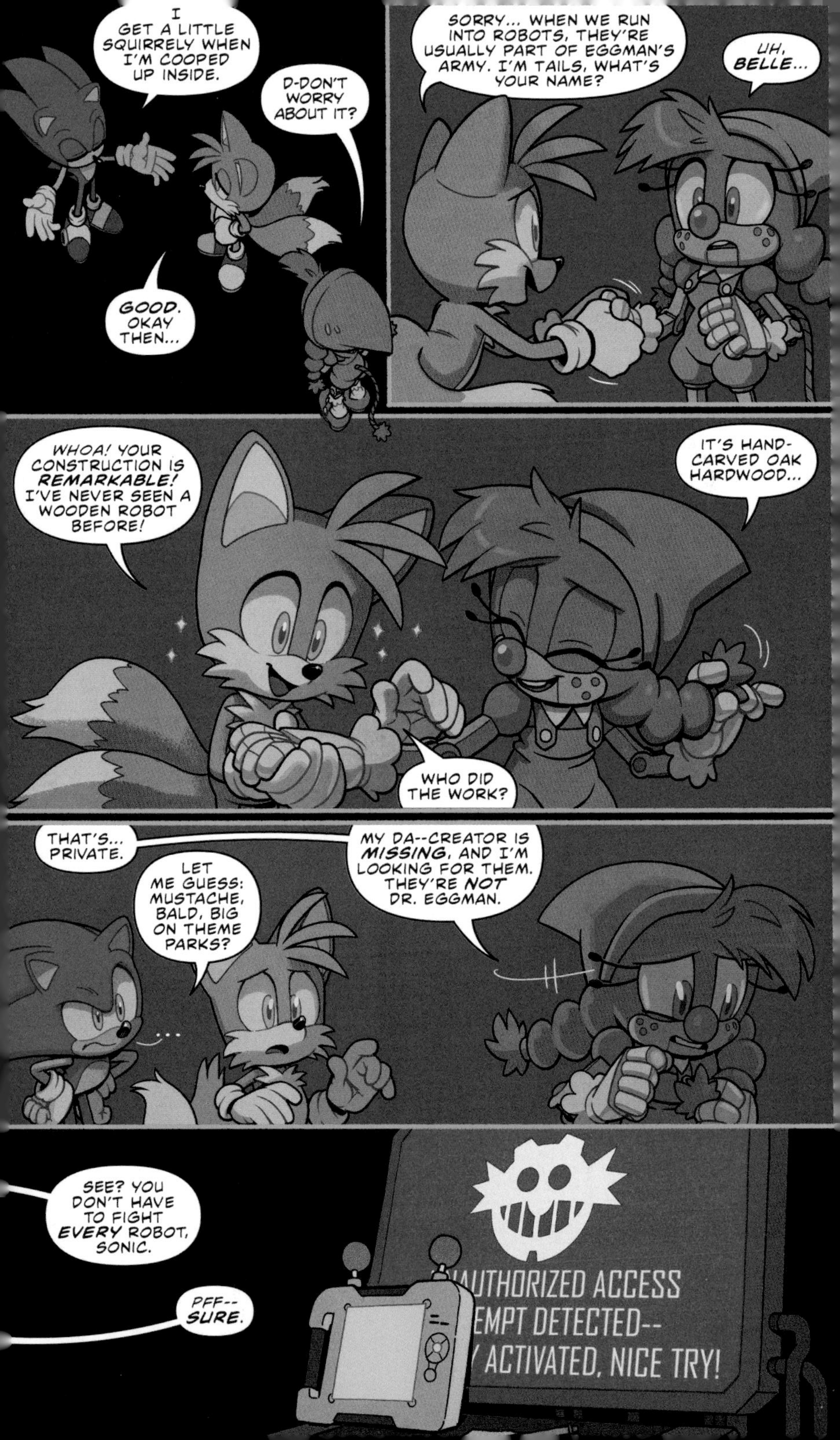
I GET A LITTLE SQUIRRELY WHEN I'M COOPED UP INSIDE.
D-DON'T WORRY ABOUT IT?
GOOD. OKAY THEN...
SORRY... WHEN WE RUN INTO ROBOTS, THEY'RE USUALLY PART OF EGGMAN'S ARMY. I'M TAILS, WHAT'S YOUR NAME?
UH, BELLE...
WHOA! YOUR CONSTRUCTION IS REMARKABLE! I'VE NEVER SEEN A WOODEN ROBOT BEFORE!
IT'S HAND-CARVED OAK HARDWOOD...
WHO DID THE WORK?
THAT'S... PRIVATE.
LET ME GUESS: MUSTACHE, BALD, BIG ON THEME PARKS?
MY DA--CREATOR IS MISSING, AND I'M LOOKING FOR THEM. THEY'RE NOT DR. EGGMAN.
...
SEE? YOU DON'T HAVE TO FIGHT EVERY ROBOT, SONIC.
PFF-- SURE.
AUTHORIZED ACCESS
EMPT DETECTED--
ACTIVATED, NICE TRY!

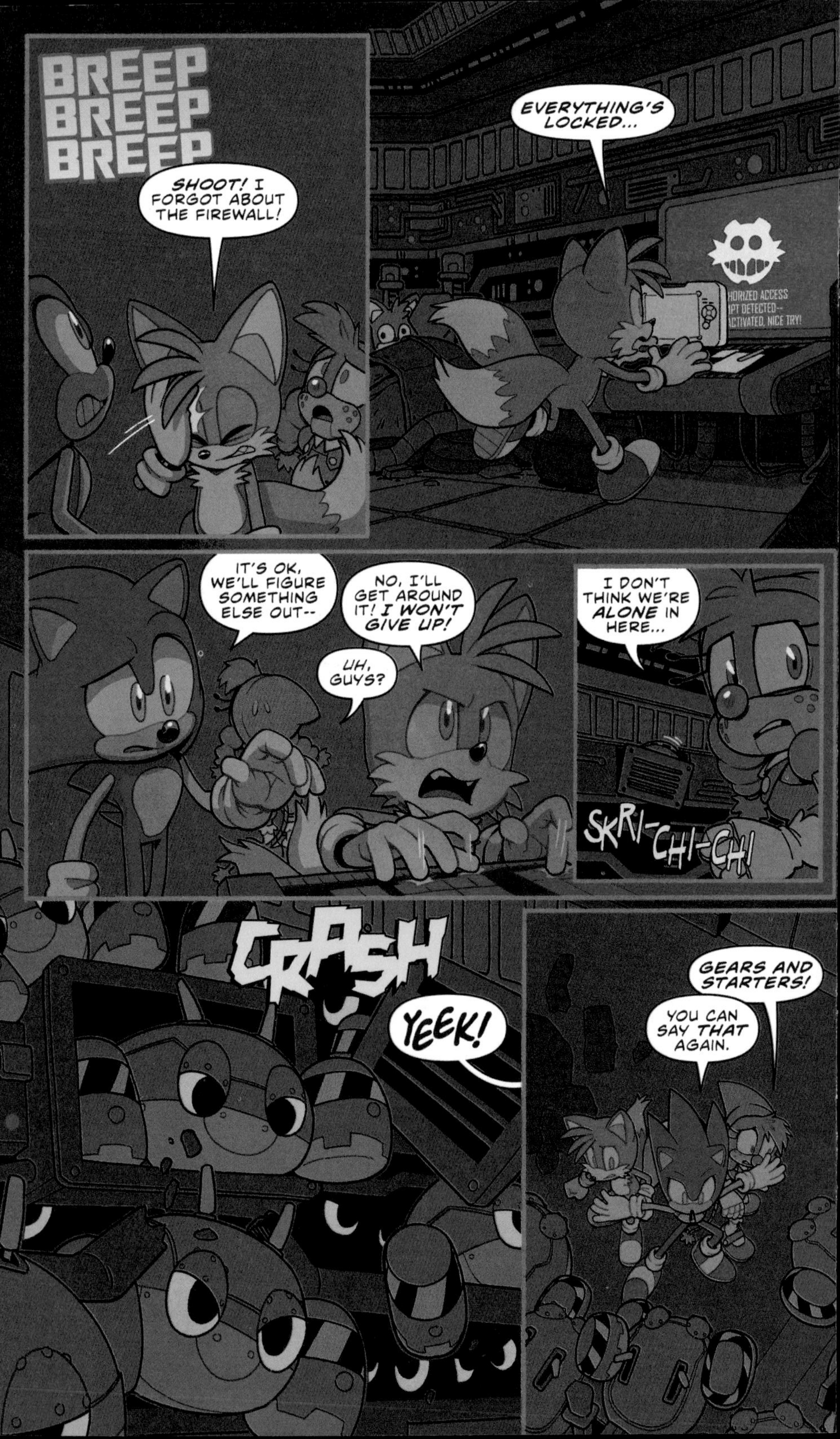

BREEP
BREEP
BREEP
SHOOT! I FORGOT ABOUT THE FIREWALL!
EVERYTHING'S LOCKED...
HORIZED ACCESS
PT DETECTED--
CTIVATED. NICE TRY!
IT'S OK, WE'LL FIGURE SOMETHING ELSE OUT--
NO, I'LL GET AROUND IT! *I WON'T GIVE UP!*
UH, GUYS?
I DON'T THINK WE'RE *ALONE* IN HERE...
SKRI-CHI-CHI
CRASH
YEEK!
GEARS AND STARTERS!
YOU CAN SAY *THAT* AGAIN.

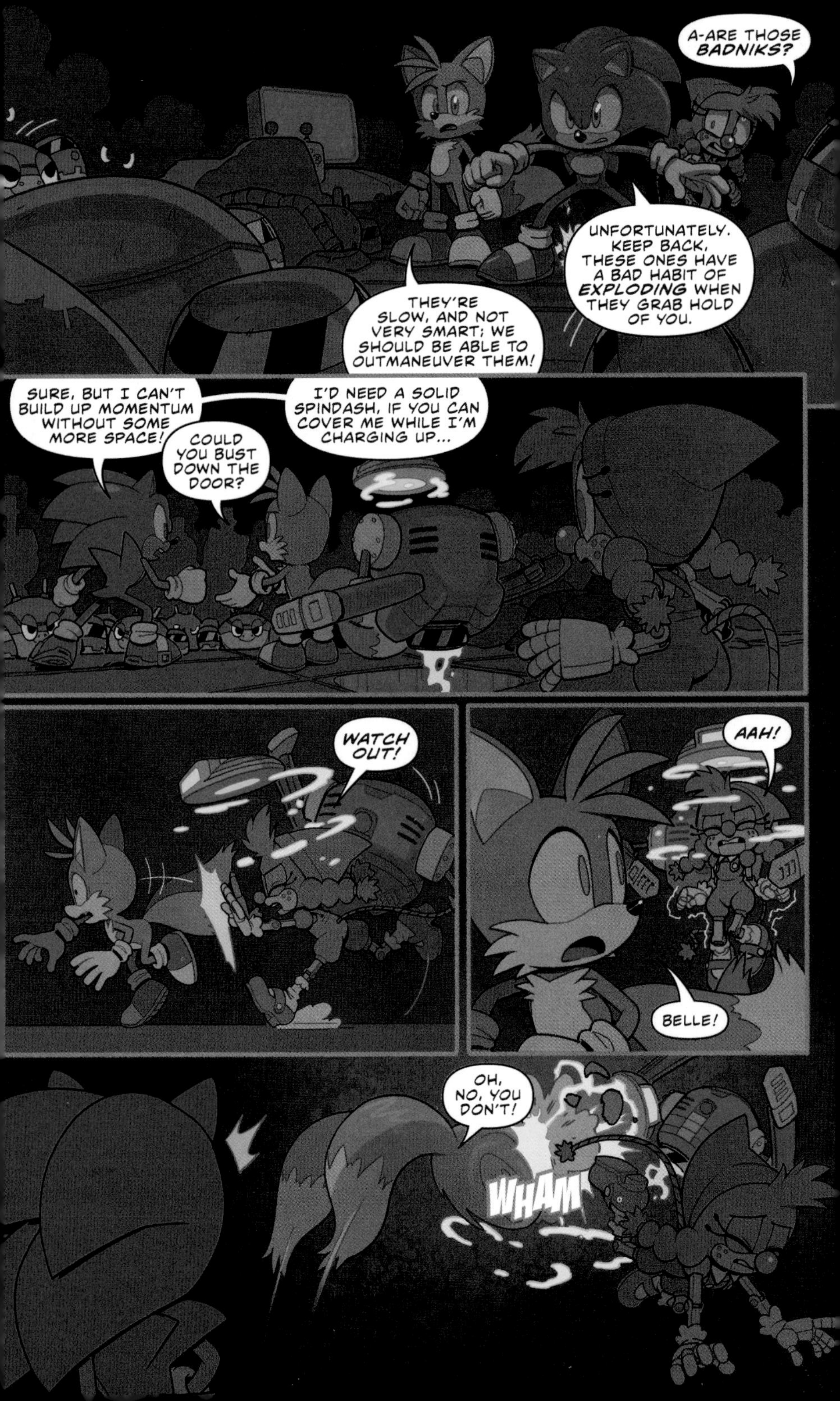
A-ARE THOSE BADNIKS?
UNFORTUNATELY. KEEP BACK, THESE ONES HAVE A BAD HABIT OF EXPLODING WHEN THEY GRAB HOLD OF YOU.
THEY'RE SLOW, AND NOT VERY SMART; WE SHOULD BE ABLE TO OUTMANEUVER THEM!
SURE, BUT I CAN'T BUILD UP MOMENTUM WITHOUT SOME MORE SPACE!
COULD YOU BUST DOWN THE DOOR?
I'D NEED A SOLID SPINDASH, IF YOU CAN COVER ME WHILE I'M CHARGING UP...
WATCH OUT!
AAH!
BELLE!
OH, NO, YOU DON'T!
WHAM

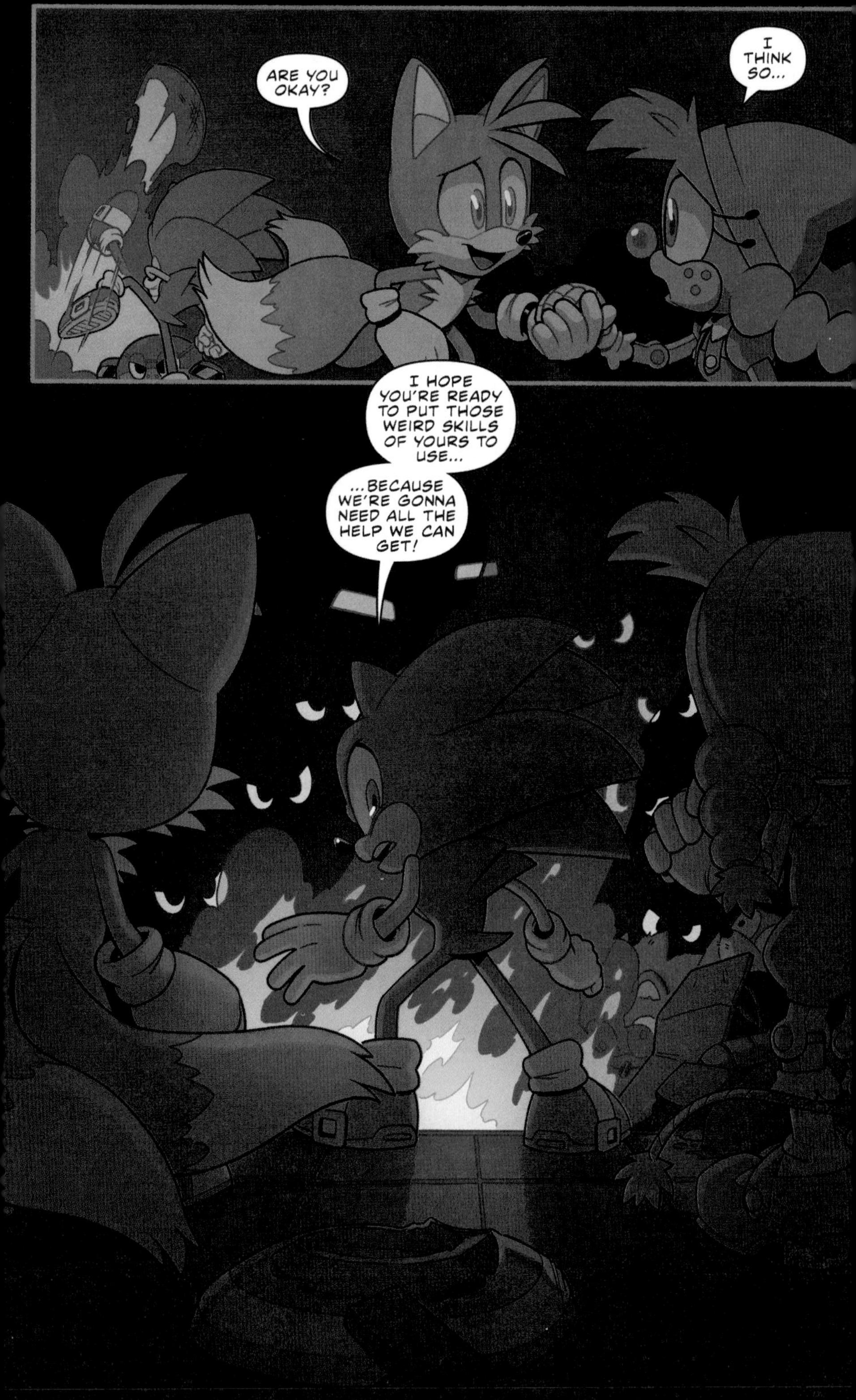
ARE YOU OKAY?
I THINK SO...
I HOPE YOU'RE READY TO PUT THOSE WEIRD SKILLS OF YOURS TO USE...
...BECAUSE WE'RE GONNA NEED ALL THE HELP WE CAN GET!

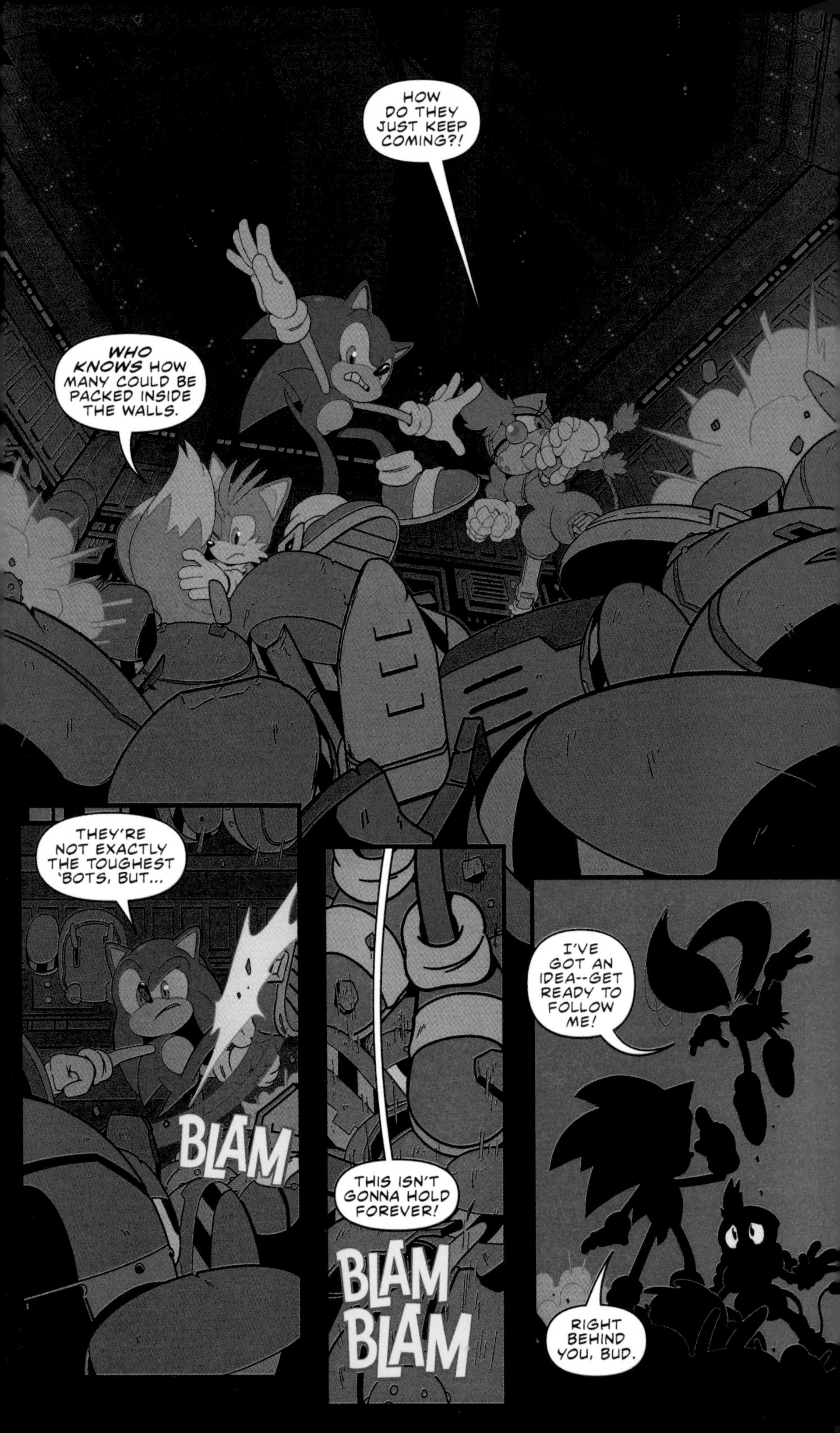
HOW DO THEY JUST KEEP COMING?!
WHO KNOWS HOW MANY COULD BE PACKED INSIDE THE WALLS.
THEY'RE NOT EXACTLY THE TOUGHEST 'BOTS, BUT...
BLAM
THIS ISN'T GONNA HOLD FOREVER!
BLAM
BLAM
I'VE GOT AN IDEA--GET READY TO FOLLOW ME!
RIGHT BEHIND YOU, BUD.

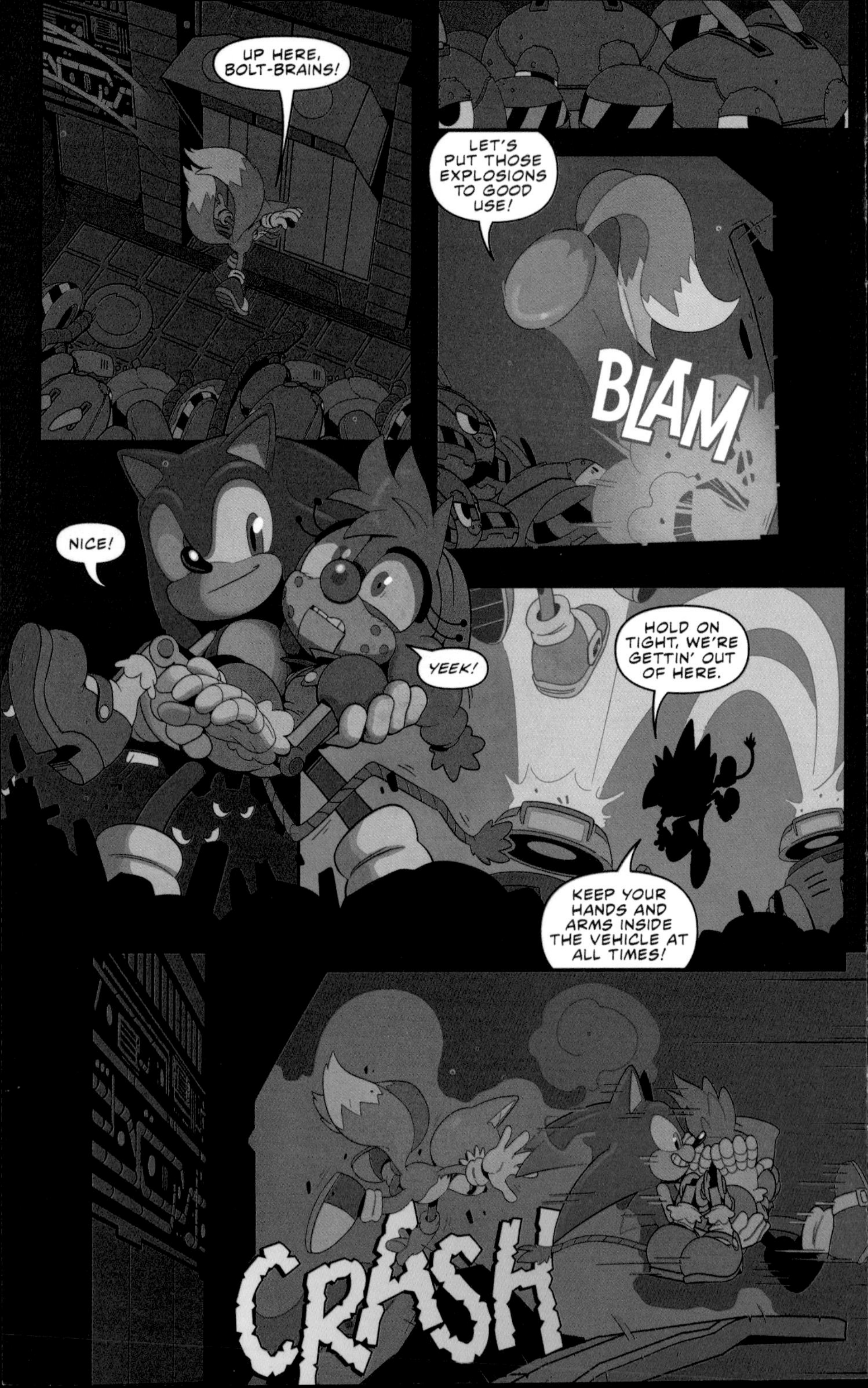
UP HERE, BOLT-BRAINS!
LET'S PUT THOSE EXPLOSIONS TO GOOD USE!
BLAM
NICE!
YEEK!
HOLD ON TIGHT, WE'RE GETTIN' OUT OF HERE.
KEEP YOUR HANDS AND ARMS INSIDE THE VEHICLE AT ALL TIMES!
CRASH

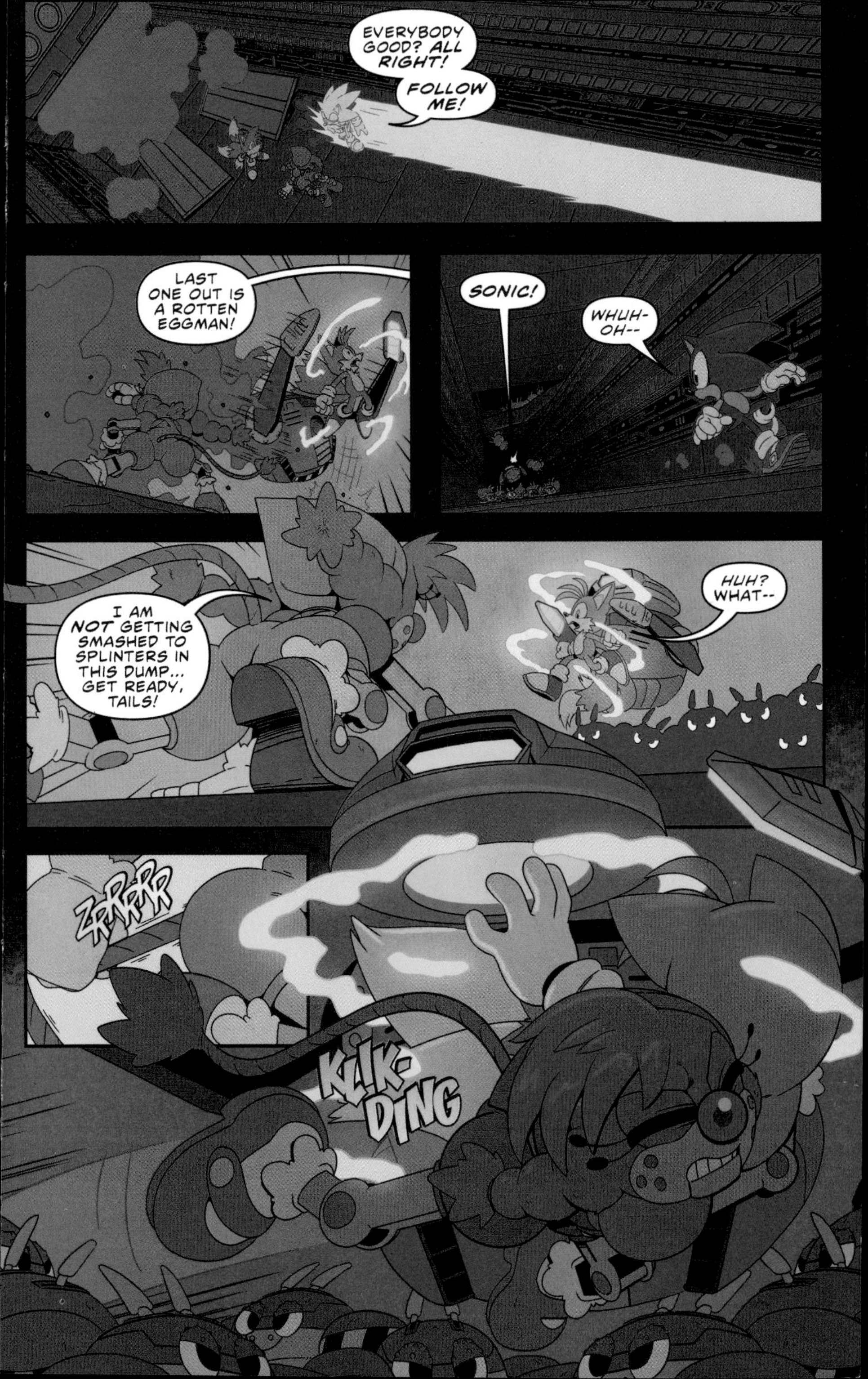
EVERYBODY GOOD? ALL RIGHT!
FOLLOW ME!
LAST ONE OUT IS A ROTTEN EGGMAN!
SONIC!
WHUH-OH--
I AM NOT GETTING SMASHED TO SPLINTERS IN THIS DUMP... GET READY, TAILS!
HUH? WHAT--
ZRRRRR
KLIK-DING

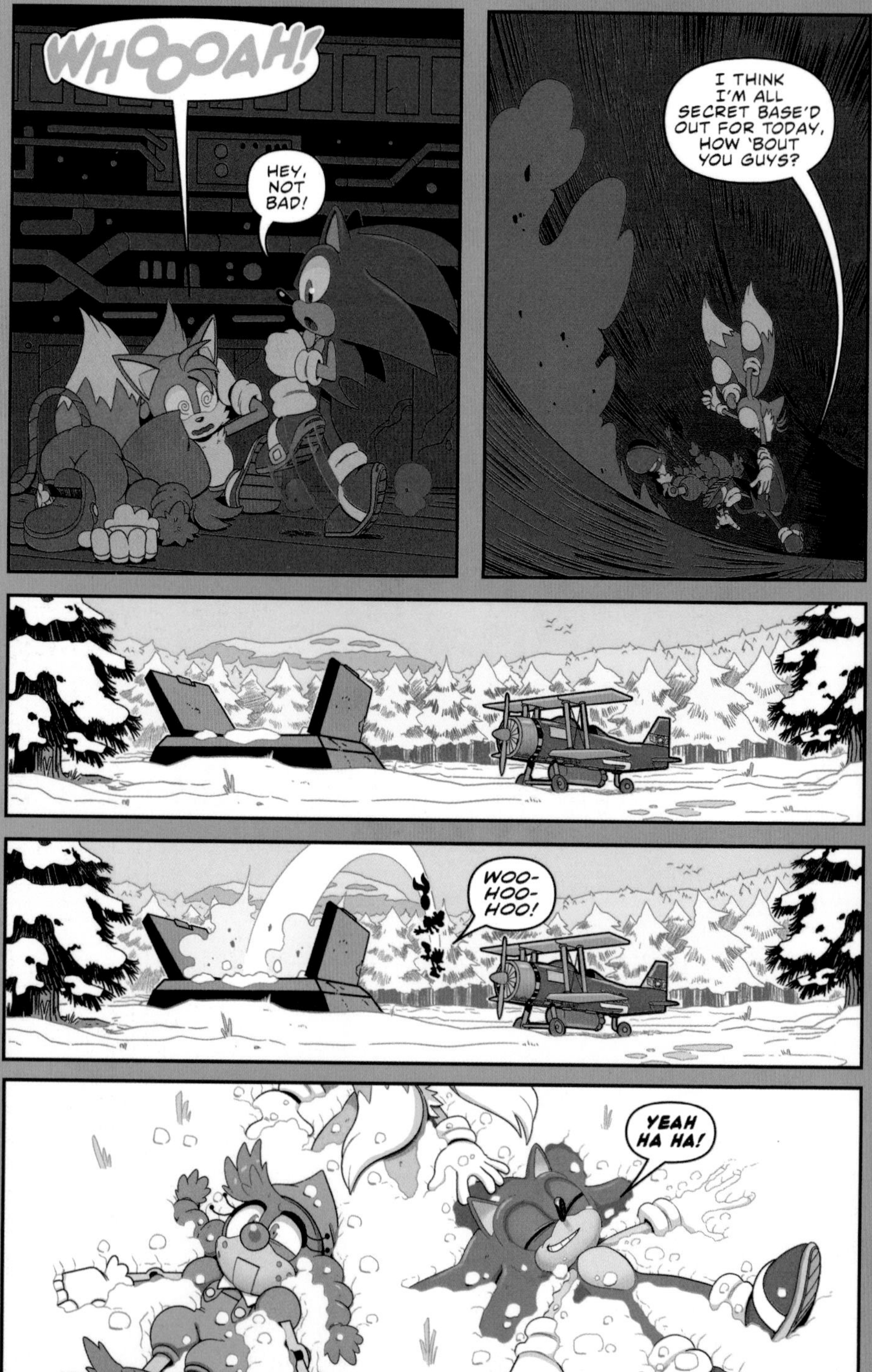
WHOOOOAH!
HEY, NOT BAD!
I THINK I'M ALL SECRET BASE'D OUT FOR TODAY, HOW 'BOUT YOU GUYS?
WOO-HOO-HOO!
YEAH HA HA!

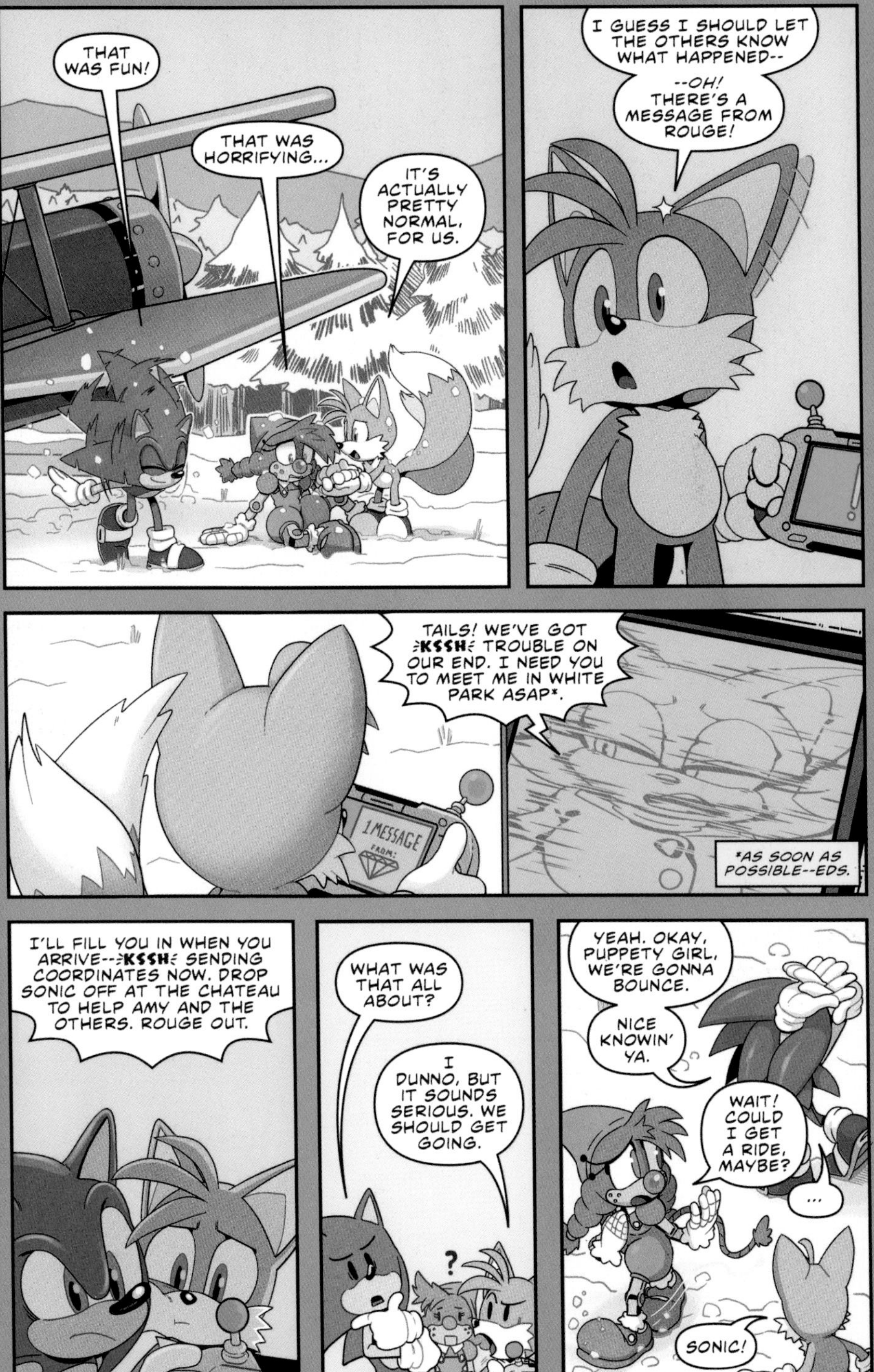
THAT WAS FUN!
THAT WAS HORRIFYING...
IT'S ACTUALLY PRETTY NORMAL, FOR US.
I GUESS I SHOULD LET THE OTHERS KNOW WHAT HAPPENED--
--OH! THERE'S A MESSAGE FROM ROUGE!
1 MESSAGE FROM:
TAILS! WE'VE GOT KSSH TROUBLE ON OUR END. I NEED YOU TO MEET ME IN WHITE PARK ASAP*.
*AS SOON AS POSSIBLE--EDS.
I'LL FILL YOU IN WHEN YOU ARRIVE--KSSH SENDING COORDINATES NOW. DROP SONIC OFF AT THE CHATEAU TO HELP AMY AND THE OTHERS. ROUGE OUT.
WHAT WAS THAT ALL ABOUT?
I DUNNO, BUT IT SOUNDS SERIOUS. WE SHOULD GET GOING.
?
YEAH. OKAY, PUPPETY GIRL, WE'RE GONNA BOUNCE.
NICE KNOWIN' YA.
WAIT! COULD I GET A RIDE, MAYBE?
...
SONIC!

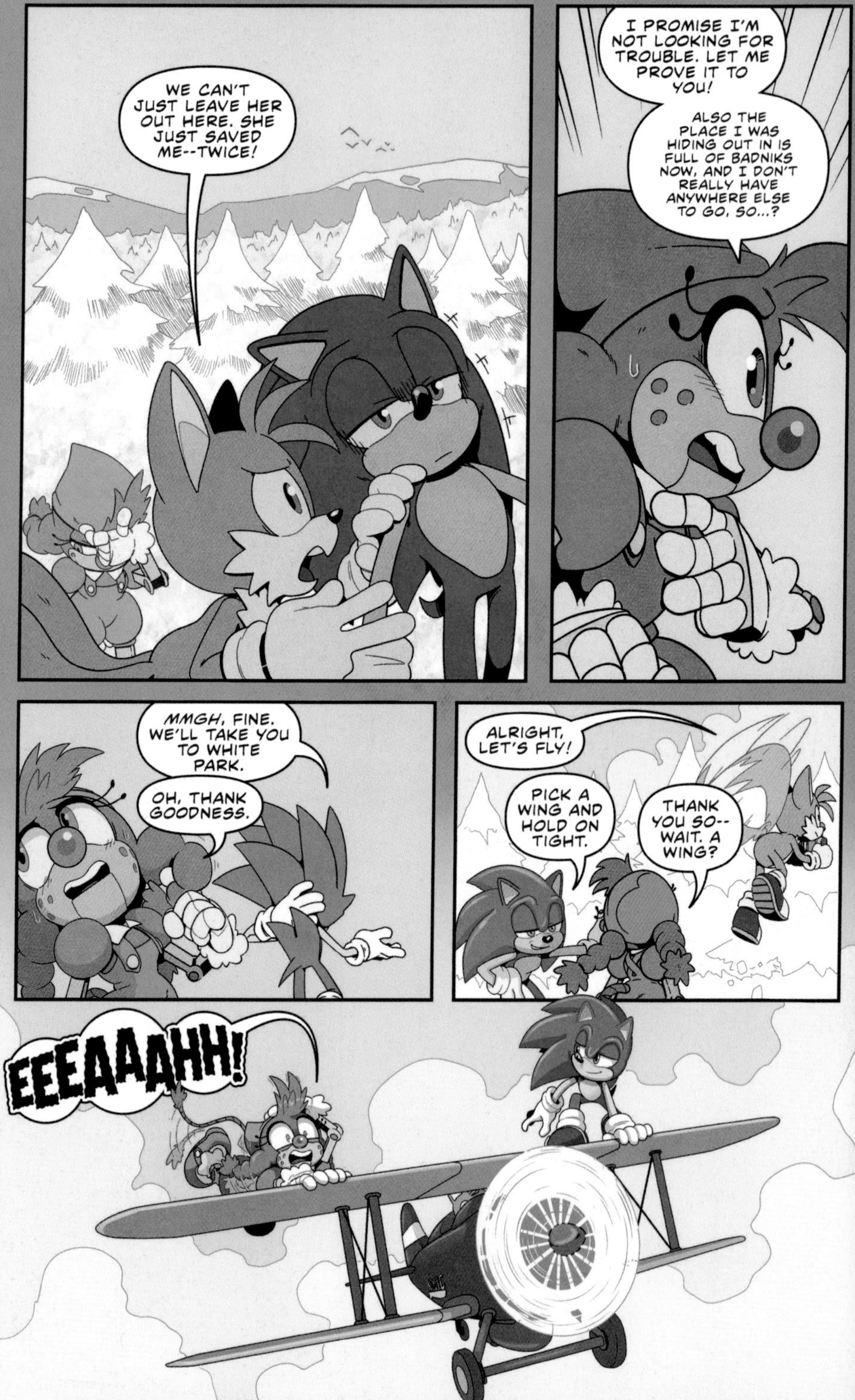
WE CAN'T JUST LEAVE HER OUT HERE. SHE JUST SAVED ME--TWICE!
I PROMISE I'M NOT LOOKING FOR TROUBLE. LET ME PROVE IT TO YOU!
ALSO THE PLACE I WAS HIDING OUT IN IS FULL OF BADNIKS NOW, AND I DON'T REALLY HAVE ANYWHERE ELSE TO GO, SO...?
MMGH, FINE. WE'LL TAKE YOU TO WHITE PARK.
OH, THANK GOODNESS.
ALRIGHT, LET'S FLY!
PICK A WING AND HOLD ON TIGHT.
THANK YOU SO-- WAIT. A WING?
EEEAAAHH!

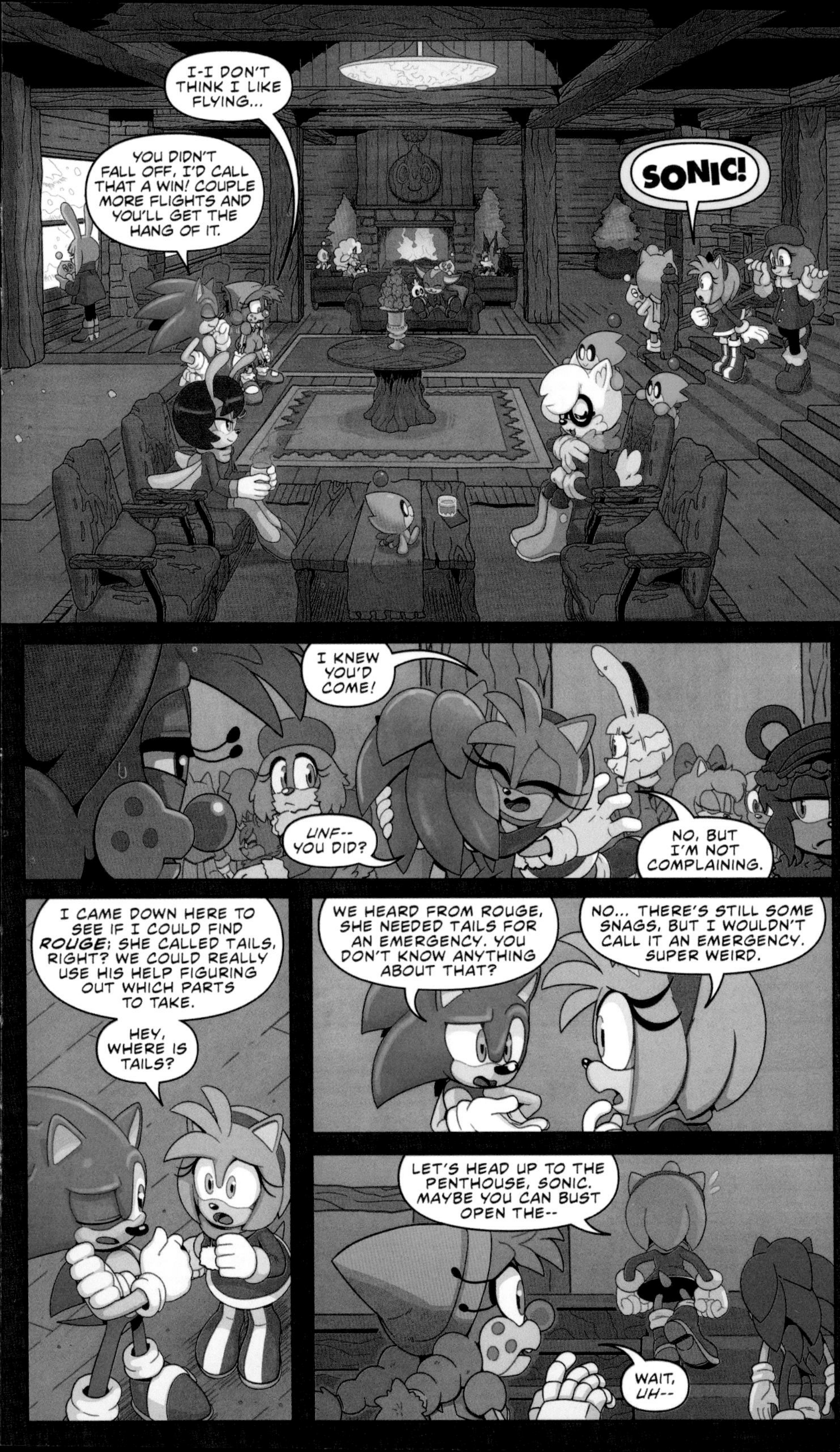
I-I DON'T THINK I LIKE FLYING...
YOU DIDN'T FALL OFF, I'D CALL THAT A WIN! COUPLE MORE FLIGHTS AND YOU'LL GET THE HANG OF IT.
SONIC!
I KNEW YOU'D COME!
UNF-- YOU DID?
NO, BUT I'M NOT COMPLAINING.
I CAME DOWN HERE TO SEE IF I COULD FIND *ROUGE*; SHE CALLED TAILS, RIGHT? WE COULD REALLY USE HIS HELP FIGURING OUT WHICH PARTS TO TAKE.
HEY, WHERE IS TAILS?
WE HEARD FROM ROUGE, SHE NEEDED TAILS FOR AN EMERGENCY. YOU DON'T KNOW ANYTHING ABOUT THAT?
NO... THERE'S STILL SOME SNAGS, BUT I WOULDN'T CALL IT AN EMERGENCY. SUPER WEIRD.
LET'S HEAD UP TO THE PENTHOUSE, SONIC. MAYBE YOU CAN BUST OPEN THE--
WAIT, *UH*--

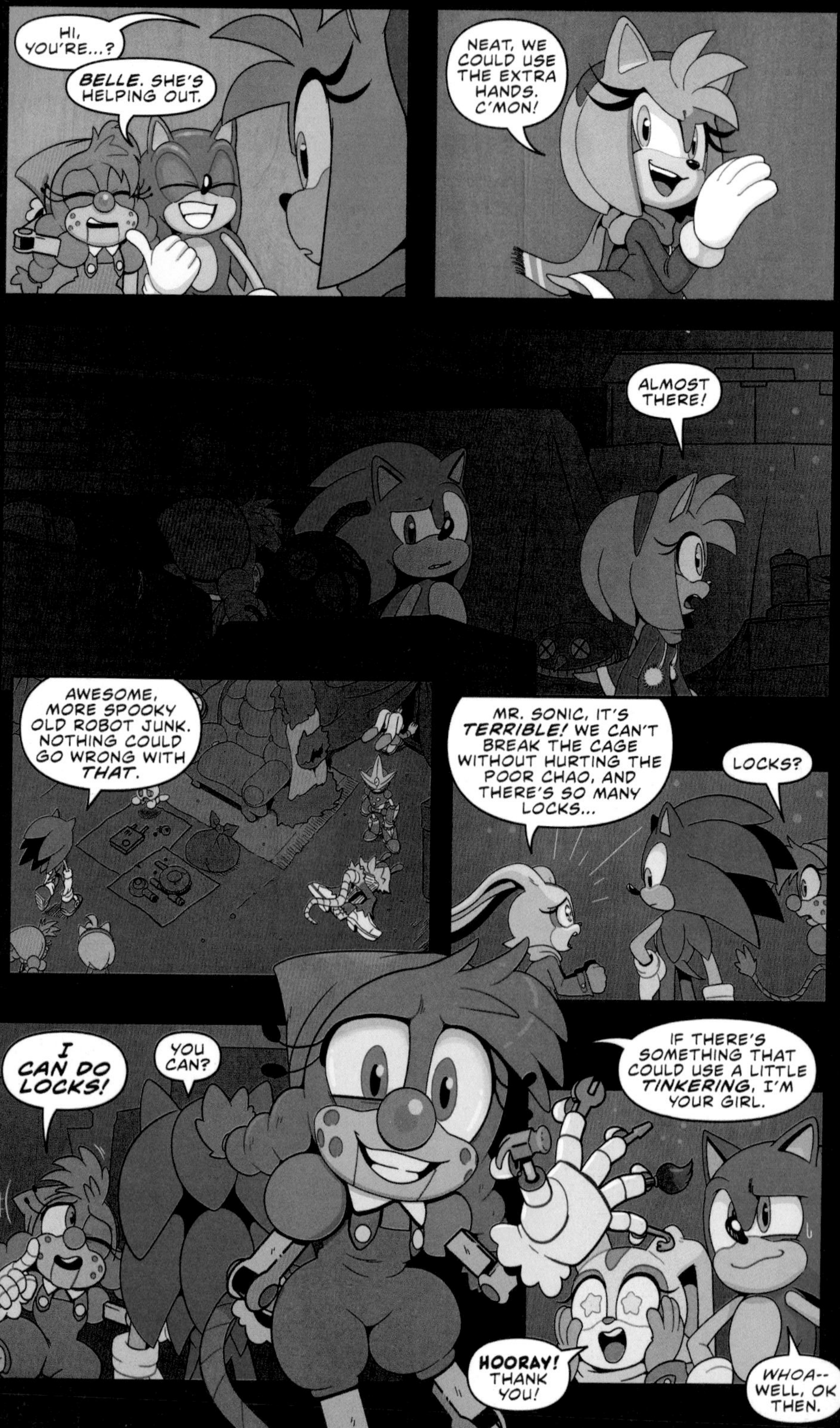
HI, YOU'RE...?
BELLE. SHE'S HELPING OUT.
NEAT, WE COULD USE THE EXTRA HANDS. C'MON!
ALMOST THERE!
AWESOME, MORE SPOOKY OLD ROBOT JUNK. NOTHING COULD GO WRONG WITH *THAT*.
MR. SONIC, IT'S *TERRIBLE!* WE CAN'T BREAK THE CAGE WITHOUT HURTING THE POOR CHAO, AND THERE'S SO MANY LOCKS...
LOCKS?
I CAN DO LOCKS!
YOU CAN?
IF THERE'S SOMETHING THAT COULD USE A LITTLE *TINKERING*, I'M YOUR GIRL.
HOORAY! THANK YOU!
WHOA-- WELL, OK THEN.

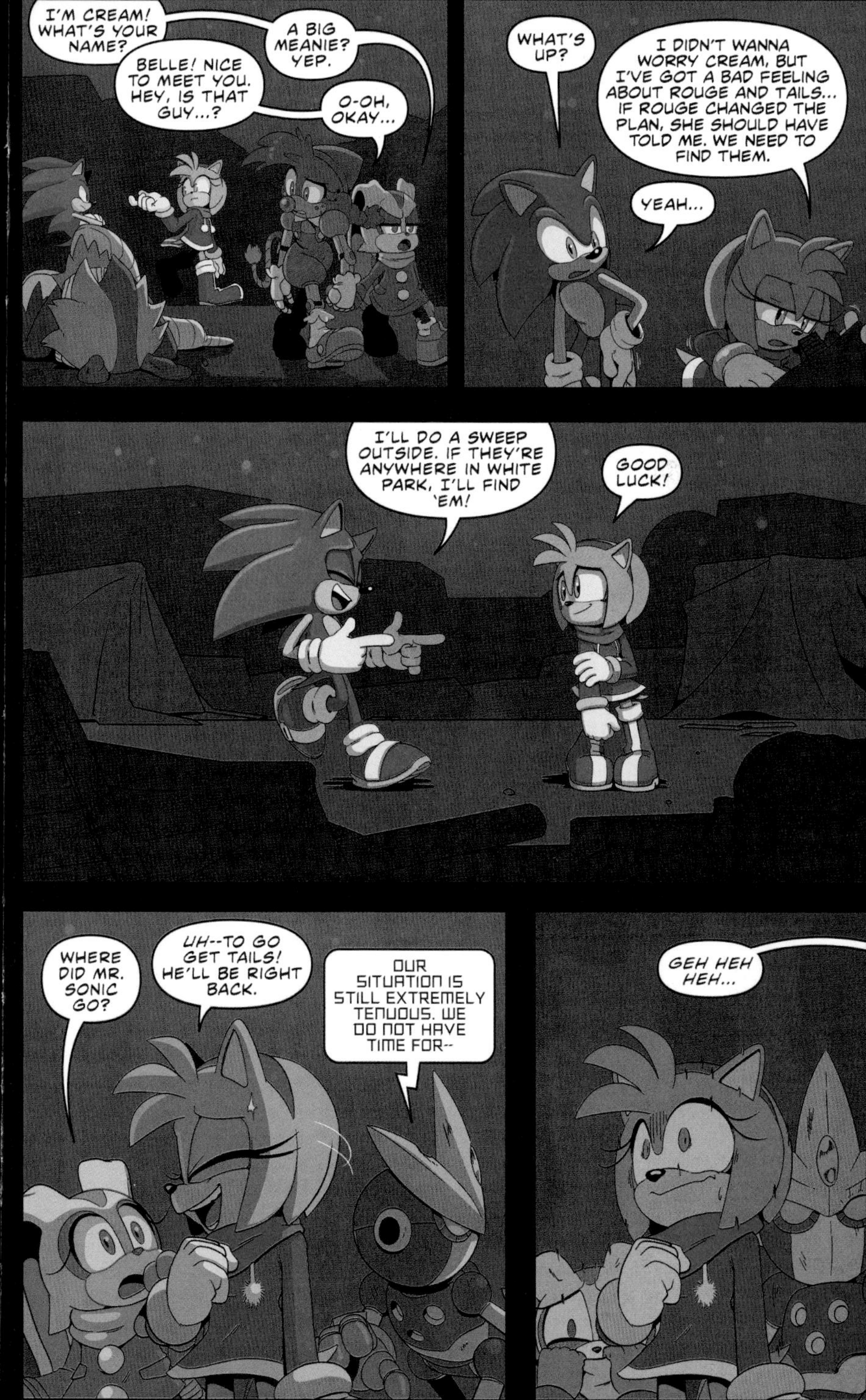
I'M CREAM! WHAT'S YOUR NAME?
BELLE! NICE TO MEET YOU. HEY, IS THAT GUY...?
A BIG MEANIE? YEP.
O-OH, OKAY...
WHAT'S UP?
I DIDN'T WANNA WORRY CREAM, BUT I'VE GOT A BAD FEELING ABOUT ROUGE AND TAILS... IF ROUGE CHANGED THE PLAN, SHE SHOULD HAVE TOLD ME. WE NEED TO FIND THEM.
YEAH...
I'LL DO A SWEEP OUTSIDE. IF THEY'RE ANYWHERE IN WHITE PARK, I'LL FIND 'EM!
GOOD LUCK!
WHERE DID MR. SONIC GO?
UH--TO GO GET TAILS! HE'LL BE RIGHT BACK.
OUR SITUATION IS STILL EXTREMELY TENUOUS. WE DO NOT HAVE TIME FOR--
GEH HEH HEH...

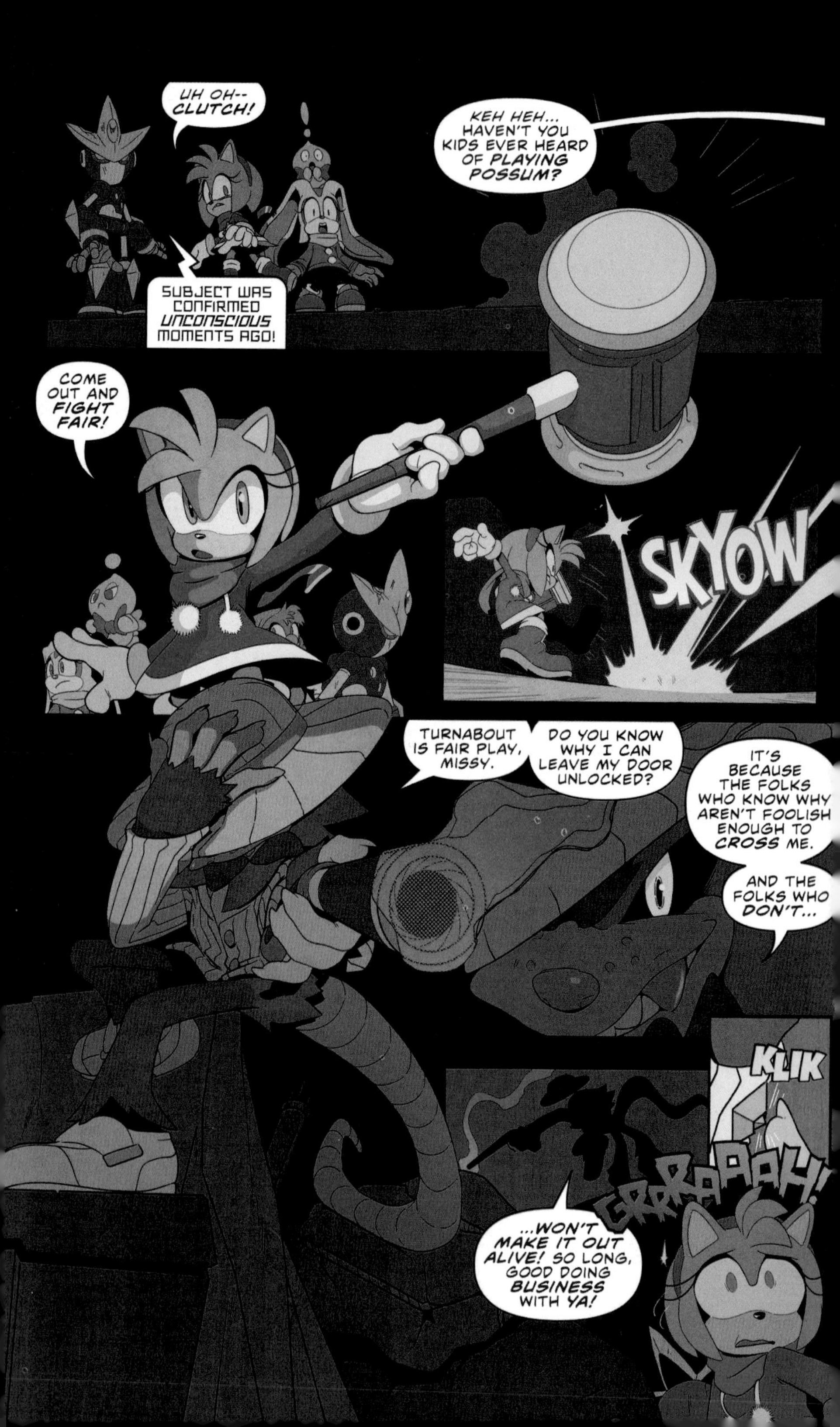
UH OH-- CLUTCH!
SUBJECT WAS CONFIRMED UNCONSCIOUS MOMENTS AGO!
KEH HEH... HAVEN'T YOU KIDS EVER HEARD OF PLAYING POSSUM?
COME OUT AND FIGHT FAIR!
SKYOW
TURNABOUT IS FAIR PLAY, MISSY.
DO YOU KNOW WHY I CAN LEAVE MY DOOR UNLOCKED?
IT'S BECAUSE THE FOLKS WHO KNOW WHY AREN'T FOOLISH ENOUGH TO CROSS ME.
AND THE FOLKS WHO DON'T...
KLIK
GRRAAAAH!
...WON'T MAKE IT OUT ALIVE! SO LONG, GOOD DOING BUSINESS WITH YA!

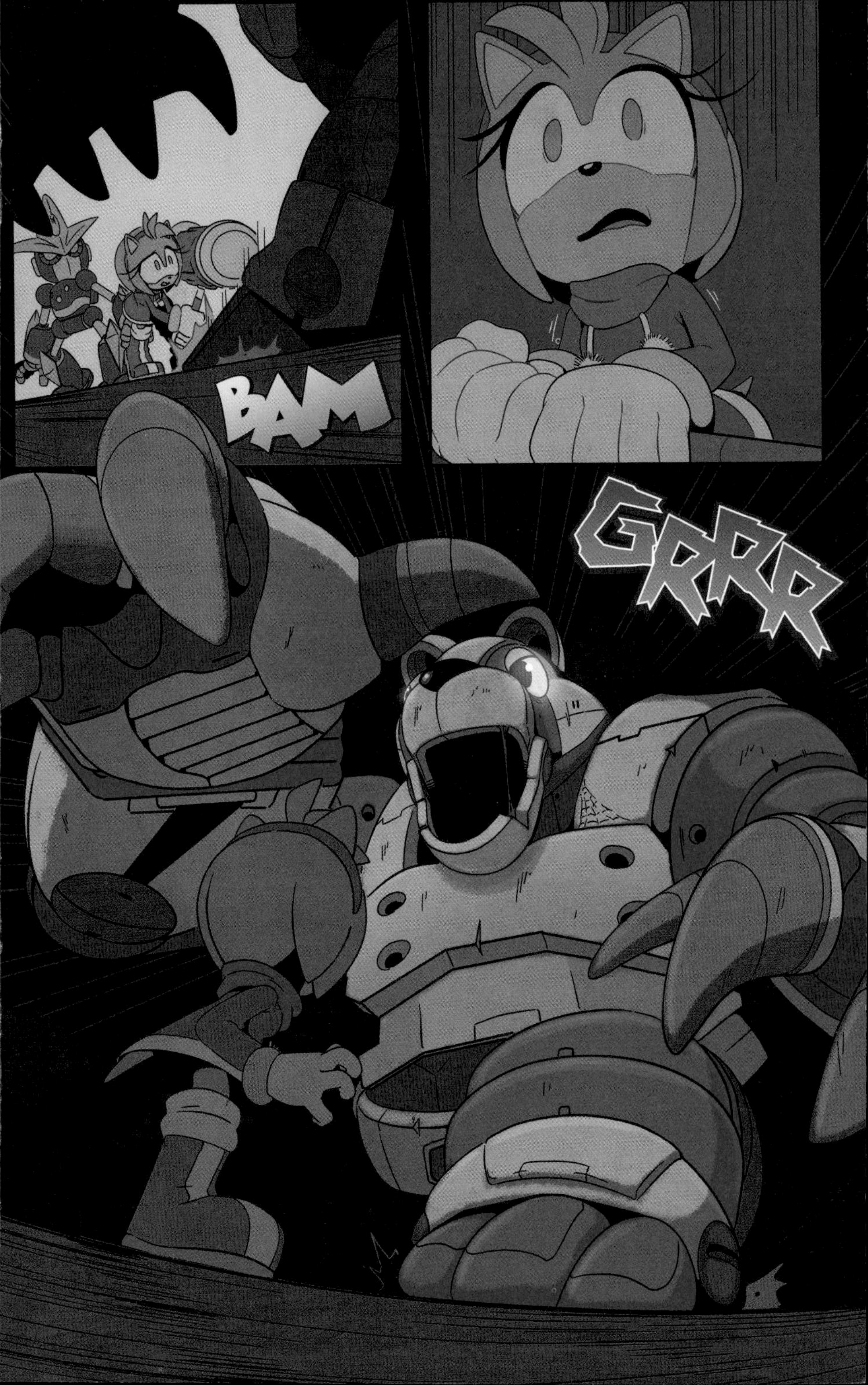
BAM
GRRR

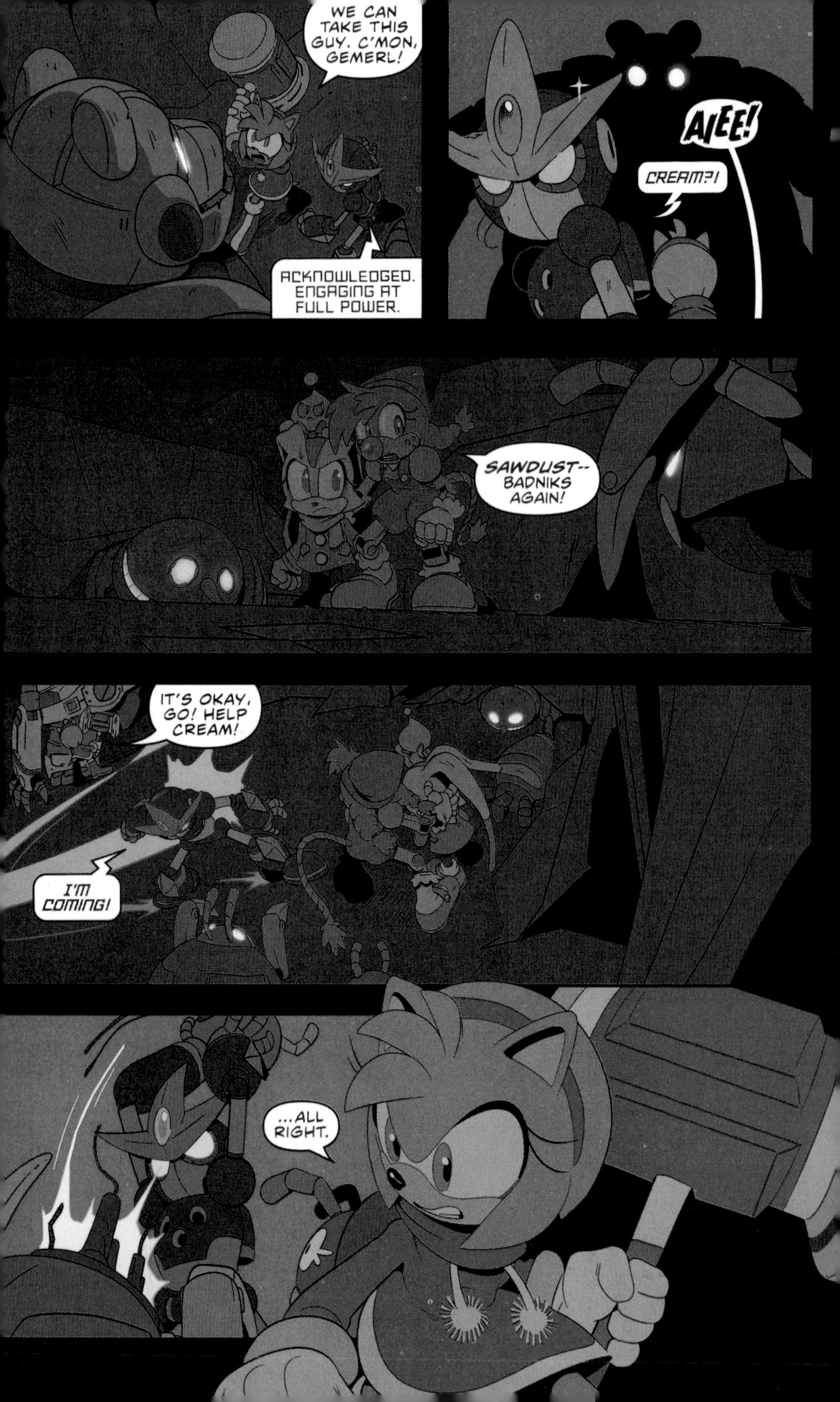
WE CAN TAKE THIS GUY. C'MON, GEMERL!
ACKNOWLEDGED. ENGAGING AT FULL POWER.
AIEE!
CREAM?!
SAWDUST-- BADNIKS AGAIN!
IT'S OKAY, GO! HELP CREAM!
I'M COMING!
...ALL RIGHT.

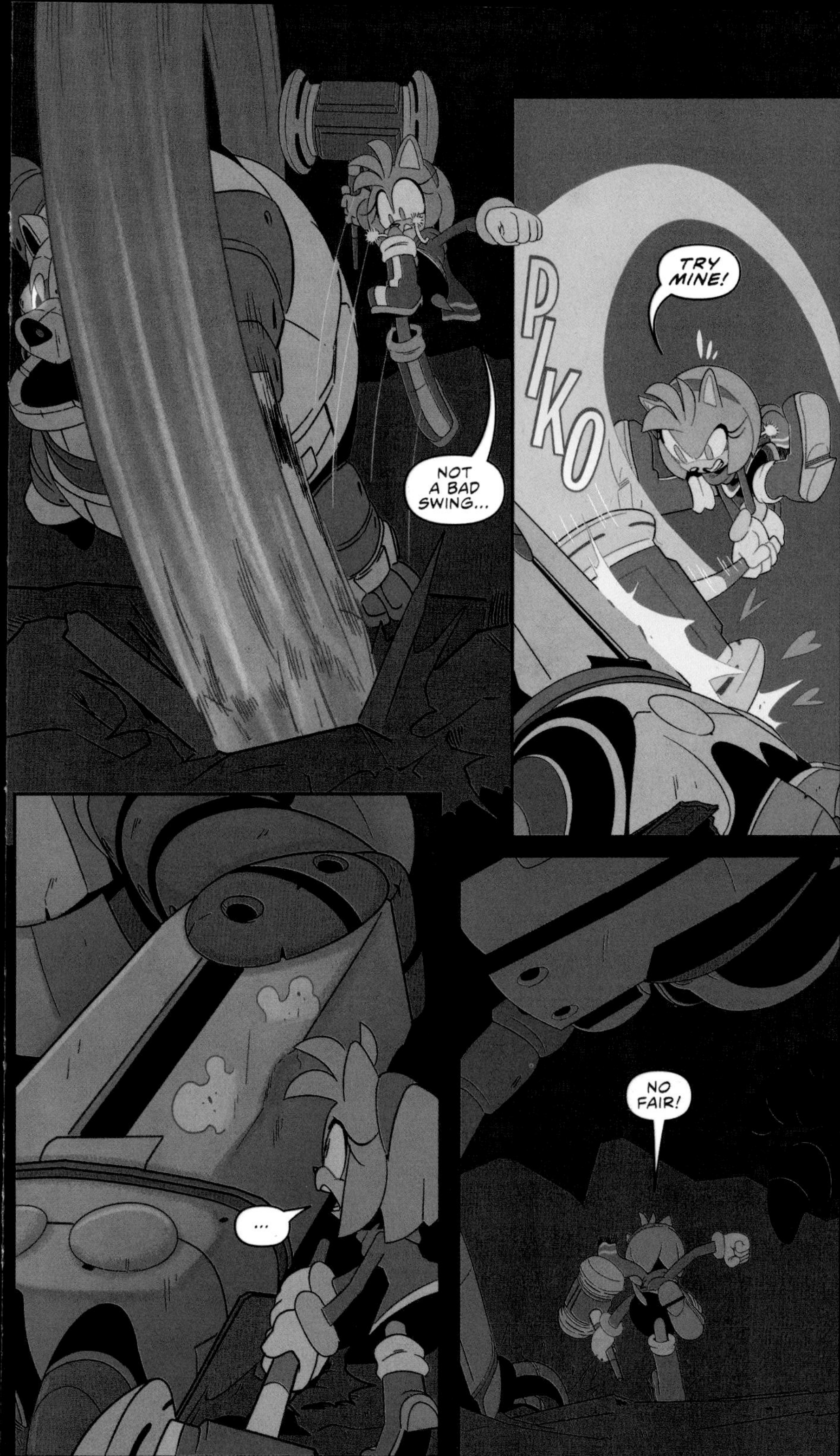
NOT A BAD SWING...
PIKO
TRY MINE!
...
NO FAIR!

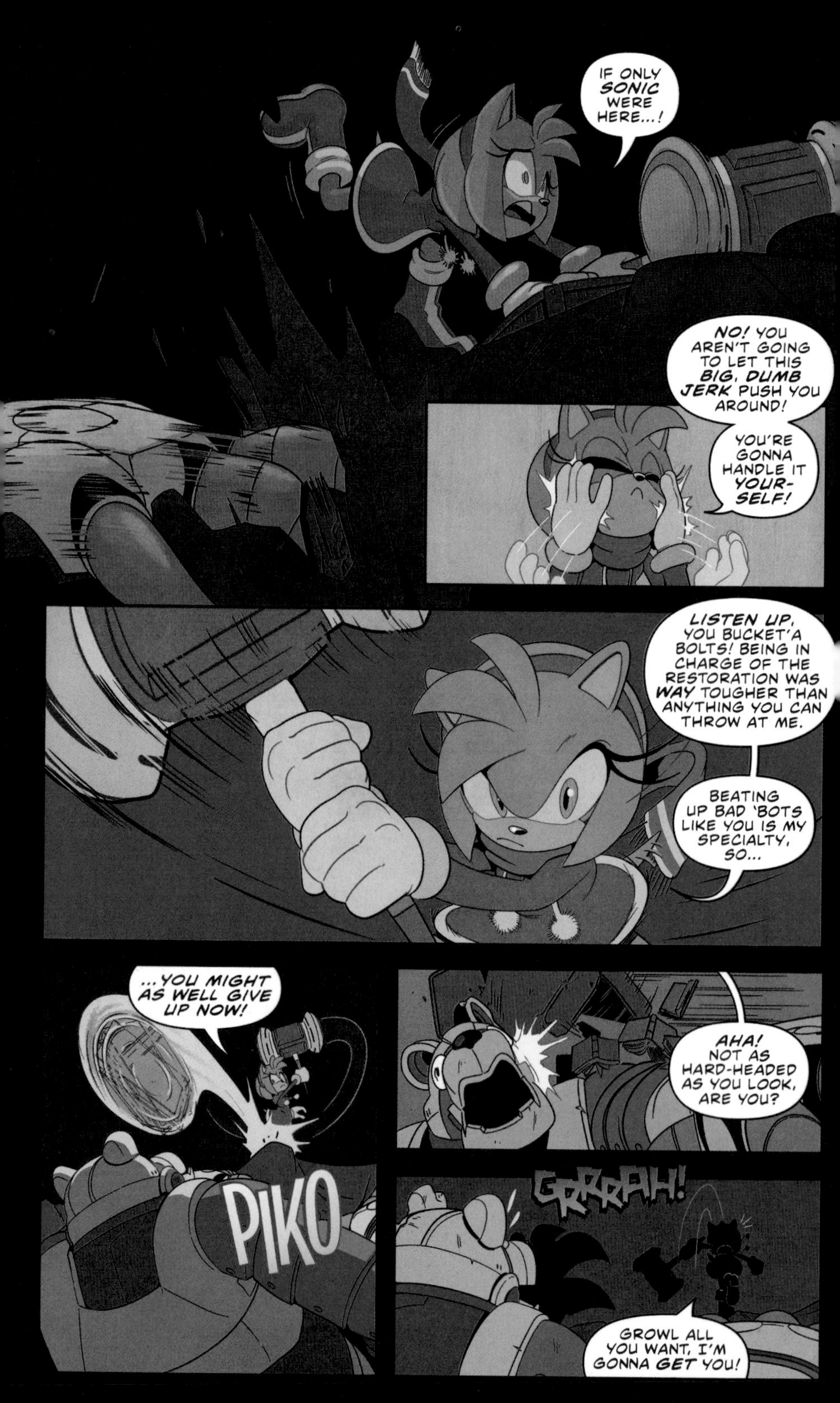
IF ONLY SONIC WERE HERE...!
NO! YOU AREN'T GOING TO LET THIS BIG, DUMB JERK PUSH YOU AROUND!
YOU'RE GONNA HANDLE IT YOURSELF!
LISTEN UP, YOU BUCKET'A BOLTS! BEING IN CHARGE OF THE RESTORATION WAS WAY TOUGHER THAN ANYTHING YOU CAN THROW AT ME.
BEATING UP BAD 'BOTS LIKE YOU IS MY SPECIALTY, SO...
...YOU MIGHT AS WELL GIVE UP NOW!
PIKO
AHA! NOT AS HARD-HEADED AS YOU LOOK, ARE YOU?
GRRRAH!
GROWL ALL YOU WANT, I'M GONNA GET YOU!

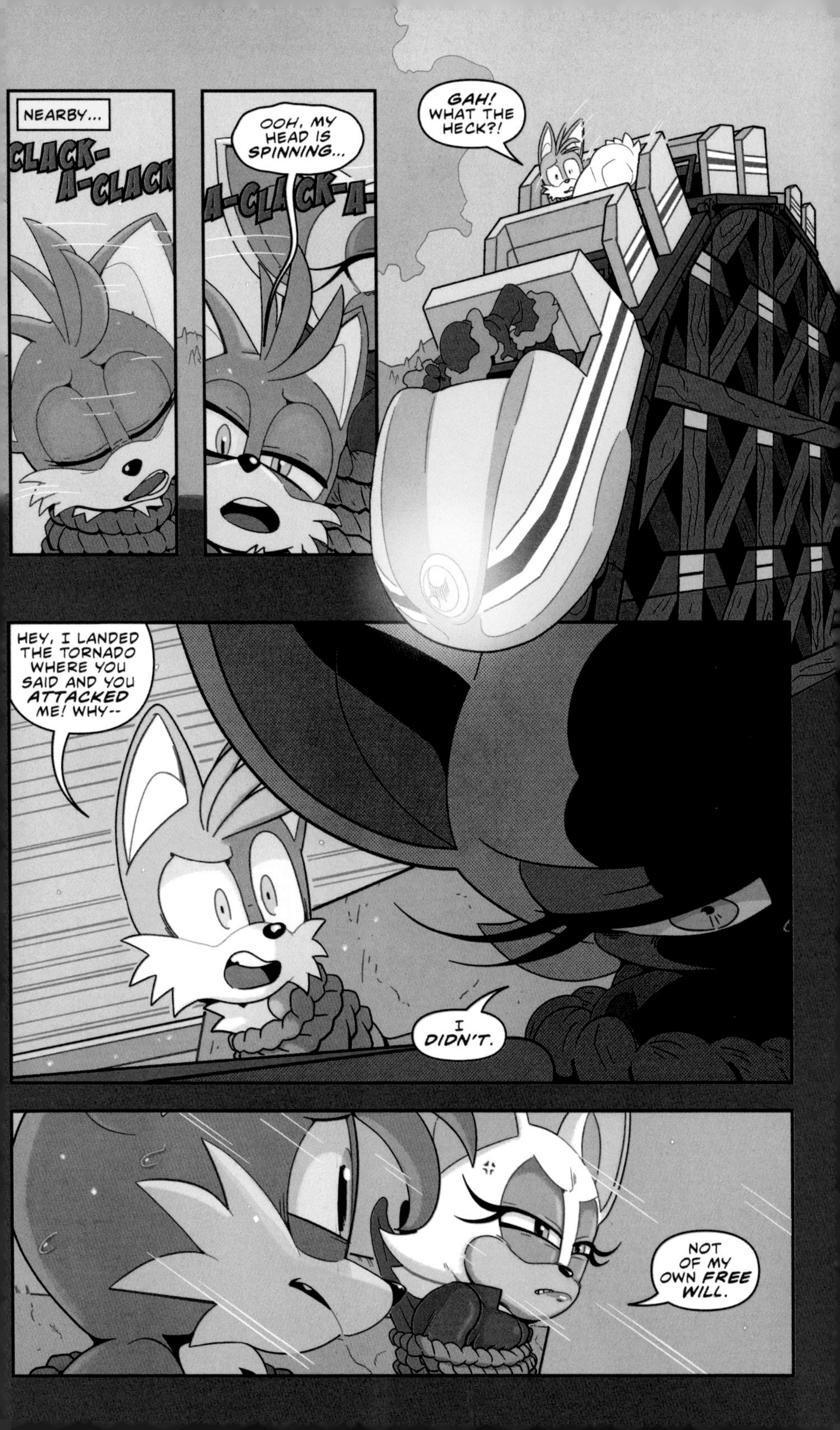
NEARBY...
CLACK-A-CLACK
OOH, MY HEAD IS SPINNING...
A-CLACK-A-
GAH! WHAT THE HECK?!
HEY, I LANDED THE TORNADO WHERE YOU SAID AND YOU ATTACKED ME! WHY--
I DIDN'T.
NOT OF MY OWN FREE WILL.

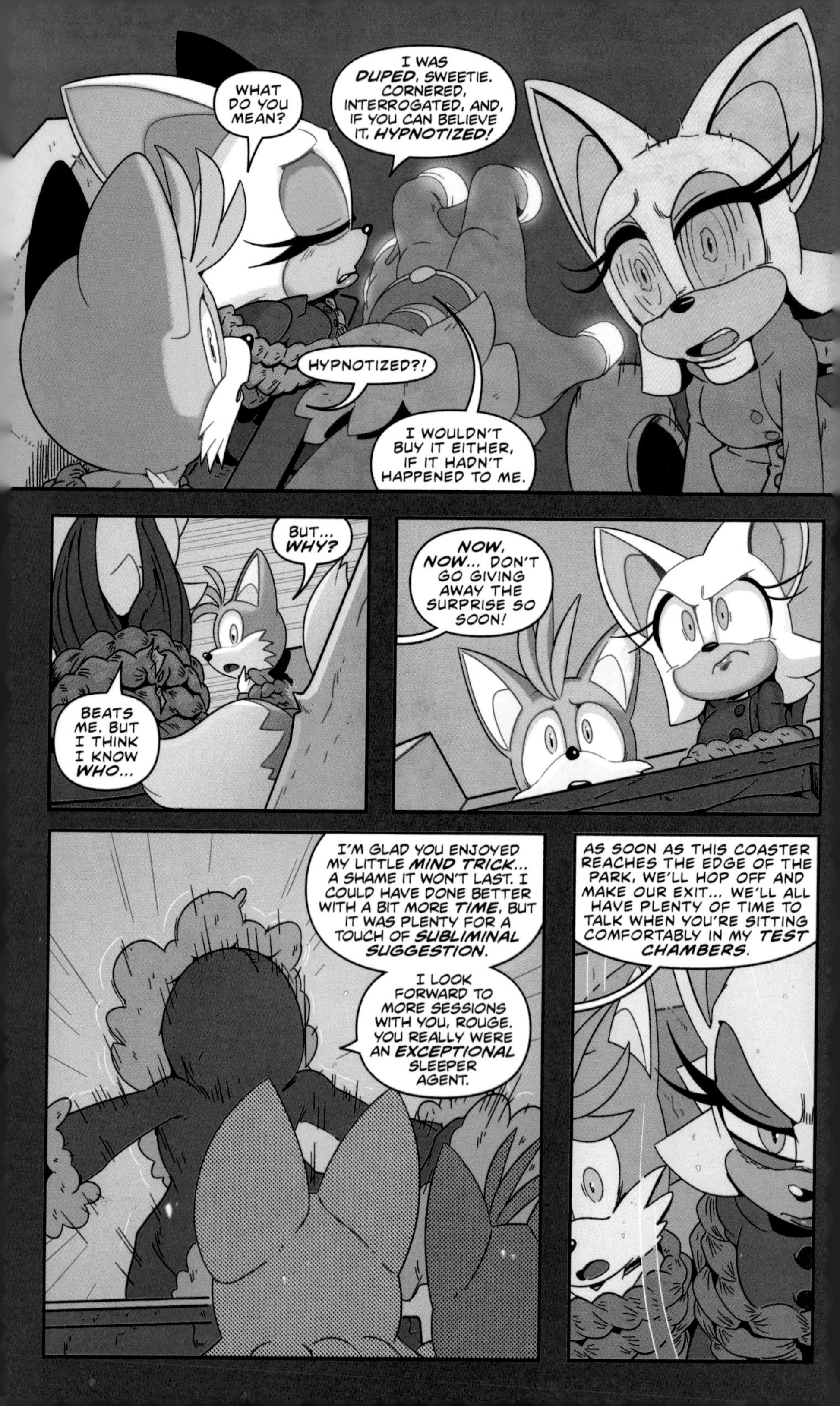
WHAT DO YOU MEAN?
I WAS DUPED, SWEETIE. CORNERED, INTERROGATED, AND, IF YOU CAN BELIEVE IT, HYPNOTIZED!
HYPNOTIZED?!
I WOULDN'T BUY IT EITHER, IF IT HADN'T HAPPENED TO ME.
BUT... WHY?
BEATS ME. BUT I THINK I KNOW WHO...
NOW, NOW... DON'T GO GIVING AWAY THE SURPRISE SO SOON!
I'M GLAD YOU ENJOYED MY LITTLE MIND TRICK... A SHAME IT WON'T LAST. I COULD HAVE DONE BETTER WITH A BIT MORE TIME, BUT IT WAS PLENTY FOR A TOUCH OF SUBLIMINAL SUGGESTION.
I LOOK FORWARD TO MORE SESSIONS WITH YOU, ROUGE. YOU REALLY WERE AN EXCEPTIONAL SLEEPER AGENT.
AS SOON AS THIS COASTER REACHES THE EDGE OF THE PARK, WE'LL HOP OFF AND MAKE OUR EXIT... WE'LL ALL HAVE PLENTY OF TIME TO TALK WHEN YOU'RE SITTING COMFORTABLY IN MY TEST CHAMBERS.

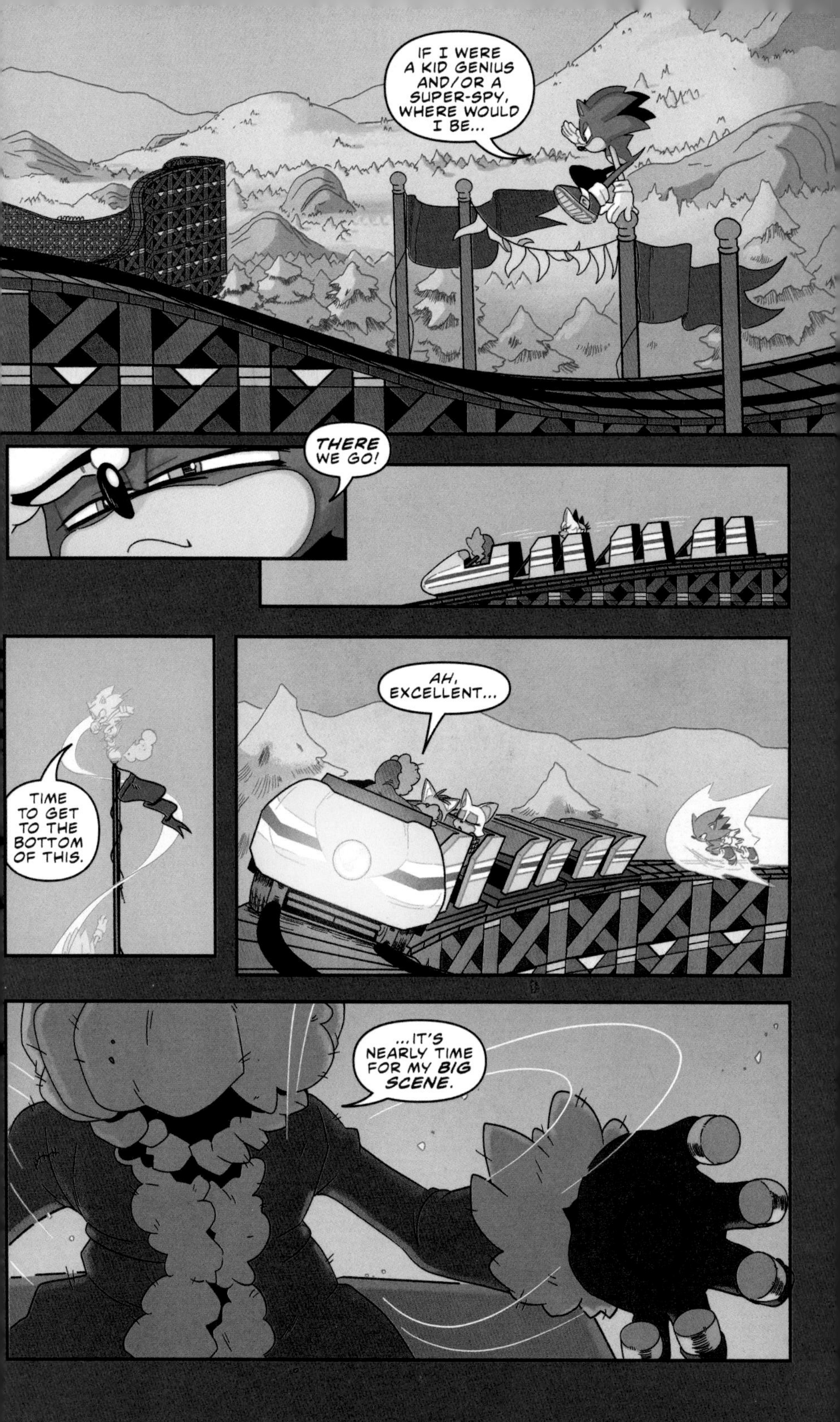
IF I WERE A KID GENIUS AND/OR A SUPER-SPY, WHERE WOULD I BE...
THERE WE GO!
TIME TO GET TO THE BOTTOM OF THIS.
AH, EXCELLENT...
...IT'S NEARLY TIME FOR MY BIG SCENE.

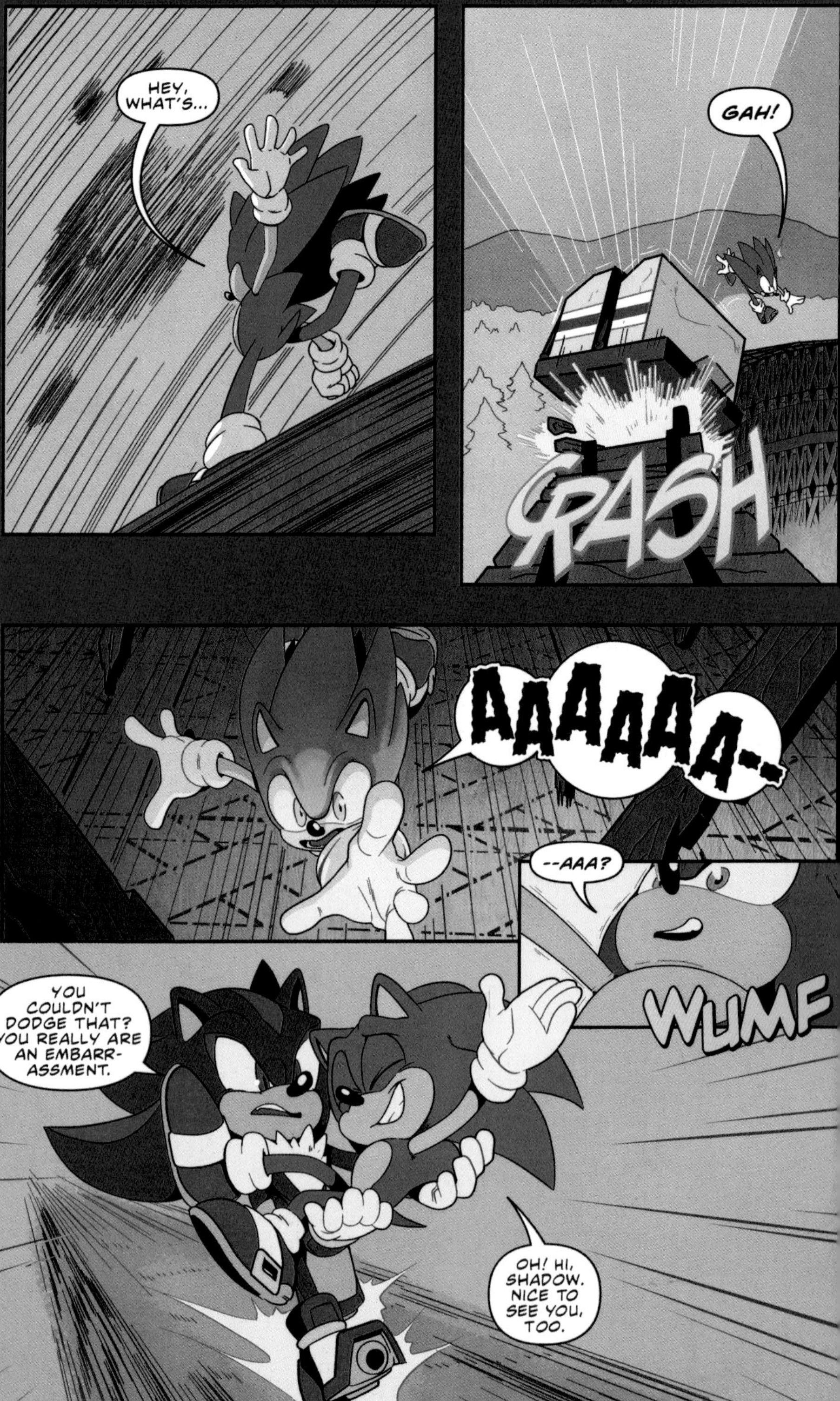
HEY, WHAT'S...
GAH!
CRASH
AAAAAA--
--AAA?
WUMF
YOU COULDN'T DODGE THAT? YOU REALLY ARE AN EMBARR-ASSMENT.
OH! HI, SHADOW. NICE TO SEE YOU, TOO.

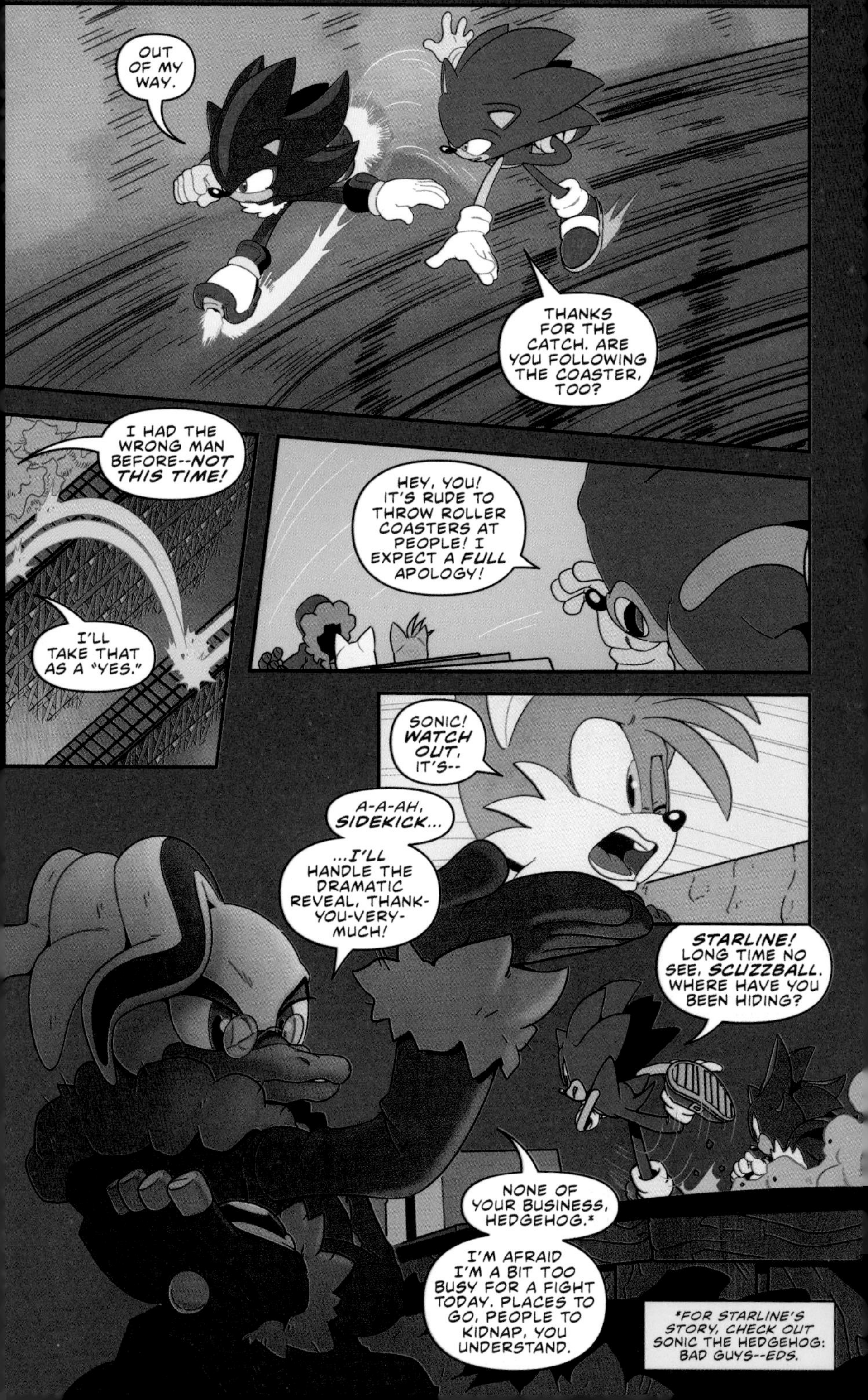
OUT OF MY WAY.
THANKS FOR THE CATCH. ARE YOU FOLLOWING THE COASTER, TOO?
I HAD THE WRONG MAN BEFORE--NOT THIS TIME!
I'LL TAKE THAT AS A "YES."
HEY, YOU! IT'S RUDE TO THROW ROLLER COASTERS AT PEOPLE! I EXPECT A FULL APOLOGY!
SONIC! WATCH OUT, IT'S--
A-A-AH, SIDEKICK...
...I'LL HANDLE THE DRAMATIC REVEAL, THANK-YOU-VERY-MUCH!
STARLINE! LONG TIME NO SEE, SCUZZBALL. WHERE HAVE YOU BEEN HIDING?
NONE OF YOUR BUSINESS, HEDGEHOG.*
I'M AFRAID I'M A BIT TOO BUSY FOR A FIGHT TODAY. PLACES TO GO, PEOPLE TO KIDNAP, YOU UNDERSTAND.
*FOR STARLINE'S STORY, CHECK OUT SONIC THE HEDGEHOG: BAD GUYS--EDS.

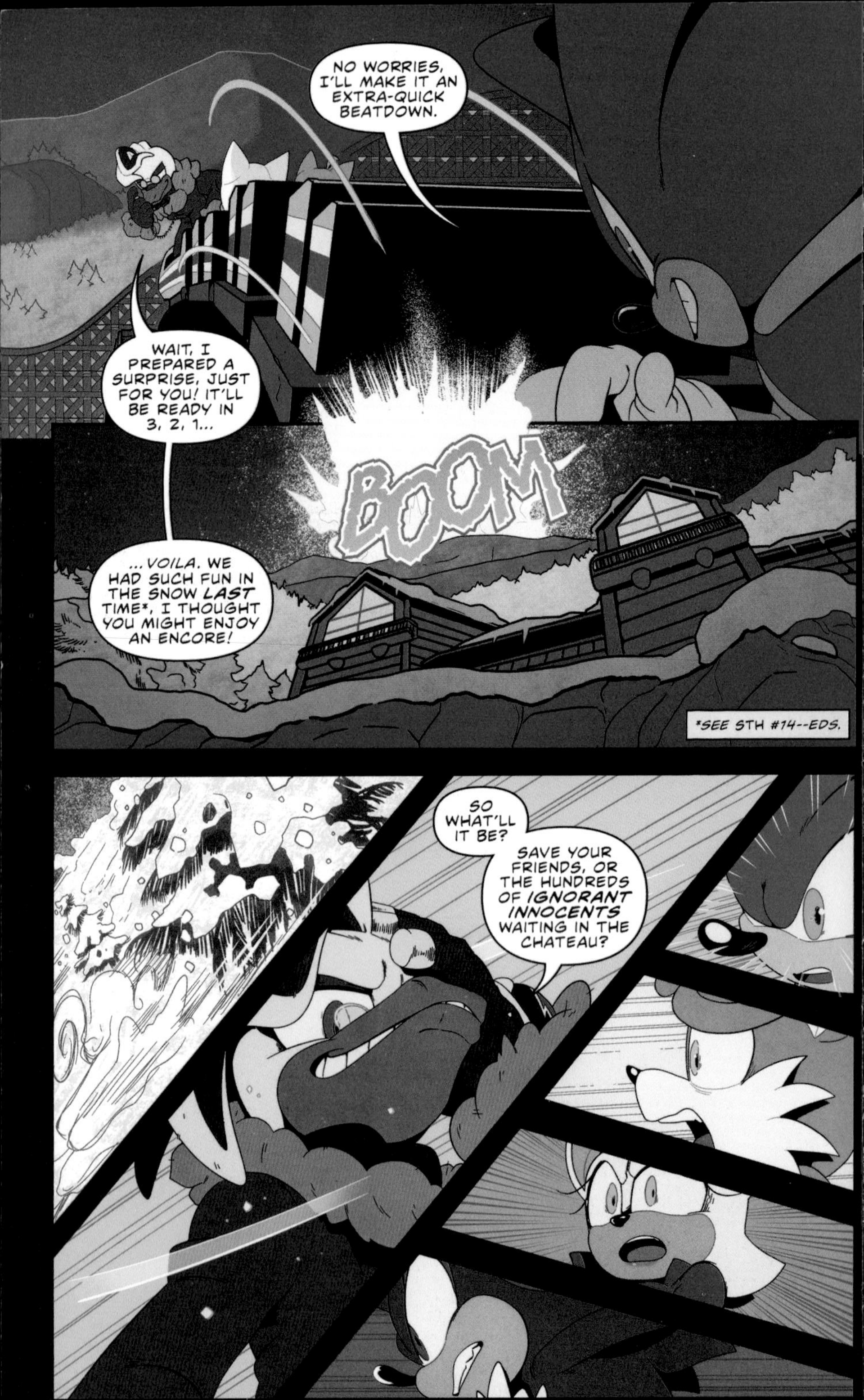
NO WORRIES, I'LL MAKE IT AN EXTRA-QUICK BEATDOWN.
WAIT, I PREPARED A SURPRISE, JUST FOR YOU! IT'LL BE READY IN 3, 2, 1...
BOOM
...VOILA. WE HAD SUCH FUN IN THE SNOW LAST TIME*, I THOUGHT YOU MIGHT ENJOY AN ENCORE!
*SEE STH #14--EDS.
SO WHAT'LL IT BE?
SAVE YOUR FRIENDS, OR THE HUNDREDS OF IGNORANT INNOCENTS WAITING IN THE CHATEAU?

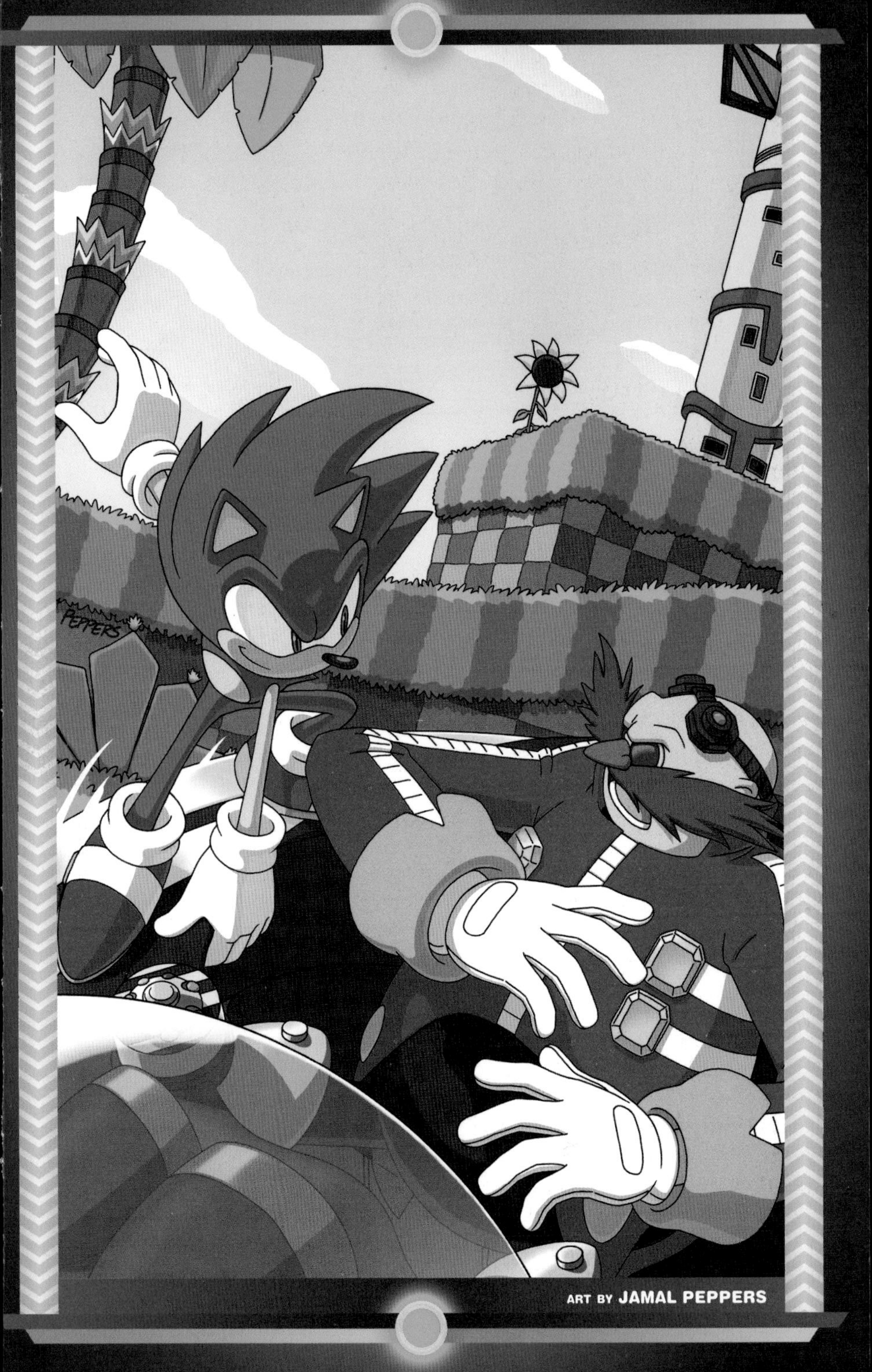
PEPPERS

ART BY JAMAL PEPPERS

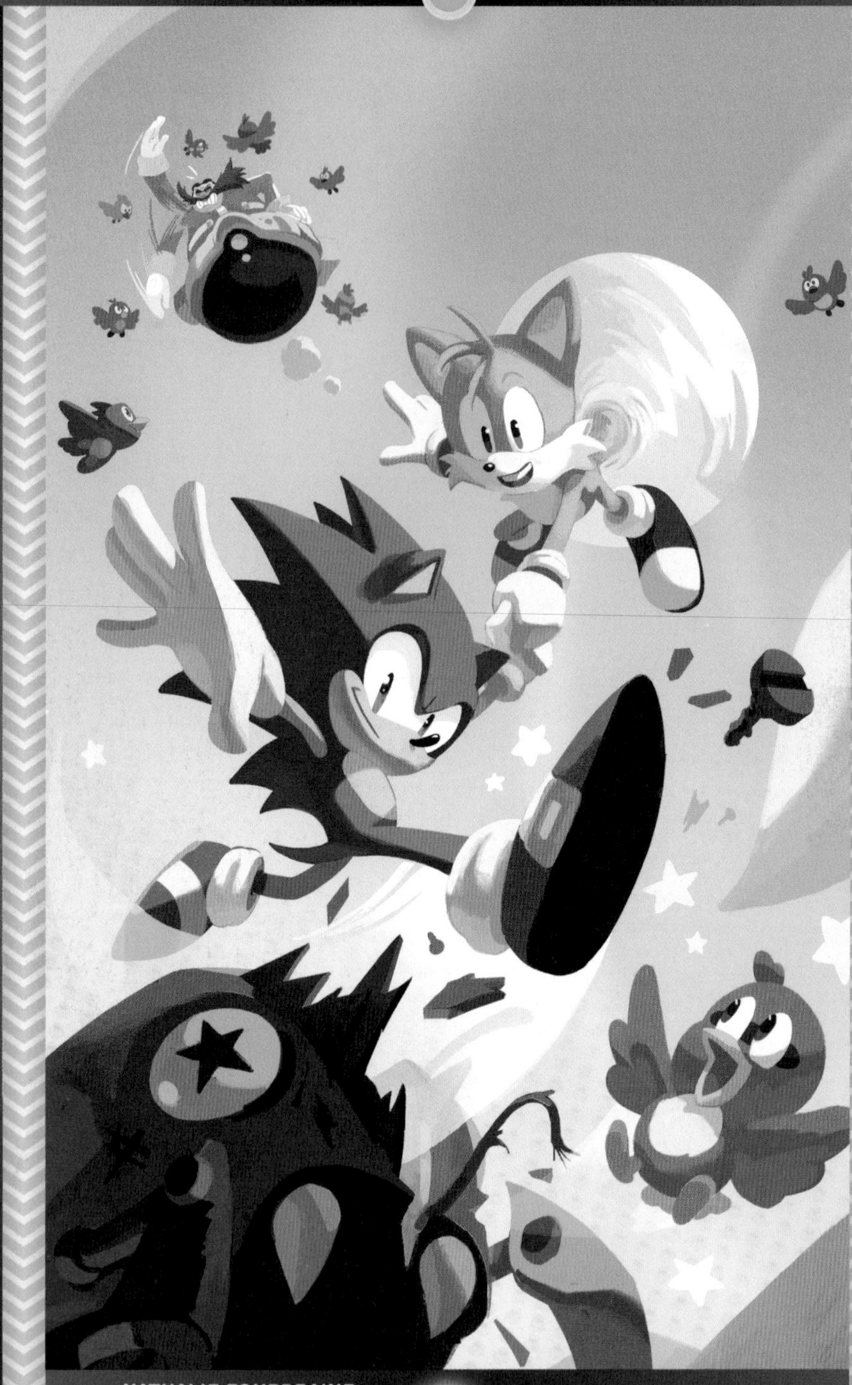

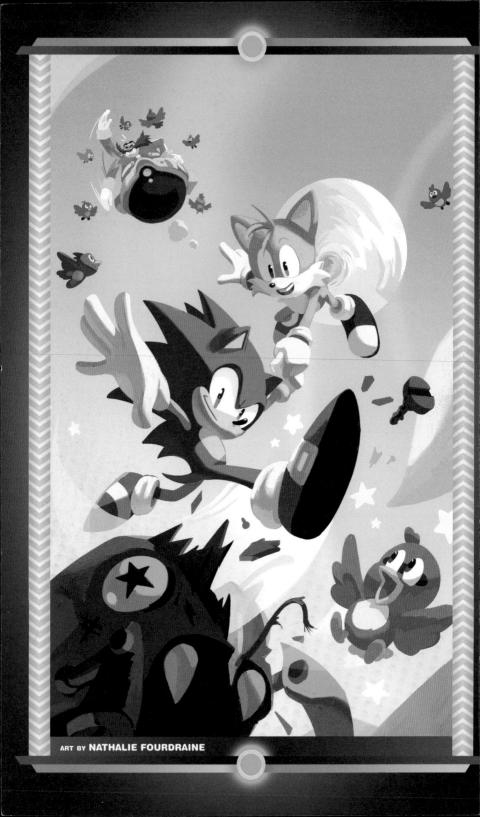

ART BY NATHALIE FOURDRAINE

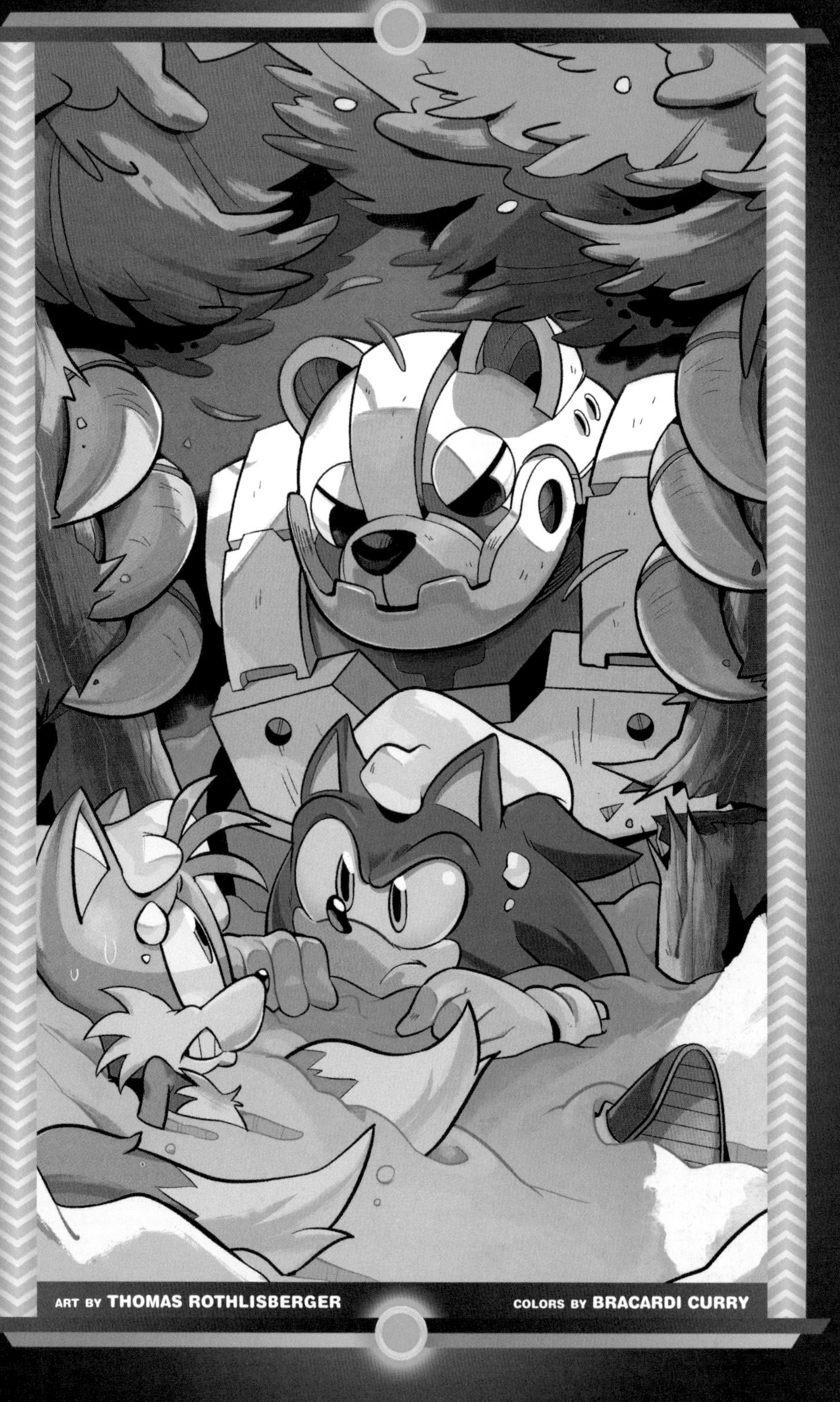

ART BY THOMAS ROTHLISBERGER COLORS BY BRACARDI CURRY

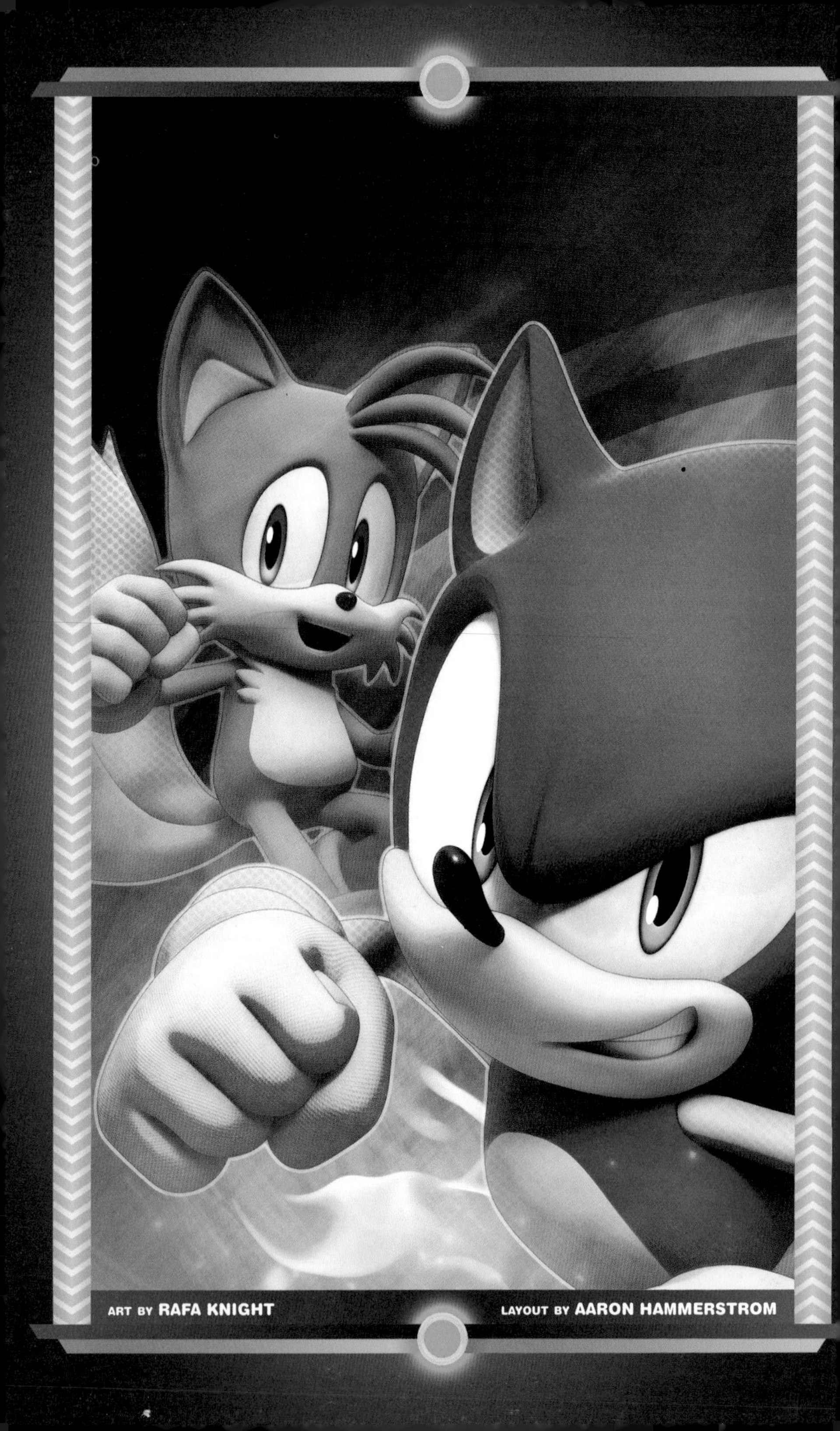

ART BY RAFA KNIGHT

LAYOUT BY AARON HAMMERSTROM